To Simon and Conall, for all your love, laughter and support

DEADLY INTENT

DEADLY INTENT

Anna Sweeney

This first world edition published 2014
in Great Britain and the USA by
SEVERN HOUSE PUBLISHERS LTD of
19 Cedar Road, Sutton, Surrey, England, SM2 5DA.
Trade paperback edition first published
in Great Britain and the USA 2014 by
SEVERN HOUSE PUBLISHERS LTD.
Originally published in Irish as *Buille Marfach*
by Cló Iar-Chonnacht in 2010 under the name Anna Heussaff.

British Library Cataloguing in Publication Data

Sweeney, Anna, author.
  Deadly intent.
  1. Murder–Investigation–Ireland–Beara Peninsula–
  Fiction. 2. Detective and mystery stories.
  I. Title
  891.6'235-dc23

ISBN-13: 978-07278-8369-8 (cased)
ISBN-13: 978-1-84751-513-1 (trade paper)

Except where actual historical events and characters are being
described for the storyline of this novel, all situations in this
publication are fictitious and any resemblance to living persons
is purely coincidental.

All Severn House titles are printed on acid-free paper.

Severn House Publishers support the Forest Stewardship Council™ [FSC™],
the leading international forest certification organisation. All our titles that
are printed on FSC certified paper carry the FSC logo.

MIX
Paper from
responsible sources
FSC® C013056

Typeset by Palimpsest Book Production Ltd.,
Falkirk, Stirlingshire, Scotland.
Printed and bound in Great Britain by
TJ International, Padstow, Cornwall.

ONE

Maureen lay sprawled on a rough track in the country-side. She was in the shadow of an old stone wall where it was difficult to see her. Night was falling and the surrounding hills had become black shapes hunched over the fields.

Slowly and gently, Nessa moved the torchlight onto her face. Maureen's mouth was open, and her lipstick was smeared as if she had been dribbling. Nessa wished she could wipe her clean with a handkerchief. But the ambulance and the local garda sergeant were on their way. Everything had to be left exactly as it was.

'Look, just there, on her head, that's where the wound is . . .'

'Is she still bleeding? Could you see properly when you found her first?'

'See this large stone beside her, I think that was how . . .'

Three people were talking at once. Nessa's teenage daughter, Sal, was crouched beside her, and their neighbour, Darina, who had found Maureen, was standing behind them. She had been out for an evening stroll when she glimpsed a figure on the ground as she passed nearby. She had recognised Maureen as one of a group staying at Nessa's guesthouse, and phoned her to raise the alarm.

Nessa passed the torch back to Sal and took the injured woman's hand. Her heart pounded. Darina was too upset on the phone to explain things properly and Nessa had not known what to expect. She had had to concentrate on the practicalities first, making emergency calls, gathering supplies, and ensuring that the rest of her guests were fine. She had asked Sal to take a shortcut on foot from their house to meet Darina as soon as possible, while she herself drove the longer way around.

Maureen was alive; that was what mattered. Bending over

her, Nessa could feel her breath on the cool air. Her guest was in her early forties, but she was a thin, nervy sort of person, and smoked a lot. She would hardly have survived a night out on a cold, damp hillside.

Nessa released her hand for a moment and pulled an emergency blanket out of her bag, a lightweight aluminium covering that would help to conserve Maureen's body heat. Questions crowded her mind but she pushed them aside. In the torchlight, she could see a shiny streak of blood in Maureen's hair. She had to be kept warm, that was the priority until medical help reached them. It was mid-September and a chill wind blew in from the sea.

'It took you ages to get here in the car,' Sal complained to her mother. 'Darina was in a real state.'

'It took me a while to contact you, just trying to get a phone connection,' said Darina. 'I was afraid I'd have to run all the way to your house. It's such a curse that we don't have a reliable mobile signal everywhere.'

'Her pulse seems OK, so let's hope for the best.' Nessa did her best to keep her voice calm. Darina was clearly shocked, her arms clutched around her chest. She was in her early twenties, and Sal was just eighteen.

'Look at this stone on the ground,' said Darina, pointing with her foot. 'I think it must have caused the main wound.'

'You mean Maureen fell over it, or maybe fainted and hit her head on it?' Nessa gestured to Darina not to touch anything. She was worried that they had already disturbed the ground around Maureen.

'No, Nessa, what I mean is, that it wasn't an accident. I thought I'd explained that on the phone. Did you not notice her clothes? I covered her with my jacket, because she was really cold to the touch. But I left her skirt just as it was.'

Nessa had just put the blanket over Maureen, but she lifted it and removed the jacket carefully, handing it to Darina. Maureen's skirt was rumpled and torn in a few places. Two buttons on her silky blouse were open and the buckle on her wide belt was loose. When she covered her again, Nessa added a small rug on top of the blanket. She tried to keep a new wave of anxiety at bay.

'You were right not to touch her clothes, Darina,' she said quietly. 'But we can't be certain what happened.'

Darina pulled on her jacket forcefully. 'Well, it's disgusting that anyone would attack a woman out in an isolated spot like this. I mean, it could've happened hours ago, in the middle of the day, and poor Maureen was left lying here ever since.'

'I'm sure Sergeant Fitzmaurice will have his own ideas when he gets here. But we're very lucky that you saw Maureen at all, considering this track is a dead end.'

'Darina was walking along the little road at the top of the track, up where you parked,' said Sal, who didn't like to be left out of a conversation. 'But you told me it wasn't dark at that stage, Darina, and that's how you managed to spot her?'

'Yes, that's it. I suppose it was a bit dusky, but I think . . . I stopped at the corner and just happened to glance down this direction. I'd stopped to pick a few blackberries, as a matter of fact, and I was wondering if I'd get more of them down here.' Darina hesitated as she tried to describe the sequence of events. 'I think it was her shiny blouse that caught my eye, but I'd no idea I'd find someone unconscious.'

'Anyway, we took a few photos of Maureen while the light was fading,' said Sal, clicking through the menu on her phone. 'That was actually my idea, because I reckoned they'd make, like, handy evidence if there was a police investigation. But they're not great pics, I'm afraid. The camera on my phone isn't the best.'

Sal sounded more excited than shocked. Her mother could well imagine the sort of *CSI* television images playing in her head, now that she had a lead role in the action. Life's cares didn't weigh heavily on her as they did on Darina.

Nessa looked at her watch. The ambulance had to come from Castletownbere, over ten miles away on narrow country roads, and she hoped she had given them clear directions. There was a network of byroads or boreens, as they were known locally, winding and criss-crossing each other between the coast and the mountains. It would be all too easy to take a wrong turn.

She willed herself to be patient. Help was on the way. If Maureen had not been found in time, it might have been impossible to send out search parties before daybreak. Nessa's guests were taking part in a week of guided walks and other activities on the Beara peninsula on Ireland's rugged southwest coast. On Thursdays, however, they were free to do as they liked, and Maureen had been out since mid-morning. When she had not returned for dinner at seven o'clock as agreed, Nessa made a few calls to check whether she was in the nearest pub or hotel. But if Darina's call had not alerted her soon afterwards, she might have waited a few hours longer before becoming seriously concerned.

'So what about Dominic? I presume you got onto him when Maureen didn't turn up for dinner? And I hope you phoned him back with the news?'

'Of course I did,' said Nessa. She pretended not to notice her daughter's needling tone. 'He was out fishing all day but he left me a message a short while ago.'

'And is he rushing to the scene, or what?'

'Who's Dominic? I don't remember his name.' Darina had crouched by the drystone wall, and was turning a small stone over and over in her hand.

'He's Maureen's husband,' said Nessa. 'He'd said this morning that he wouldn't join us for dinner, and I think his phone must have been switched off when I tried to get hold of him.'

'I don't remember meeting him when Maureen and the others came to the Barn on Tuesday?' Darina was working to establish herself as an artist, and Nessa had brought her guests to visit her studio and those of other local artists. 'But he must be worried sick by now.'

'I don't know about that,' said Sal. 'The story is that he and Maureen broke up for a while earlier this year. And from what we've seen all week, they won't be nominated for a Happy Couple of the Year award any time soon.'

'I'm sure Dominic is very worried about her,' said Nessa.

'Worried about money, more like,' said Sal. She turned to Darina and grinned. 'Thing is, Maureen scooped a big Lotto win a few years ago. She bought a pub with the proceeds, or so she told us the other evening. Then she was, like, "I should've invested in a toyboy for myself while I had my chance". She was totally serious about it too. And there's Dominic beside her, pretending not to notice while she blabs away—'

'Please, Sal, that's enough.' Nessa stroked Maureen's cold hand. Her skin was clammy, like fish just out of the fridge. It had become painfully clear during the week that she was vulnerable, with little sense of when to keep her mouth shut.

She studied her face. Maureen cultivated a young woman's looks quite successfully, but the signs of age showed under the harsh torchlight. The corners of her mouth were puckered, and her jet black hair was thinning. The bright cheerful mask she liked to show the world had slipped.

'Why is the ambulance taking so long?' Darina stood up and looked out into the darkness. 'Once they turn off the main road and then up from the village, they should be here in no time.'

'What I was wondering,' said Sal, 'is why Maureen made her way to this secluded spot in the first place? It wasn't really her thing, was it, rambling around the countryside on solo outings? And anyway, why was she walking along a dead end?'

'She wasn't wearing walking shoes either,' said Darina. 'So if she had to run from her attacker . . .'

'I think she was drinking,' said Sal. 'I'm pretty sure I got a whiff of alcohol from her, so maybe she fell when she tried to run. In fact, maybe she wasn't attacked at all, and just fell.'

'Poor woman, she could have screamed for help and nobody would have heard her. The nearest house must be five or ten minutes walk away.'

Sal lifted the edge of the blanket and gazed at Maureen's high heels. 'Well, whatever happened, you'd have to actually ask yourself what brought her to Beara in the first place. We're not exactly famed for the type of shopping and karaoke holiday I reckon she'd be into.'

Nessa let go of Maureen's hand and stood up. She held her counsel, but she had learned through her business that the reasons for people's holiday choices were not always obvious. If their relationship was strained, Maureen and Dominic may have decided to spend a week with a group of strangers rather than face each other silently across a hotel table each night.

'I'm going to switch on the car's lights,' she said then. 'I should have thought of it when I arrived, so that the ambulance people can damn well see where we are.'

A ribbon of sea shimmered between Beara's dark coastline and the Iveragh peninsula to the north. Nessa stood alone by the car for a few minutes, troubled by the evening's events. Large pale stones were scattered on the hills nearby, and in the glare of the headlights they appeared to her like bare bones protruding from the earth's skin. She shivered as she thought of how differently things might have turned out.

She looked back at the two young women lit up in the middle of the boreen. Their heads were bent towards one another as they talked. Sal was tall and shapely, her dark skin displaying her father's African origins. Next to her, Darina looked slight and washed out, her pale translucent skin framed by thick sandy hair. The landscape's black shadows encircled them.

Nessa's husband Patrick had left Ireland that very morning to travel to Malawi in southeastern Africa, where he had grown up. Whatever had befallen Maureen, and whatever its consequences, Nessa would have to deal with them alone. She also had several other guests to look after until Saturday morning. But meanwhile, it occurred to her that once Maureen was on her way to hospital, she should bring Darina back to the house to make sure she was OK. Then she could try to figure out her own ideas on what had happened.

Her solitary musings ended when the arrival of the ambulance and garda car broke the night's silence. The medics got to work quickly, organising a stretcher to carry Maureen the short distance to the top of the track. Meanwhile, the police busied themselves with photographs and measurements of the location. Just as the ambulance left and Nessa was hoping they could return home, Sergeant Conor Fitzmaurice started on a round of questions. What time had Maureen agreed to return for the evening meal? What time had Darina found her injured? Was there any reason beforehand that such an incident could happen?

They were still talking when a car door slammed loudly nearby and a man got out. They saw Dominic blinking in the lights, trying to take in the scene. He was heavily built, his belly flopping over his belt, and was out of breath as he hurried towards them.

'I tried to phone her earlier,' he said. 'I did my best to phone Maureen this afternoon.' He stared at the faces around him. 'I should've gone looking for her when I heard nothing back. I should've known something was wrong.'

The sergeant stepped towards him. 'Would you mind if I asked you a few quick questions before you head off to the hospital? I'm sure you'd like to be on your way—'

'What I'd like right now is a proper explanation.' Dominic looked around again and then pointed a finger at Nessa. 'I went off on my own for one day, that's all. One lousy day for myself, madam, and in my innocence I trusted *you* to keep an eye on your guests!'

Nessa had no chance to reply before Dominic launched into a longer tirade. 'But then again, you had other things on your mind this week, isn't that so? You had a big shot visitor staying in your fine house, and you and your husband spent the week licking his boots, as far as I could see. You didn't give two damns that your gentleman visitor was whispering softly in Maureen's ear and that she started to believe, God help her, that he fancied a roll in the bushes with her? And now look what's happened!'

The sergeant tried to interrupt but Dominic had not finished. His lower lip quivered as he spoke. 'You'll be hearing more about this, I promise you. It's not what I expected when I brought Maureen here on holiday. I call it negligence, and I'll tell my solicitor all about it if I have to.'

TWO

C louds were swelling in the western sky. Large and fat, they filled and billowed as they rose from the horizon. A bright sliver of moonlight separated them from the night's blackness.

Nessa watched a single cloud sweep ahead on its own. When the clamour of her guests got to her, she liked to escape to an unseen corner of the back garden. Just enough time to gaze at the sky and at the outstretched branches of the trees. Time to slow her thoughts, which were fizzing like demented flies tonight. She had spent the last hour and a half trying to get information from the district hospital in Bantry, attending to the rest of her guests and arranging for them to give statements to Sergeant Fitzmaurice, and all the while worrying about the implications of the episode.

Her eyes followed the course of her solitary cloud, swift and buoyant across the dark backdrop of the sky. But she was unable to shake off Dominic's outburst. She told herself it would come to nothing. He was upset, naturally enough, and needed to vent his feelings, but he was also clearly gripped by jealousy. Nessa was well aware of his target when he described a fellow guest as 'a big shot visitor'. Oscar Malden was a wealthy businessman – and unlike Dominic, he was also a pleasant and courteous individual. It was hardly Nessa's business if he and Maureen had been flirting under Dominic's nose. What is more, if Dominic was so concerned about his wife, why did he go off fishing on his own?

But Nessa still wished she had paid more attention to Maureen, who had been hanging around the house that morning, moody and unsure of how to spend the day. Nessa was very busy, and she was also feeling the end-of-season weariness that September brought. So she had been relieved when Maureen finally reappeared from her room dressed to the nines and happy to accept Nessa's offer of a lift to the local village of Derryowen, half a mile down the hill. Nessa told her to text if she wanted a lift back later, but was quite glad to hear nothing more from her all day.

When Maureen had not turned up for dinner, two other guests reported seeing her at the Derryowen Hotel earlier, while they were drinking mid-morning coffee on the sea-facing terrace. Maureen had greeted them but went indoors, and soon afterwards, they saw Oscar arrive. Through a window, they noticed the pair having a conversation, but then Oscar left on his own. Maureen was still in the hotel bar a while later when the other two guests went off walking, so it was anybody's guess whether she and Oscar had agreed a rendezvous in the countryside. The whole thing was based on supposition – but if the very worst had happened and Oscar assaulted Maureen on the boreen, it was difficult to see how Nessa or anyone else could have prevented it.

As adults, all of the guests were responsible for their own safety, and in any case, they had been strongly advised not to go walking alone in unfamiliar places. So Dominic's accusation of negligence was way off the mark. But it was not the legalities that concerned Nessa so much as a feeling that if the week turned out badly, she and her husband Patrick had failed in their job to keep their guests as safe and as happy as possible.

She watched as the lone cloud drifted out of sight. A multitude of questions still weighed her down. How bad were Maureen's injuries? How soon could she give her own explanations to the gardai? Had Oscar been involved in the incident?

Nessa decided to allow herself five more minutes outdoors. She sat under a big oak tree, on a wooden seat Patrick had given her many years earlier as a present from Malawi. It was made of two pieces of dark wood elegantly fitted together, and as she stretched against its firm support, she reminded herself that at least she was not in a hospital waiting room with Dominic for company – eyes bulging with anger and garish jersey stretched tightly across his belly. She had offered to go to the hospital, of course, but Sergeant Fitzmaurice said that a colleague from Bantry station could call in instead, and pass on any news. But so far, Nessa had had no word from the colleague.

She took out her phone to write a text to Patrick, who had been on her mind all evening. His aunt in Malawi had been ill for several months and he had waited the whole summer for an opportunity to visit her. He had lived in Ireland for over twenty years, and indeed, his father's mother had been white and Irish, but most of his relatives were in Malawi. He had originally booked flights for the following Sunday – most of the guests would have left by then, and he would have no more guided walks to organise until the October bank holiday weekend.

But he was forced to change his booking at the last minute, because of a threat of strike action at an airport en route. His new flight from Cork airport was at eight o'clock on Thursday evening, three days earlier than planned. He had some business to do on his way to Cork and had left Beara in a hurry that morning. Nessa told herself it was pointless wishing he had delayed until after the weekend – that if only he had been at home, she might have paid more attention to Maureen.

'I'd rather not leave you holding the fort on your own, Nessa,' he had said as he pored over internet timetables. 'We're both so tired after the summer.'

'You know I'll be absolutely fine,' she had replied. 'You've been hopping with impatience for weeks so please don't think twice about it.'

She was acutely aware of how important the journey was to him. As an only child whose parents had been involved in political struggle, Patrick's earlier life had been difficult. His father had died in traumatic circumstances when he was a teenager and his aunt had been his rock of support. He had fretted about her ever since she became ill, and Nessa knew that the sooner he got on a plane the better.

The back garden sloped down to the house, which was called Cnoc Meala, an Irish name that translated as 'honey hill' and also 'sweet hill'. They had picked the name when they heard that a previous owner used to keep bees in a field above the garden. Nessa always felt a surge of pride when she contemplated the house, which they had renovated completely after buying it almost three years earlier.

Moving from Dublin to the far reaches of the southwest coast had been an upheaval for the whole family: swapping her career as a newspaper journalist and Patrick's as a graphic artist for the uncertain demands of tourism, and parting their two children, Sal and Ronan, from the familiar routines of urban living. For almost two decades, Nessa had loved her work in Dublin, and had made quite an impact with a number of investigative stories; but one morning soon after her mother's death, she had been struck by an overwhelming feeling that life was too short to spend it all in one place. She and Patrick had occasionally fantasised about living in a scenic and rural community, and while figuring out the move took them some time, Nessa was sure that Cnoc Meala was now their home for life. They had decided to use the same name for their holiday activity business, and in spite of setting it up in the teeth of economic recession, they had survived and paid the bills so far.

It was easy to praise the attractions of the Beara peninsula in their publicity blurb. Splendid mountains and panoramic seascapes, hidden valleys and hedgerows sweet with birdsong were all to be found in abundance between the great bays of Bantry and Kenmare. Even the unreliable weather could be portrayed as part of nature's colourful drama. The hard part was to convince tourists to base themselves a good distance from airports and major roads. There was also the challenge of group holidays that was not spelt out in any brochure – getting a random assortment of strangers to gel together and enjoy each other's company for a week.

When things went really well, laughter and chat filled the house until late into the evenings. At other times, Nessa and Patrick settled for a general sense of contentment in the group. But once or twice a year, they found themselves with a few cantankerous guests who could spoil the fun for everyone, and who had to be diverted, humoured and quietly managed all week long.

However, Nessa had had no inkling of trouble ahead when eleven people met for drinks in the living room on the previous Sunday. She had certainly wondered whether Oscar Malden would be difficult to please, because as a well-known entrepreneur and man-about-town, he might find Cnoc Meala rather low-key for his tastes. She had noticed straight off how readily he became the centre of attention. He was not tall or flashy in his appearance, but he had that magnetism that drew others to him and made them feel he was paying special attention to every word they uttered. Of course, he was an old hand at working a room, meeting, greeting and making conversation. Little wonder, really, that Dominic was jealous.

Nessa heard the wind rustling in the oak leaves. It was time to return to the fray. She told herself again that everything would be fine, just as soon as Maureen recovered and Oscar could show that he had played no part in her mishap. Most of the guests seemed to be enjoying their holiday – eight of them in the house, along with a family of three in a self-catering lodge in the grounds – and until tonight's events, nobody had hinted at a complaint.

Sal called out to her from the back door of the house. Nessa looked back over the text she had jotted to her husband. His plane should have landed at Schiphol airport in Amsterdam by late evening, and he would probably check his mobile before his overnight connection to Johannesburg. She did not want to worry him, however, so she had just said that Maureen had an accident but that everything was under control. In a day or two, she could fill him in on the outcome of police enquiries.

It was clear, in any case, that Dominic was ignorant of one salient fact. Oscar had already left Beara. He had checked out of Cnoc Meala that morning, telling Nessa that an unexpected business problem had come up, forcing him to return to his native County Tipperary. He assured her he was very sorry to leave early, and that he would stay in the area until lunchtime, to take a last walk along the coastal path. His grown-up son, Fergus, who had come down with a minor stomach bug the previous day, would stay on in Beara for the last two days of the holiday.

Nessa reflected that if the gardai required a statement from

Oscar, they would have to contact him in Tipperary. And if they learned that he had arrived home while Maureen was still in full health, Dominic's claims would come to nothing.

'Where did you get to? You shouldn't disappear without a word, I've told you loads of times . . .'

Sal spoke as if she were the parent issuing a reprimand. Nessa kept her lips tightly closed. Her daughter was barring her way at the door until she had her say. Darina sat at the table inside, clasping a teacup.

'A policeman phoned from Bantry,' said Sal. 'His name is Redmond something, and he's at the hospital now. He and his inspector want to come over to see you tomorrow. They're anxious to clarify the details of the incident, as he put it, and to enquire into all the circumstances of the case. You know the way gardai talk.'

'OK, love, I'm sorry I missed his call. But did he mention how Maureen is now?' Nessa smiled, remembering Sal's earlier needling. 'I presume you didn't forget to ask about her?'

'You presume . . .? Ha, ha, don't be smart, of course I asked about her. He said Maureen is as comfortable as can be expected. Whatever that might actually mean.'

'It's always the same bland line, isn't it?' said Darina, who was still pale, but seemed less strained than earlier. 'I hate the way hospitals tell you nothing on the phone.'

Nessa decided that she would look in on her son Ronan, who had gone to bed late, and then get back to the garda in Bantry. But as she noted the garda's number, she remembered her daughter's homework. Sal had just started her final Leaving Certificate year at school, and had promised to stick to a strict programme of study. But unsurprisingly, she had not opened a schoolbook all evening.

'Could I give you a lift home in about ten minutes, Darina?' Nessa glanced out at the garden. 'I think it's about to rain.'

Sal gave their young neighbour a meaningful look. 'Well, are you still on for Kenmare, Darina? I wouldn't mind joining you, and I'm sure you'd like company tonight—'

'Hold your horses now, Sal,' said Nessa. 'If you think you're going anywhere on a weekday night, you can forget it. I'm sorry, Darina, I hadn't realised that we'd upset your plans for the evening.'

'It doesn't matter now,' said Darina. 'I'd just mentioned earlier that I might go to a music session in a pub in Kenmare. But really, I don't feel like it.'

'OK then, but tomorrow night is definitely on, Darina, isn't it?' Sal looked defiantly at her mother. 'Friday night, see? We're both invited to a big party and you can't possibly, like, lock me up for the weekend, can you now?'

A knock on the kitchen door prevented Nessa's reply. It was opened cautiously and Fergus Malden stood looking at them. Unlike his father, he was shy and rather quiet.

'Excuse me,' he said uncertainly. 'If things are too busy . . . But my stomach is still upset and I thought, maybe . . .?'

'Come in,' said Nessa. 'I'm sorry you're not feeling any better.' Earlier in the day, she had accompanied him to the nearest town, Castletownbere, to go to a chemist. It was one of the reasons her day had been so busy.

'I can wait until the kitchen is quiet.' He seemed about to close the door again. 'I was going to heat up some milk but if I'm in your way . . .'

'It's no problem, Fergus, please come in and I'll do it for you.' Nessa opened the fridge. 'You know you're welcome to whatever you'd like.'

'I wonder if I could ask you . . .?' Darina removed her jacket from the back of her chair and spoke quickly. 'I'm Darina O'Sullivan, we met over at my studio on Tuesday and I spoke to your father again this morning, down in the village. He told me he might call in to the Barn before he left Beara, but as he didn't make it . . .' She bit her lip as she continued, 'I hope you won't mind my asking, because I'd hate to be pushy—'

'You'll have to up your sales pitch, Darina,' said Sal with a laugh. 'What you're really trying to say is that you'd love Fergus's dad to commission a painting or a portrait from you. The great Oscar Malden as rendered by Darina O'Sullivan, isn't that your idea? But now you're afraid you've missed your chance?'

'Of course, whatever I can . . .' As Fergus spoke, Nessa

noticed how grey he looked. For her own sake as well as his, she hoped fervently that he would recover by Saturday. She could hardly wait to put her feet up.

'Well, that's it, I actually did a drawing for him today, just a little thing on a card, but I'd like to put a few finishing touches to it.' Darina hesitated at the sink, cup in hand. 'I didn't have time this evening, but tomorrow . . .'

'That's OK. I'll give it to him and I'm sure . . .'

Fergus had a habit of tailing off his sentences, and Sal joined in again. 'You could bring it over in the evening,' she said to Darina, 'when you come to collect me for the party.' She winked conspiratorially at their neighbour, and in spite of her worries about homework, Nessa was glad to see them becoming friends. There were very few young people in the immediate area, and as a result, Sal often pestered her parents to be allowed to gad about further afield. As for Darina, Nessa suspected that her life was rather solitary – she had lived alone since her mother, barely into her forties, had died of cancer a few years earlier.

Nessa poured warmed milk into a cup. She felt exhausted, and did not argue when Darina turned down a second offer of a lift home. As their neighbour was leaving, Sal gave her a big hug.

'Thanks *so* truly much,' she said with a giggle. Their plans for the following night were clearly well-advanced. 'Or what do they say in Spanish? *Muchas gracias, mi amiga*!'

Fergus retreated and Nessa went upstairs to her son's bedroom. At twelve years old, Ronan had a very active imagination and had plied her earlier with questions about Maureen and the ambulance. Now he was asleep with a book on his chest, so she turned out his light and tried to phone the garda in Bantry, a large town over forty miles away. She had forgotten whether his first name or surname was Redmond, and when his answerphone came on, Nessa just left a message to say that she could meet himself and his inspector at Cnoc Meala the following afternoon.

Sal was busily working her phone in the kitchen. 'The others have gone down to Derryowen for a drink,' she said. 'The French couple, that is, and the two sisters – Zoe and whatshername, the quieter one. No doubt they're discussing this evening's excitement over their pints.'

'Not the kind of excitement we advertise, unfortunately.' Nessa poured wine for herself. She could arrange for her guests to get a lift back from O'Donovan's pub in Derryowen, if they decided against the long walk up the hill.

'By the way, have you heard the rumour?' Sal paused in her fingerwork. 'The latest on Maureen's love life?'

Nessa took a slow sip of her drink. She was in no mood for new dramas, and just wanted to escape to her room with a comforting glass and a book. A good night's sleep would renew her habitual curiosity about her fellow human beings.

'She was seen upstairs last night,' Sal continued. 'Maureen, that is, while Dominic and a few others played cards in the living room. And the big rumour is – wait for it – that she got lucky in her love quest.'

'You'd better spell it out for me, love. Is this about Maureen and Oscar, or is there another entanglement I haven't heard about?'

'It's about Maureen going into Oscar's bedroom. One of the two sisters – not Zoe but the other one, Stella, isn't it? – went upstairs at about half ten, to look for a book she'd mislaid or something. Oscar's room is opposite theirs and who does Stella see going in to him but Maureen? How about that now?'

'Maureen might have been inviting him to join her husband's card game,' said Nessa drily.

Sal smirked in response. 'Yeah, right. But the thing is, she wasn't in a hurry about it, because according to Stella's account, Maureen was still in Oscar's room when Stella came downstairs at least, oh, ten or fifteen minutes later.'

THREE

The beguiling Beara peninsula, as the guidebooks had it. Craggy purple mountains and soft green farmland, not to mention the usual touristy stuff about boats bobbing on the waves. And, of course, hospitable people who loved to welcome strangers.

Redmond Joyce was not enticed by the image, no matter what others told him. All he could see of Beara was a low sky and persistent grey drizzle on his windscreen. He was on his way from Bantry, outside the peninsula, to Castletownbere, its main town, and from there to Derryowen. He was always amazed that people chose to spend their holidays in such places – bare and lumpy mountains, roads twisting across an empty landscape, nothing in sight but bleak loneliness.

It looked better in sunshine, of course. But even so, it would not attract him. To him, one mountain was the same as the next, and staring at a jumble of stones and water was not his idea of a good time. As for the people, he would run a mile from their kind and hospitable attempts to make conversation. What he wanted on holidays was to escape to one of the world's great cities – Berlin, Singapore, New York, Rio de Janeiro – where he could feel the ceaseless throb of activity on all sides. Noisy crowds, a clamourous din and, best of all, not a soul who knew him.

But his visit to Beara was not a holiday outing, it was part of his job as a garda. He had been posted to Bantry station six months earlier, after a few stints in small towns in the midlands. In his own mind, he was marking time while he awaited a move to a city station. His dream job was to be a detective in one of the troubled suburbs of Dublin or Limerick, abuzz with action and danger.

'I'd like to deal with this business in Derryowen as quickly

as possible.' His companion, Detective Inspector Trevor
O'Kelleher, was shuffling through a pile of notes as he spoke.

'I made the arrangement as you requested, inspector, and
Nessa McDermott is expecting us at three o'clock. But if you
wish to amend the timetable—'

'Jesus, I don't wish to amend anything, as you put it. All I
mean is that I'd like to leave time to sniff around the quay in
Castletown later.' The inspector spoke quietly, but Redmond
noted the impatience in his voice. He found it hard to hit the
right tone with his senior officer.

He also felt too much of an outsider to use the local
abbreviation of the fishing port's name. 'What's happening in
Castletownbere?' he asked after a moment.

'There's trouble brewing with that Russian ship at the quay,'
O'Kelleher replied. 'It's been there for weeks, so it's obviously
been abandoned by its owners.'

'I remember hearing something on the local news a few
days ago. But surely the owners have legal obligations?'

'Well, if they do, you can bet they're trying to dodge them.
They must be some shower of blaggards, to leave a crew of
men stranded without as much as a loaf of bread to feed
themselves.' O'Kelleher turned a few pages of his notes.
'Anyway, our man Conor Fitzmaurice has covered a lot of the
ground for us in Derryowen so I don't think we'll be detained
there too long.'

Redmond nodded politely. In his view, there was little
substance to the incident reported from Beara the previous night.
But he was always keen to accompany Detective Inspector
O'Kelleher on his rounds, in the hope of displaying his own
abilities. Bantry station was the garda district headquarters and
as a senior officer, O'Kelleher kept regular contact with a number
of smaller stations in west Cork.

There was also a built-in bonus to the day's outing. Redmond
was curious to get his own impressions of Nessa McDermott.
He knew of her reputation as an investigative journalist, supposedly relentless in her pursuit of the unpopular or unsavoury
facts. Indeed, according to a quick online search Redmond had
done the night before, it had caused some surprise in media
circles when she had left it all behind for the good life. But

O'Kelleher seemed to be wary of her, judging by his comments in Bantry that morning. 'Our lads in Castletown are checking out this business on the hillside,' he said. 'But I wouldn't mind having a look for myself. After all, who knows what trouble we may have on our hands, when our friend in Cnoc Meala is involved.'

'So tell me, Redmond, what did you think of Maureen Scurlock?'

Redmond delayed his answer for a moment, his eyes on the traffic in the centre of Castletownbere. He was also reluctant to admit that he could not make up his mind about the patient he had interviewed in Bantry hospital that morning.

'She says she has no clear memory of what happened,' he said, once he had negotiated the narrow turning beside the port town's supermarket. 'But even the details she claims to remember seem unreliable.'

'Did she admit, by any happy chance, that she and Oscar Malden had arranged to meet up in the hills?'

'She said they were on friendly terms, but she was adamant that she didn't see him again after he'd left the hotel premises.'

'She swore to whatever she'd like her husband to hear, most likely. And what about the doctors, could you get anything useful out of them?'

'I regret to say I couldn't.' Redmond put the car in second gear as they climbed a steep hill. He could see the town's chimneys and the harbourside ships in his rear-view mirror. 'I spoke to just one doctor, and according to him, Mrs Scurlock's injuries were consistent with an accidental fall. But he said he was also unable to exclude the possibility of an assault.'

'God, give me patience with the medical profession, and the great wads of money we pay them for their exclusions and inclusions! Surely they can tell us what happened?'

'The doctor did say that Mrs Scurlock's wound is not very deep. But it seems that its location at the back of her head makes both possibilities valid – that she tripped on a few stones accidentally, or that she was deliberately assaulted.'

Redmond glanced quickly at his companion, whose
expression was difficult to read. He wished his own words did
not sound so measured and stiff. But he thought there was no
point in jumping to conclusions when there were so few facts
available.

'As you know,' he added, 'they found evidence of alcohol
in her blood, but it wasn't possible to identify the precise time
she'd been drinking.'

'No, heaven help us, and I'm sure it also wasn't possible
to identify the precise quantity of booze she'd swallowed all
day. But the young lad working in the hotel bar told Conor
Fitz that Maureen bought just two coffees and then an orange
juice.'

'She may have been drinking on her own while she was
out walking, I suppose?'

'She may indeed, or she have been glugging with her desirable
friend, Oscar Malden. He left the hotel up to half an hour ahead
of her, and he'd chatted to the barman about his plans for a
walk.' O'Kelleher paused to look down at his notes. 'He was
heading for one of those waymarked trails that are signposted
for tourists – Coomgarriff Walk, it's called. But the bold Maureen
wasn't as innocent as she made out to you, because when she
was paying her bill, she enquired from the young barman how
to get to the selfsame place.'

'And is that where she was found? I don't remember the
name Coomgarriff being mentioned.'

'No, indeed, she was found in a different spot, say ten
minutes walk away, where there are no helpful little signposts.
So we don't know whether she lost her way, or maybe went
there purposefully for a private encounter with Malden. When
the track was searched, there were three or four fresh cigarette
butts on the ground, which we may have to send to forensics,
depending on how things go.'

'What about Dominic Scurlock? Suppose he met his wife
out there and they had a row?'

'Dominic's story is that he spent the day fishing at Pooka
Rock, a bit of a way down the coast from Derryowen Hotel.'
The detective inspector flipped back to an earlier page. 'Yes,
here it is. Dominic says he saw nobody all day, not a solitary

sinner apart from a few holidaymakers who passed him in a boat. He says he waved at them a few times but otherwise all was peace and tranquillity.'

Redmond fell silent as he gazed at the countryside. The blanket of cloud was slowly lifting from the hills. He saw a grey-green streak of sea ahead as they reached the far side of the Beara peninsula. Another seven miles or so to Derryowen, he thought. He had his own GPS device, but had decided not to use it in case the inspector had a low opinion of gadgets.

'It's a tangled tale, right enough,' said O'Kelleher after a while. 'Let's hope Malden himself will be able to straighten it out for us.'

'I made three or four attempts to contact Mr Malden this morning. But his mobile phone is off, and his secretary has heard nothing from him either.'

'Nor indeed has his son Fergus. That's if he's been telling the truth to Conor Fitz.'

'Don't you think it's suspicious, inspector? Not hearing back from Malden?' Redmond thought he should make up for his earlier reticence. 'Most businessmen keep their phones on day and night, surely? It suggests to me that he may have a reason to avoid us.'

'The snag is that whether he has or he hasn't, we can hardly haul him to court for turning off his mobile phone. And Fergus Malden claims that his father has just such a habit when it suits him.' O'Kelleher smiled faintly. 'What's more, Fitz has his own particular theory on the matter.'

The young police officer glanced quickly at his passenger. He felt a stab of jealousy each time Inspector O'Kelleher referred approvingly to Castletownbere's sergeant.

'Fitz had a quiet word with a source of his earlier today, a man who knows Oscar Malden fairly well. What he learned was that our businessman friend goes incognito whenever he finds a fair maiden who'll spend a day or two under the duvet with him. And that's hardly a crime in this day and age.'

As Redmond drove into Derryowen, he noticed a signpost on the left for the hotel, down towards the sea. The village itself appeared straggly, with no real centre, unlike the picturesque multicoloured villages that adorned Beara's postcards.

He turned right at a second signpost, up a winding road that brought them to Cnoc Meala.

Redmond decided to venture another opinion before they arrived at the house. 'I suppose Mr Malden could make things difficult for us. His public image will hardly sit well with an accusation of assaulting a woman with a rock.'

'I presume you're hinting at another reputation of his – that he has friends in high political circles? And you're worried we'll come under pressure to handle him with care?' To Redmond's relief, O'Kelleher laughed softly. 'If Oscar Malden can provide us with satisfactory answers, he and his important friends will have nothing to worry about. And if not, who knows how interesting this particular job may turn out to be.'

The house at Cnoc Meala was hidden behind trees, and Redmond was halfway up the drive before it came into view. It was old-fashioned, built in a style favoured by gentry a hundred years earlier: wide stone steps up to the front door, which had imposing windows on either side of it; and ivy in autumn colours clambering on its squat two-storeyed walls. Just what foreign tourists would like, he thought.

'Blast and damnation!' Inspector O'Kelleher spoke suddenly. 'We're not the only visitors today. Pity I didn't see the fecker in time.'

A silver sports car was parked near the front door, where two people stood.

'I'm sorry, who are you talking about?'

'Jack Talbot, that's who. Look at the showy Merc over there – that's not your cheaper class of motor, I promise you.'

'I've heard his name before, but I'm not sure . . . Is he a journalist?'

'Yes, indeed, and a proud member of the nasty slimebag school of journalism at that. Surely you read the gospel he proclaims to the faithful every Sunday in his highly opinionated column?'

'So what's he doing here? If he writes for a national paper, why would he bother?'

'He has a well-appointed holiday cottage a few miles from ourselves in Bantry. I have to admit I hadn't pictured him as one of Nessa McDermott's bosom pals. But then again, she worked in the media for many years, and who knows the kind of favours given or received.'

Jack Talbot came striding towards the garda car, beaming at the occupants. O'Kelleher opened the door, unfolding his long lanky frame as he got out.

'Don't utter a word about our business here,' he said quickly. Redmond saw him arrange a smile on his face. 'Let's decipher the lay of the land first.'

'What a pleasant coincidence!' Talbot grasped O'Kelleher's hand before it had been offered. 'It's a delight to see an old friend out here in the wilds. I hope you haven't come bearing bad news?'

'I hope you're not suffering from overwork, Jack, to find yourself so far from home on a Friday afternoon?'

'Oh, don't get me started on overwork, *mon ami*. Sweat and toil is our daily lot, that's the sad truth of the matter.' Talbot clearly did a strong line in flattery. 'But meanwhile, if there's any assistance I could offer you, inspector, please say the word. The fight against crime is most certainly the concern of every decent citizen.'

Nessa McDermott waited at the front door. Redmond's internet search had also told him that she was in her mid-forties, and a native of Dublin. What he noticed immediately was the way she gesticulated vigorously as she spoke, and the spiky style of her short auburn hair.

As soon as introductions were made, she resumed a conversation she had clearly been having with Talbot. 'I appreciate your interest, Jack, but I think the best thing at this stage is to contact Oscar's public relations office.' She glanced at the two gardai with an air of unease. 'Unfortunately, I've a lot on just now.'

'I'm sure you have, my dear.' Jack gave a small tinkling laugh. 'But all the same, you and I know that real journalists don't waste our time dealing with PR types.'

He turned to O'Kelleher and Redmond, smiling graciously. 'What I have in mind, my friends, is a feel-good feature on one of our shining knights of Irish industry, to highlight his unselfish support for Ireland's niche-tourism, as demonstrated by his choice of holiday here.'

Redmond watched his senior officer carefully, appalled that McDermott and Talbot appeared to be concocting a plan to present a rosy image of Oscar Malden's stay in Beara – in a desperate attempt, presumably, to forestall bad publicity for Cnoc Meala.

'Listen, Jack, we'll discuss it anon, but I can't promise you anything.' Nessa spoke briskly, and Redmond thought she was hoping to convey distance between herself and her old colleague. 'As I said, I do appreciate the suggestions you've made.'

Nobody moved after she'd spoken, until Inspector O'Kelleher indicated to Talbot that he would like a word in his ear on a different matter. They walked off from the door, leaving Nessa and Redmond to regard each other in silence.

'I'm sorry to have delayed you,' she said then. 'I'd like to help in whatever way . . .'

Redmond thought it was best to be formal. 'We're grateful for your assistance, Mrs McDermott, and I'm sure you appreciate the need to leave the investigation in the hands of the gardai. The role of the media in such a situation . . .'

Nessa looked at him wide-eyed. She probably had that arrogant belief, all too common among journalists, that their work carried an inviolable authority.

'What I'd like to say,' continued Redmond, 'is that it hardly seems advisable to publish stories about last night's incident while the relevant facts are as yet quite unclear.'

FOUR

J ust one more day, Nessa had said to herself when she awoke in the morning. One more day of putting other people first and anticipating her guests' needs before they were even aware of them. Mostly, she relished the stimulation of having strangers under her roof, but sainthood was not on her to-do list, and by mid-September, after several months of working around the clock, fighting irritability could be a losing battle.

The day so far had certainly been flush with irritations. The only information from the hospital was that Maureen was not well enough for visitors. A morning visit to Derreen Gardens, a place Nessa usually loved to go, was overshadowed by a recurring problem with the minibus she had hired. Sal was supposed to clean the kitchen after school on Fridays, but she had been shut away in her bedroom for hours, getting ready for her night out.

And worst of all, Jack bloody Talbot. Nessa had run into him several times during her media career, but she had no time for his style of journalism. His Sunday newspaper column was full of malice and snide commentary masquerading as substance. He had also gained attention for his interviews with public figures, in which he drooled and fawned at their achievements while enlightening his lucky readers with some choice secrets he claimed to have extracted from them.

When Nessa opened the front door to him that afternoon, he reminded her of a greyhound. His face was long and thin, and he seemed to pant excitedly as he spoke. His dress was as affected as his speech: a country gentleman's tweeds set off by a cheery cravat. Becoming a star in the media circus was at the expense of his own dignity, she decided.

He had his snout in the door before she could shut it on him, full of his planned feature on Oscar Malden and the alleged benefits flowing to Cnoc Meala as a result. It did not take long for Nessa to recall a conversation with Patrick a few days earlier, about a journalist's request to interview Oscar. She had not realised then that Jack Talbot was the journalist in question, but as far as she knew, Patrick had passed on the request to Oscar and nothing had come of it.

But now here was Talbot at the door, brashly presenting his credentials. She decided instantly to stay quiet about Oscar's early departure from Beara, not to mention Maureen's episode and Dominic's accusation. The less he knew the better. But Talbot refused to drop the bone between his teeth. His photographer was down at the hotel, he sallied, and really, there was no hurry. Nothing would please him more than to relax in the delightful environs of Cnoc Meala until Oscar returned from his afternoon outing.

Nessa filled the dishwasher in the kitchen and turned it on. Damn Jack Talbot and his silky pleadings, and damn the policemen too, for arriving while he was there. She could see Jack sniffing the air for a juicy story as soon as he set eyes on them. It was a relief when the garda inspector somehow encouraged him to leave. But then off he drove at full throttle to Derryowen, knowing well that the owner of the village pub and shop, Caitlín O'Donovan, was also a stringer for a local radio station, supplying them with snippets of news. When Jack quizzed her, she had little choice but to tell him the basic facts of Maureen's accident. Caitlín was a good friend of Nessa's, and as she recounted to her afterwards, he left the pub with tail aloft, eager to ferret out further details wherever he could find them.

Nessa pulled out a sweeping brush and got to work. In September, Cnoc Meala employed a cleaner only at weekends, so she would have to do Sal's share, and wait until the morning to phone Patrick. She had texted him several times since the previous night, and was surprised to have heard nothing back. Of course, there might have been a delay between connecting flights, or maybe his mobile battery was low. But she would love to hear his calm and sensible voice, and clear up her confusion about Jack's enquiries. For example, had Patrick promised to try again to persuade Oscar to do the interview, as Jack claimed at the front door?

She was thumping the floor with the brush as she swept. She was annoyed at that young garda from Bantry station; that was another thing. Redmond Joyce must be some fool if he really thought she would try to cover up Maureen's accident with a fluffed-up feature article. The more she thought about him, the more self-righteous the young garda seemed. Boyishly handsome, for sure, but only if you were taken in by that clean-scrubbed, shiny look – the very picture of a policeman with a mission to purge the community of its sins.

Just some coffee pots to clean and table napkins to iron. Nessa's plan was to get to O'Donovan's pub by nine o'clock at the latest. Most of the remaining guests were already ensconsed, eating their evening meal and looking forward to Friday's music session, but Fergus Malden had opted to stay in bed for the evening.

'OK, tell me what you think!' Sal bounced into the kitchen in party mode. She was wearing shorts over black tights, topped by a shimmery dark green tunic on which red apples appeared to peep amid lustrous foliage. Her jet-black hair was her crowning glory, and was draped in twirly tresses interweaved with crimson ribbons.

Before Nessa got to say anything, Sal cut in again. 'Hold the negative vibes, if you don't mind.' She grinned cheekily. 'Your lovely Salomé is *so* going out on the town tonight, but the outfit only works with the right kind of energy, know what I mean?'

'The colours really suit you, I must say.' Nessa had to smile at her warm, bubbly daughter, who was indeed lovely, even if the look had taken hours to achieve. She had changed in the previous year from a diligent, almost prim schoolgirl to an exuberant teenager intent on making up for lost time. She usually disdained her full name, Salomé, which had been chosen for her by her African grandmother, but perhaps it suited her newfound craving for pleasure.

'So will your hairdo stay in place, or does that take more—?'

'Careful! You're about to say it, aren't you? That I've already spent *way* too much time upstairs? But you see, if I rushed the *GHD* appliance on my hair, the results would be seriously tragic!'

'And what about getting a lift home from the party?'

'Everything is under control, like I told you already. Darina will be driving us there in her bockety old van, which means she'll get me home too, so what could be simpler? It's not exactly the coolest carriage for a hot thing like me, mind you, but the point is that Darina won't be drinking, so you can delete that particular worry from your list.' Sal spoke to her reflection, examining her hair in a handheld mirror. 'And by the way, it's just possible that we'll be a teensy bit later than midnight, so don't stress yourself out by sitting up late, OK?'

Sal's flurry of chatter told Nessa what she already suspected, that her daughter's hopes for the party involved an attractive young man. She could only hope that Sal would fail in her pursuit, as she had heard rumours of who the likely target was.

His name was Marcus and she had seen him hanging out in the village. Tall, with long dark hair combed onto his face, he had lived in Spain for a few years, where his parents' property investments had reportedly gone bad. Since his return, he had taken over the family's hackney service, and was also managing some holiday cottages they owned near Derryowen. Nessa had booked his taxi for guests a few times but had not been impressed by his casual air. Caitlín O'Donovan had also told her he liked to flash his money in the pub, so encouraging Sal to stew over her books would hardly be his style.

But Nessa decided it was too soon to say anything about him. She wiped the last coffee pot and put aside the ironing till early morning. She was famished at the thought of the dish of spicy lamb awaiting her in the pub. And if Caitlín got a break from serving at O'Donovan's bar, she would listen sympathetically to her worries.

Sal called her out to the hall when Darina arrived. Their neighbour's style of dress contrasted sharply with Sal's – vintage clothing in flowing layers, complete with a long scarf and gypsy earrings. She handed a card to Nessa as well as a box of eggs for the guests' breakfast, freshly laid by the hens she kept. Darina had grown up in Cork city, but she fitted in well with the hippy image still to be found in parts of west Cork. She also worked extremely hard, however, and if she and Sal got on so well, maybe she would infect Sal with her dedication and cancel out whatever malign influence Marcus might exert.

As Nessa waved them off she heard the house phone. She winced as she recognised Jack Talbot's smooth tones on the answering machine.

'I was disappointed in you today, Nessa. I offered you the sort of publicity that money can't buy, or certainly not your sort of money. But now I hear your VIP guest has fled home to Tipperary, and that a poor woman is lying injured in hospital. Needless to say, I have a duty to keep my readers informed on these matters. *Au revoir, ma chérie!*'

It was a sly threat, probably aimed at extracting more information from her. Nessa suppressed her anger and decided not to grace his message with a response. Jack probably had Oscar's mobile number – no doubt they crossed each other's paths at the celebrity events they both frequented in Dublin. It was quite likely that Oscar had already refused to do the interview, and that Jack's purpose at Cnoc Meala had been to waylay him in person.

Nessa picked up the card Darina had given her for Fergus. Getting Oscar's patronage would be a great coup for her, even if she and Fergus matched each other in their apologetic conversation about it. Darina had done a drawing in fluid ink on both sides of the card, to advertise her style of work to Oscar – on one side, a close-up profile of him, probably designed to flatter his vanity, and on the other, an impression of Beara's dramatic mountain scenery, with a standing stone in the foreground, one of the innumerable monuments to life and death long ago that were dotted all over the area. Nessa studied it for a moment, and felt a surge of pride in the wonderful peninsula she had made her home. She would stand firm against insinuations and the fear of criticism. Cnoc Meala was a good business, offering its visitors a genuine cultural experience, including hill walks, archeology, garden visits, food and contemporary art. Whatever mischievous garbage Jack might write would be forgotten in a week or two.

Twenty to nine, time to join the outside world. The house was so quiet that Nessa could hear each hollow tick of the old wooden clock in the hall. Ronan was staying overnight with one of his school pals, so the usual hum of television and computer games was missing. She was unused to being on her own indoors.

She heard a creaking noise – most likely a window somewhere in the house. In Dublin, she had always locked each window before going out, but in the country it was different.

She had just left the eggs in the kitchen when she heard it a second time. A sharp creak that continued three or four seconds, coming from the guests' sitting room. One of the double doors to the garden must have been left open. She went in, reaching for the light switch on the wall. And then she froze.

Somebody else was in the room, she was absolutely certain of it. The room was dark but she felt a presence close by.

Time stopped as she stood immobile, her hand glued to the wall. She got a whiff of something unpleasant but her mind was unable to make sense of it.

Then she heard again the sound that had drawn her in, a whine from one of the double doors shifting in the breeze. The night's damp air was on her skin. She awoke from a trance of fear and slammed her fist on the switch, lighting up the room in a white glare.

Her heart almost stopped for a second time. She could see nobody.

'Who the hell are you?' She shouted out loud, fear quenched by the light. 'I'll call the gardai!'

A man bore down on her from behind the door, heavy and roundbellied. It was Dominic.

'Don't you threaten me with the guards,' he said, 'or you'll be sorry you ever opened your mouth.' He grabbed her elbow and a sickly smell filled her nostrils, a mixture of alcohol and sweaty armpits.

'Guards this and fuckin' guards that!' His face twisted into a smile. 'Tell me something now, before you run along to your bullyboy friends.' His eyes bulged as he spat out the words. 'Why bother being nice and helpful when smarmy superintendents and their lackeys don't believe a single word you tell them?'

Dominic was pushing against her. She had dealt with drunken guests a few times before, but nothing like this. Drops of his spittle hit her face.

'Oh yes, I can spot their little game a mile away. Blame the husband, that's the fuckin' answer every time, isn't it? They think I landed my own wife in hospital, but they won't say it out straight. So maybe you'll answer me this if you can – why would I hurt Maureen, when I'm the one who has to protect her from other men?'

Dominic's words slowed to a halt. Breathing loudly, he stared at Nessa. His eyes were clamped on her breasts, their shape hardly concealed by her light shirt.

'Oscar loverboy Malden, he's the man of the moment, isn't he?' Dominic leered. 'I'm sure you fancy him yourself, just like all the women? You'd like a rub of his paws on your lovely paps, fuckin' sure you would.'

Nessa couldn't breathe. His eyes sucked and devoured her. She felt suffocated, helpless, empty.

He laughed out loud all of a sudden. Then he stepped back unsteadily, still keeping his grip on her arm.

'You think I'm going to seize my chance, lady, now that the two of us are nice and cosy here together?' He scanned her body up and down. 'Just like your garda buddies, you believe the very worst about me, isn't that it?'

He licked his lips, his tongue moving slowly. His hand reached towards her neck.

'Get out of here, right now!' The words exploded from Nessa at last. She pushed Dominic's bulky weight away from her.

'Don't you touch me again! Don't you dare!' She tried to focus her shattered thoughts but random images floated into her mind. His face was pale and soft, like a plate of mushy rice. His lips were strips of fatty meat.

'I'm not alone,' she heard herself say. 'One of the visitors is here in the house.' She was afraid to name Fergus in case it set off another rant. 'I'm going to call out to him now . . .'

Dominic backed away from her, and sat down on the sofa with a bump. His expression turned sulky. 'All I wanted was my bag. Just to collect my bag from my room.' He darted a glance at her. 'You took me by surprise, coming into the room in the dark.'

'You could have knocked on the front door, that's what everyone else does. It's no excuse – no excuse at all for what you did just now.'

Nessa held her arms across her chest to hide her shaking

from him. If she bolted, he could follow her. Why had she let him know there was only one visitor in the house? She did not really believe Fergus would hear her call out. His room was on the ground floor, but a long way from the hall.

Dominic was muttering from the sofa. 'You wouldn't understand . . . I'd say you've always had a grand easy life . . .'

Nessa kept her eyes on him. If only she had her mobile in her pocket, she could phone Caitlín, or her nearest neighbour down the road. Five or ten minutes at the most, for someone to arrive.

'I can tell the type you are, you and your fine African fella, living it up in this big house.' Dominic's voice rose as he pursued a new train of thought. 'There's one word the likes of you wouldn't understand – it's a dirty, mean little word that gets you no respect in this world.' His lower lip jutted out in self-pity. 'Failure, that's the word I'm talking about. You see, I'd hoped to achieve something in my life, did I mention that during the week, when we were all so nice and pally together?'

Nessa shook her head, pretending to listen to him. As long as he stayed put on the sofa, she could figure out what to do and take back the control she had lost in her own house.

'Oh, yes, I had high hopes at one time, stupid fool that I was. I set up my own enterprises – dancehalls and bingo and what have you, music and bloody dancing to keep everyone happy. I tried to make it in business but where did it get me, that's the question. And the answer is, nowhere at all, because you see, I didn't have the right contacts, not the sort your friend Oscar has. I never learned the *plámás* talk that gets you places in this rotten crummy country . . .'

Nessa remembered she had two keys in her pocket. If Dominic attacked her again, she could jab him under the chin with her keys. She took a step towards the door.

'That's how it went,' he continued, 'and now I'm a laughing stock wherever I go! No proper job and no pitter-patter of children either, which was most likely my fault too. Nothing at all to show for my stupid sorry life.' Dominic was talking to himself now. 'But what's your problem, Dominic? Didn't Maureen swoop the pot of gold in the Lotto, and wasn't that the answer to everything? She was able to buy us a fine old public house, where the pair of us can drink our days away. Our own best bloody customers, and the whole town sneering at us!'

He looked up at Nessa, his eyes focussing on her again. She gripped the doorhandle. She could lock herself in the kitchen until help arrived.

'So then we come here for a bit of a break, but it's the usual story, everybody tittering behind their hands at us.' Dominic swayed onto his feet, his lips wet with spittle. He dug into one of his trouser pockets. 'A smug little group of people, they are, and your oh-so-polite husband, not to forget Oscar the ladies' darling . . .'

'Sit down . . .' Nessa swallowed the words as she said them. Dominic held a pocket knife in his hand and opened it with a quick flick.

'Now, here's a thing you weren't expecting, eh? Dominic's had enough of being a nice boy to everyone, d'you get me? He's sick of people making fun of him, that's his little problem.' Nessa stood petrified, her eyes fixed on the shiny blade turning to and fro. 'You pay attention to me, Lady Muck, for a change.' Dominic's voice sharpened. 'You still don't believe that Oscar got his hands on Maureen, do you?'

Nessa heard a footstep in the hall. She forced herself to look at Dominic's face instead of the knife. Willpower was her only defence. Even if Fergus was outside the door, she could not rely on him to save her.

'I'm the *amadán* that said we should come on holidays here, same place we came when I was a child. My mother was from Beara, did I tell you that?' Dominic shifted his weight and fell back on the arm of the sofa, his lower lip quivering again. 'But even here I couldn't get away from my old enemies. Failure and despair – they're the boys that lie in wait for me wherever I go, so now it's time for me to face up to them for once and all.'

He opened out his palm and placed the tip of the blade on his skin. Nessa watched as a bright red drop of blood spread from its centre. When Dominic turned his eyes to her again, they were filled with loathing.

FIVE

Redmond had a day off work but the last thing he wanted was to hang around at home. He could not stand solitary idleness, as he had long ago realised. So he had just spent an hour in the hotel gym close to the garda station, and was wondering whether to continue his workout in the station's own fine facility, or to pass an hour in the hotel pool. But either way, he would have nothing to do by lunchtime.

He was tempted to sidle in to his desk in the station, as he often did in his spare time. The snag was that his colleagues had begun to joke about it. On Thursday evening, he had been lingering late at his desk when the call about Maureen Scurlock came in – and next morning, he overheard sniggering voices while he was closeted in one of the station toilets. 'The country would be rid of the scourge of crime,' said one, 'if we were all as diligent as Garda Redmond Joyce!' 'No doubt about it,' said the other, 'and the buckos in government would be over the moon, with all the fuckin' overtime money they'd save!'

Redmond drained the last of his takeaway coffee, bought in the shop next door to the station. The cashier had asked him whether he was on his way to Castletownbere port, where a big crowd was expected at a protest that afternoon. News bulletins had reported that the owners of the Russian ship were bankrupt and would not pay their employees. The controversy was hotting up, with calls for action and negotiation, while the men on board relied on food donated by local people.

Redmond told himself he had a great excuse to go into work, as Inspector O'Kelleher might well need extra gardai for the protest. It would make a change from the usual duties: complaints about pub licences, late-night fights between local youths, and the repeated full-colour, close-up horror of road accidents. All of them reminders, to Redmond's mind, of the country's collective addiction to alcohol.

He kept his back to the station while he made up his mind. It was a sunny morning and he had a fine view of the Beara peninsula's vigorous spine of mountains on the far side of Bantry Bay, but a day's rambling on his own was definitely not on his agenda. He reminded himself that he had genuine work to do, making phone calls about the Derryowen incident two days earlier. Fergus Malden had booked a taxi for two o'clock on Thursday, to drive his father home to Tipperary; but Fergus also said that Oscar had contacted him at the last minute to cancel the booking. Redmond was trying to track down the taxi driver, having failed so far to make contact with Oscar Malden himself.

He had googled the businessman on the internet and found plenty of photographs, showing a man with clear, even features and a wide smile. His light-coloured hair was turning grey, but it was that attractive silvery grey that wealthy people always achieved. According to one Sunday newspaper, he was ranked at number sixty-eight on Ireland's rich list, and was lauded by politicians and pundits alike for his entrepreneurial spirit. He had made his money on security installations such as electronic gates for apartment blocks, and then countered recessionary losses by expanding his business interests in Russia and the Middle East. He was also highly regarded as a patron of contemporary art and music, and known for persuasive public commentary on cultural issues. Hardly the type to do a runner after assaulting a helpless woman on a remote laneway, as most gardai in the station agreed.

Redmond crumpled his takeaway cup in a bin, and crossed the edge of Bantry's attractive main square to the police station. He squared his shoulders as he pushed open the door. Just inside, Trevor O'Kelleher was in conversation with the district superintendent.

'I've ten lads down in Castletown already,' said the inspector to his superior, 'and I've others getting ready to join them. This caper could go on until nightfall.'

The young garda managed to catch O'Kelleher's eye. He reckoned he was in with a chance.

'Redmond, good man yourself,' said O'Kelleher. 'I've been

looking around for someone to follow up a call that just came in.'

The inspector stepped away from the superintendent and spoke rapidly to Redmond. 'It's a bit of a nuisance, to be honest. Something about a dead animal on a roadside over in Beara, getting in the way of motorists. We'll have to find out who dumped it and follow up on the legalities. I believe it's somewhere near Adrigole, but you'll get all the details over at reception.'

Redmond got caught in traffic in Glengarriff, a popular tourist town twelve miles west of Bantry and a gateway to the Beara peninsula, which stretched another thirty miles out into the Atlantic. A few coach buses had stopped to disgorge their passengers to the craft shops, and Redmond cursed as he waited. He would have been better off at home than searching for a dead sheep in the mountains. He was damned sure that Dublin-based gardai did not spend their time on such pursuits.

He smoothed down his hair and grimaced at his reflection in the rear-view mirror. He had always resented his baby-face looks, with the soft skin of a child – they made it so much harder for him to be taken seriously, he felt. Indeed, most people assumed that he had joined the gardai after leaving school or college, and had no idea he was already into his thirties, having worked in computing for several dreary years. His worry now was that he had made a mistake moving to Bantry, instead of applying for a city posting.

During his garda training, what he had loved most was the period of three months he spent in a suburban station in Dublin. Much of his time was taken up with routine jobs, but he also got a glimpse of a different and enormously exciting world: officers on tenterhooks as they played a deadly game of hide-and-seek with local drug gangs who were forever on the ready to execute anyone looking sideways at them, and garda camaraderie intensified in the glare of fear and danger. Redmond had often fantasised about that world since then, and how it would cater to his own addiction to a drug freely and legally available – adrenaline, the wonderful buzz brought on by constant stress and pressure.

But he knew that his innate caution meant he was not a natural candidate for such a life, and feared that jumping in at the deep end would expose his pathetic limitations. Meanwhile, Bantry station had advantages over most small-town postings. As a district headquarters staffed by about thirty officers, its brief went well beyond the humdrum. And the southwest coast of Ireland, notched as it was by innumerable remote inlets, was on the front line in the long war on illegal drugs. Boats laden with toxic packages made forays to shore, all part of a multibillion trade controlled from South America, Spain and Amsterdam. Sooner or later, Redmond would get the kind of investigative experience that would bolster his chances of getting his dream job in the future.

He told himself that he should make the most of his time in Bantry. The golf clubs he carried in the boot of the car were not going to get used, he realised that by now. But as he neared Adrigole village, he noticed a signpost to a sailing centre. He could call in on his way back – enrolling for a new activity had to be better than living in fear of his free time, and being superfit could earn him extra points with those who noticed such things.

His mobile phone beeped with a new text message and he stopped by the seashore to read it. It was from Sergeant Fitzmaurice, about a disturbance involving Dominic Scurlock at Cnoc Meala the night before. Redmond smiled as he texted back that he would be in Castletownbere in an hour or so. Once he had sorted out the roadside carcass, he could meet the sergeant and see the quayside protest as a bonus.

His satnav directed him to turn right towards the famous Healy Pass road that crossed the craggy middle of the peninsula. Houses and trees petered out a short distance inland. The sun went in, and soon he was surrounded by stony mountains and gathering clouds. His spirits sagged at the bleakness of the place – a nightmare vision of emptiness, he thought. His car seemed tiny and insignificant, like a beetle scuttling across the floor of a cave.

He could imagine the mountain valley as a location for a horror film, devoid of humans and over run by monsters tearing up the landscape, wrenching bare purple-grey stones out of the depths of the earth and hurling them all over the hills.

'Be careful! We were afraid to go down.'

Three or four people stood at an old stone bridge over a

wide stream, their cars parked nearby. The road continued up to the mountain pass high above them.

As he approached, Redmond realised that the dead animal was not at the side of the road. It was lying on rough grass by the stream, wrapped in a black plastic bag. The air was filled with the squawking of gulls, but several other birds were tearing at the bag itself. Redmond knew little about nature but thought they could be rooks or hooded crows. They pulled at the plastic with their powerful beaks, all the while beating their wings to keep the gulls away from their booty.

'We'll have to phone the police.' One of the watching group pulled out his mobile as he said it. 'I don't believe that's a dead sheep or a dog down there.'

Redmond understood instantly. The awful contents of the bag were being revealed as the birds tore it to ribbons.

He called out to the other people that he was a garda, as he ran to his car and pulled out the golf clubs from the boot. After handing them around, he jumped over a low wall by the roadside and down the steep slope to the bank of the stream. He waved his own club at the birds to scare them off.

He had no idea whether the birds would attack him. But they had to be driven away and the scene secured. Another man was trying urgently to get through to the Garda station. Whoever had made the original call had not understood or explained the situation.

The birds backed off gradually. One of them scraped Redmond's head with its claws but he ignored the pain. He was fighting off the nausea that assailed him as soon as he looked properly at the heap on the ground.

One leg was splayed sideways. A shoe was falling off at the ankle and the skin was exposed above a piece of ragged sock. The birds had torn into the flesh, pulling away at the trouser leg to get at their prey. In another half an hour they would have destroyed the body.

Redmond finally allowed his eyes to focus on the most awful sight of all. A bloodied hand was turned up to the sky, as if begging for mercy.

SIX

T he place was dark. A basement, maybe, or an underground den. Windowless and dark, apart from a faint light far above Nessa's head. There were steps spiralling up towards the light.

She was surprised she could make out her own hand in the darkness. She opened her palm and saw a drop of blood at its centre. The blood was a bright red colour.

She felt a knot in her stomach, a tight knot of fear. The staircase was steep and her feet were tired, so very tired. She tried to trudge up the steps but she was afraid every minute of slipping down into the blackness.

She suddenly realised that she was not alone. It was the smell she recognised, that sickly smell of stale alcohol and sweaty skin. She could not see Dominic but she knew he was there.

Then she heard a laugh. Jack Talbot was chuckling over a newspaper article he thrust out in front of her.

It was his laugh that made Nessa realise she was dreaming. She was trapped in a nightmare, down in the depths of her own mind. The laugh began to change and now she heard Dominic's self-pitying tones. His face followed her into the cold light of awakening.

She lay rigidly still, hoping the tight lump in her stomach would ease. She wished she could turn to her husband's comforting touch, but a chilly emptiness had taken his place.

The room was dark but Nessa remembered that several hours of daylight had already passed. She had been up earlier to serve breakfast to the guests, to deal with their bills as they checked out, to nod at their concerned farewells. It seemed to her now that someone else had been acting her part all morning. She had slept so little during the night that arranging eggs on plates had been a trial of endurance. Just as well that her son Ronan was still at his friend's house, or she would have had to put on a false smile for him too.

She was glad too that she had drifted off when she finally made it back to bed. An hour of dozing uneasily allowed her to escape Dominic's lingering smell for a time, before he caught up with her in her dreams. She had stood in the shower for a long time earlier but felt she could not wash him off her. Her skin prickled under the duvet as his image loomed over her again, eyes bulging and belly pushing against her as he got ready to rape her.

She turned her face into her pillow as if that would get rid of him. She could not make sense of what had happened. Her friends would have described her as tough, determined, indeed bolshie at times, and she had always assumed that she could rely on those traits to get her out of trouble, even while she valued her softer side in her own mind. She should have been able to throw Dominic out of the house instead of standing there under his malign spell, immobilized and weak, at his mercy as he twirled the glinting knife in front of her.

And then Fergus Malden came into the room. He looked bewildered but his arrival was enough to make Dominic beat a retreat to the garden. Nessa shouted at Fergus to shut the French windows, after which they rushed around the house in a frenzy of locking doors and windows. It was only when Fergus told her that Dominic's dark blue BMW was no longer outside that she attempted an explanation. By then, neighbours had also arrived and the evening became another blur of phone calls and half-conversations.

As far as she understood, a garda from Castletownbere caught up with Dominic somewhere between Adrigole and Glengarriff, about an hour after he fled the house. He was breathalysed but she was unsure of what happened after that. In the morning, however, she got a message from Bantry to say that Maureen was being transferred to Cork's Regional Hospital for a brain scan, and that her husband was making his way to the city too.

Nessa lay hunched in the darkness, wishing she could obliterate every impression left by Dominic. She knew she should get up and distract herself, but even when she heard her phone ring, she stayed under the bedclothes. Her limbs felt heavy and useless, as if she had been flattened by a falling boulder.

Just as the ringing stopped, she sat up in fright and grabbed the phone. It could be Patrick trying to get through. She had tried over and over to contact him the night before, but all she got were the same shrill beeps in her ears.

It was not Patrick's name on the screen, however, but Caitlín O'Donovan's. Her friend had phoned earlier in the morning, to reassure her that she would stay a few nights at Cnoc Meala once the guests had gone, if that would help. Nessa decided to wait a while to phone her back this time, until she had doused herself in the shower and swallowed a cup of tea. She would also have to find a few phone numbers for Patrick's cousins in Malawi, to get a message to him. He must have arrived by now, even if every airport en route was on strike. She wanted so much to hear his quiet voice, telling her he would be home soon.

Then they would have to make a decision about Dominic. As Sergeant Fitzmaurice had explained, the gardai could not investigate his actions without an official complaint from her. They would certainly keep an eye on Dominic, but could not bring him in without his consent unless she made a statement, which the sergeant encouraged her to consider. The problem was the dilemma this would involve: how would it play in the local media, for a start, if she stood up in court and swore that one of her guests had assaulted her, but was not believed by the jury? What marks had she to show for the terror she felt as Dominic breathed into her face? Suppose Jack Talbot decided to take a sniggering pleasure in her distress?

Caitlín mentioned to her earlier that Jack had an article about Cnoc Meala in the morning's paper. It's a ridiculous scribble, she said, and I wouldn't wipe my dog's backside with it, so I was in two minds whether to say a word about it at all. But I've opened my big mouth now and maybe fore-warned is forearmed.

Caitlín tried to retreat from the subject then, but Nessa made her say what Jack's headline was. On a normal day, they might have laughed out loud about it. 'Hubby awol as hols awry' was his paper's poetic effort for the day, and as Caitlín read out the piece to her, Nessa realised that the journalist still knew nothing about Dominic's accusation against Oscar. All he had was a minor tale of a holiday mishap sauced up with some innuendo, and printed in a corner of an inside page. Nessa felt more relieved than angry as she listened to Caitlín, but she was afraid that Talbot would pounce if he sniffed another opportunity.

She slid down the pillow and pulled the duvet over her. The guests had departed after breakfast, but her rosy idea of a restful weekend had disappeared too. Another ten minutes, she told herself, and she would do her best to trudge up those steep steps out of the darkness.

It was no wonder, really, that breakfast time had been such an endurance. Soon after Caitlín's phone call, Sal had arrived home. The night before, Nessa had made frantic efforts to phone her in case Dominic was still lurking in the vicinity when she and Darina returned from the party. But Sal did not answer in person, and instead, sent two brief texts. The first was probably meant to be reassuring: 'Fine, got msg, no worries'. The second, dispatched after midnight, announced a change of plan: 'Dar left way too early, gr8 buzz, best me stay here 2nite'.

Nessa waylaid her in the hall before she disappeared upstairs. She knew it was a bad time to have a row, but the words came out sharply all the same.

'What do you think you were up to last night? First you promise to come home with Darina, then you pull a fast one and wait as late as possible before you tell me—'

'It wasn't my fault! I didn't know Darina was going to do a Cinderella act and disappear just when things were warming up nicely.'

Nessa noticed the little smile her daughter allowed herself. 'Darina is shyer than you are, Sal, so I hope you didn't abandon her at the party? I assumed you'd both agree on a time to leave . . .'

'And maybe we did agree, but Darina changed her mind – did that occur to you? I mean, just because she's obsessed with her art and wants to do nothing else all weekend, you want *me* to be a party pooper.' Sal gave another infuriating glimmer of a smile. 'Besides which, if Dominic went loopy last night like you said in your messages, I thought you'd prefer me to stay away. So when you think about it, I was doing us all a favour.'

Nessa decided to give up on the argument until the family had the house to themselves. Fergus Malden was hovering to ask her something, her French guests wanted advice on the most scenic route to Gougane Barra, and the two sisters, Zoe and Stella, had just gone into the dining room. Already, Nessa could hear Zoe declaiming loudly that she was going to Castletownbere to join a protest against the owners of the abandoned Russian ship. She gritted her teeth as she approached their table with a choice of tea or coffee.

'Did you hear the argument I had the other day about those poor sailors?' Zoe turned from her sister to address Nessa. 'I had an argument with Oscar Malden, on Tuesday or maybe Wednesday.'

Nessa smiled as best she could. Zoe was an energetic young woman with an inexhaustible supply of views on many subjects. Nessa liked her greatly at first, but by midweek she felt weary of her. The problem with Zoe was that she never tired of her own opinions.

'I said it was scandalous to allow ships whose workers are treated like slaves into our ports. We should ban them, I said to Oscar – but guess what he said back to me?'

Nessa waited, aware of the glow of conviction in Zoe's eyes. She was a community worker in Dublin's inner city, and also seemed to be involved in other campaigns.

'He said that if morality was the guiding force in world trade, we'd all be as penniless as the Russian crew. Do you not realise, he said smugly, that our happy lifestyle in Ireland depends on the sweat of millions of other people? Can you actually believe he joked about that?'

'Oscar was trying to wind you up,' said Stella. Her voice was very quiet and Nessa thought that she too might be weary of the rhetoric. She was as understated as Zoe was boisterous. The two were half-sisters and had first met only six months previously. Stella was adopted as a baby and grew up in England, and Zoe was the one to track her down when she learned about their mother's first baby, born when she was single and facing the harsh condemnation that inevitably followed in that era. Not surprisingly, Zoe had a store of strong opinions on adoption issues too.

'Really, we should leave Oscar be,' Stella added more firmly. 'We're not likely to see him again, after all.'

But Zoe was not inclined to let go easily. She continued declaiming as Nessa made her escape to the kitchen. 'I'm damned sure he didn't get rich without hurting people along the way. But there he is up on a pedestal while the rest of us are supposed to bow our heads in admiration!'

Nessa closed the kitchen door, as if to shield herself against a winter's gale. She felt a turmoil of shock, anger and shame welling up in her since Dominic's assault and the events that preceded it. But at least she had managed to play things down among the guests. All she needed was for Zoe to denounce Dominic as well as Oscar from the rooftops of Castletownbere, and the world would conclude that Cnoc Meala was a place to avoid.

It was almost two o'clock by the time she was up for the second time that day, sitting at the kitchen table cradling a cup of strong tea. She was about to make her phone calls when she heard a knock on the window. She opened the door to Caitlín, and knew immediately that her friend had come with bad news.

'I'm sorry, I was going to phone you back soon. I just didn't—'

'Don't mind that now, I've come to tell you how very sorry I am.' Caitlín took her hand and led her back to the table. She was a large soft-featured woman, and settled herself slowly into a chair beside her.

'I wanted you to hear it from me first, you see, before the guards arrive to tell you.' Caitlín's voice was unsteady. 'I heard it from a friend of a friend who works at Bantry station. There's no official news yet, of course.'

'How do you mean, official news?'

'A posse of guards have been up near the Healy Pass for over an hour, and my contact is one of them.'

'I'm not sure I follow you, Caitlín. Why the Healy Pass?' Nessa was colluding with her friend's roundabout style of speech. Someone had died, she understood that much only too well, but she longed to postpone the details for another while.

'He was found near a little bridge, halfway up to the pass.' The women's eyes met and in that instant Nessa realised that they must be talking about Patrick. She had not heard from him for two days and had no confirmation of his arrival in Malawi. She bowed her head and squeezed her eyes shut. A blade of pain cut deeply into her stomach.

'He was . . . His body was found in a bag, God help us all,' said Caitlín. 'And as I say, there'll be nothing said officially until he's been identified, so that's why—'

Nessa gazed at her. Was Caitlín unable to say her husband's name? And what could she possibly mean about him being found in a bag?

'My friend's friend recognised him straightaway, and because he was one of your guests last week . . .'

It took a few seconds for Nessa to register the words just spoken. She almost cried out with relief, and had to hold on to Caitlín to steady herself.

'Oh, I'm so sorry, I don't mean, but I just thought . . .' She pulled herself away from Caitlín's shoulder and their eyes met once again.

'The guards had been trying to contact him since Thursday night, hadn't they?' Caitlín's voice had faded to a whisper. 'It's Oscar Malden, that's who they've found. He was strangled, may God have mercy on him.'

SEVEN

Saturday 19 September, 6.00 p.m.

The room was buzzing. Twenty-five, thirty people, huddled in groups, voices sharpened by the task they faced. Rumours abounding from the scene of the crime, strong opinions on all sides. Redmond was having an argument about the period of time between a person's death and the smell of decay from the corpse. Twenty-four hours, a colleague said. Up to three days, Redmond countered. Both gave examples to prove their case. Neither admitted aloud that this would be their first experience of a murder investigation.

Three senior garda officers walked in. Chairs were shuffled and the hubbub died down.

An air of solemnity settled over the room. A violent death, and a man's body tossed by a stream like a fox or a rat. The social order of a peaceful community shattered. And of course, the hunt for the perpetrator could make or unmake careers. Murder was thankfully rare in the area, but now the incident room at Bantry station was the investigation's command centre.

While Redmond shared in his colleagues' solemnity, he was aware of other feelings too. Pride at being the first garda to lay eyes on the corpse, and silent rejoicing at the prospect of doing important work at last. Anxious thoughts, too, about which tasks he would be allotted, and how well he might prove his abilities.

Tim Devane, Garda Superintendent in Bantry, was introducing his own superiors, the chief superintendent from the divisional headquarters in Bandon and the assistant commissioner for the southern region. All three were acutely conscious that the eyes of the country were on their patch.

'You're all very welcome here in Bantry this evening,' said Devane. His delivery was as solid and heavy as his appearance. 'A grave burden has fallen on us, as we understand only too well.'

Redmond sat back in his chair. No matter how urgent the work, the super would take his time making a speech.

'I'd like to mention some people who have joined us from outside our own ranks in Bantry. The investigating team will include several uniformed and detective members from Bandon, as well as two officers from Castletownbere station. We'll also be assisted by two colleagues from the County Kerry area of the Beara peninsula, who will coordinate with us on local interviews and other matters. In addition, three detectives have just arrived from the National Criminal Investigations Bureau up in Dublin.'

Devane paused, as if to allow everyone to ponder his or her status in the scheme of things. He had spent some years as a detective superintendent in the National Bureau in Dublin himself, as far as Redmond knew. 'I have been asked to lead the investigation,' he confirmed then. 'You will all receive a handout shortly, detailing your immediate tasks. Needless to say, everyone's contribution is of great importance, regardless of your experience.'

'The deputy state pathologist is still at the scene, along with forensic staff from the Technical Bureau. We will receive their official reports as soon as possible, and meanwhile, I'd like to set out a number of points.'

At last he was going to state the bald facts of the murder. Redmond noticed that many of his colleagues sat with heads bent as if in church, listening dutifully to the teachings of their pastor.

'As you've all heard, the body was found in a plastic bag. A double layer of bags, to be precise, of the type used for garden waste. The bag seems to have been thrown from the bridge some hours before it was found earlier today.'

Redmond kept his eyes on the top table. He would love to hear his own name mentioned publicly but that might be expecting too much.

'We've indications, however, that the murder took place up to a day or two before the bag was disposed of. There were clear marks of strangulation on the victim's neck, but so far, there's no evidence that he tried to fight off his attacker. Blood tests will be required, of course, to establish whether alcohol or another substance might have hindered him.'

Devane sipped slowly from a glass of water, allowing silence to hover over the gathering. Redmond felt a tense prickling on his skin. He could hardly hope, really, that Devane would single him out for public praise.

'The name of the victim is known to you all by now, and will be released officially on this evening's television news. Oscar Malden was a middle-aged man habitually resident in County Tipperary. He had been divorced from his wife for some years. They had one son, Fergus, aged twenty-three, who had come on holiday to Beara with his father. We brought Fergus to the scene a short time ago, to do the necessary identification.'

Devane wiped his temples with a handkerchief. A rumour had circulated that Fergus Malden collapsed when he saw the body. No surprise, in Redmond's view, when he remembered the awful sight by the rocky stream.

'Oscar Malden.' Devane repeated the name with slow deliberation, and Redmond imagined it carved on a headstone in large letters. 'He was a man who had achieved a significant measure of fame amongst the public, and therefore we can expect that his tragic death will attract great attention. The public will demand answers, as well they ought in all cases of murder. And media people will arrive in our midst who will probe for answers in a civil and reasonable manner.'

Devane looked around the room, his face hard and unsmiling, his voice building momentum like a train. 'But let's be in no doubt about something else that's about to happen. A pack of wolves are on their way to west Cork at this moment, dressed up in the ordinary garb of humanity and calling themselves journalists. They'll be in the grip of a ferocious hunger for stories, and will stop at nothing in their quest for satisfaction.'

Devane paused and a man seated near the front put up his hand, in which he held a newspaper. He was a detective sergeant from Bandon.

'With your permission, sir,' he said. 'I'm sure you've seen Jack Talbot's story today in which he describes problems at the guesthouse where Malden was on holiday. Do you think Talbot could have had a tip-off that Malden was in danger, or that there's any connection between his early departure from the guesthouse and injuries sustained by a female guest he had become friendly with?'

'I'm afraid you're jumping ahead of me with your specula-
tions, sergeant,' said Devane drily. Redmond heard mutterings
around him about lick-arses who were always first to ask
questions. 'Mind the colour of your tongue,' someone whispered loudly.

Devane gazed around sternly. 'I'd like to remind you all of
an important point. Two officers from the Garda Press Office
are on their way to Bantry tonight, to deal with each and every
communication with the media, whether it's reaction to gossip
such as that raised by my good friend the sergeant, or the
progress of our inquiries, or the precise hour at which we expect
a shower of rain to fall on our heads.' His words were like
bursts of machine-gun fire. 'So don't let me hear of a gang of
gardai making merry in the same hotel bar as the media mob,
or some innocent eejit among you falling for an attractive
television presenter's *plámás*.'

Heads were bent on all sides again. 'If as much as a hint
reaches my office that one of you has mishandled a piece of
information, or been careless in any other way in the course
of this job, believe you me that you will be banished out to
the wilds of the Fastnet Rock and left there to wail and cry
with the seabirds.'

Trevor O'Kelleher gave the meeting a summary of Maureen
Scurlock's incident on the hillside and all that had followed.
He checked a sheaf of notes in his hand from time to time.

'I'd like to draw your attention to a few specific points,' he
said. 'Oscar Malden came on a week's holiday to Beara, but
as you've already heard, he decided to leave last Thursday,
two days early. However, in spite of telling Nessa McDermott
that a business problem had cropped up, he showed no great
urgency about travelling home. We know, for example, that
he spent Thursday morning strolling along the coast and
drinking coffee in Derryowen Hotel, and then set off on another
walk around midday.'

O'Kelleher spoke in his usual measured way. His voice was
quiet but could be heard clearly all over the room. Redmond
envied his confidence.

'So we've to ask ourselves whether there was a particular

reason for Malden's delayed departure on Thursday. We also have to find out more about his travel arrangements from Beara to Tipperary. Fergus Malden received a text from his father at lunchtime, telling him to cancel the taxi he had booked for him. Oscar mentioned a change of plan in the text, and said he would get a lift instead. So we have to find out what brought about his change of plan, and who else was involved.'

O'Kelleher glanced at his notes. 'Malden's mobile phone hasn't yet been found, but of course we'll be trawling for evidence of its signals, and searching every ditch in Beara for it if necessary, as it will provide us with crucial information on calls he received and internet connections he may have made. But even without his phone, the texts he sent to his son's phone should give us valuable pointers. We'll also examine all of the phone companies' records to establish who was in contact with whom, and at what precise times. We can confirm however, that we've identified and ruled out the tourist whose call led us to Oscar's body.'

Sergeant Fitzmaurice put his hand up, and O'Kelleher and Devane signalled that they would take his question.

'I understand fully,' said Fitzmaurice, 'that we're obliged to delve into each and every circumstance of this terrible crime. But would it be fair to say, *cig*, that all the evidence so far points to one particular individual who has already come to our attention this week?'

Redmond eyed the sergeant resentfully. *Cig* indeed. It was a familiar form of address, abbreviated from the Irish word for inspector, *cigire,* which always sounded to him a bit like someone who was a good kicker. By using it so publicly, Fitzmaurice was putting himself on a par with a senior officer, while also conveniently reminding everyone of his own part in the earlier investigation.

Fitzmaurice continued. 'The individual I'm referring to is Dominic Scurlock, of course. He had a motive for murder, and as he demonstrated to us up at Cnoc Meala last night, he's more than capable of being violent.'

Superintendent Devane got to his feet slowly. 'I'm very grateful to you, sergeant,' he said, 'because you've just reminded me of another vital point I'd like everyone to take on board. We're at the very beginning of our work here, and we're certainly not yet in a position to identify the most likely suspects. The pathologist is still at the scene, and rather than finding answers, we're adding new questions to the list.'

Redmond glanced again at Fitzmaurice, who was sitting back with his arms folded complacently on his chest. Clearly, he was unconcerned about his colleagues' opinions of him. He was broad-shouldered and well built, with the kind of corrugated head of hair that was typical, to Redmond's mind, of seasoned Gaelic footballers, local councillors and other such pillars of the rural community.

He tuned in again to Devane's ponderous voice. 'I'd like to leave you now with some of the difficult questions we face. Why was Oscar Malden murdered in Beara, rather than anywhere else? Can we establish a link between his death and any other incident or development that took place while he was on holiday – for example, the alleged antagonism between himself and another guest at Cnoc Meala? Or alternatively, can we establish that the perpetrator followed Malden to Beara with the express intention of killing him, on account of a business dispute, or bitter rivalry over a woman, or a simple lust for money?'

Devane was milking his centre-stage role to the full. He was an old hand at detaining an audience in their seats.

'We're checking the obvious possibilities already. Did anyone with a record of violence arrive in Beara in recent days, for example, someone just released from prison, or a person known to suffer from a particularly dangerous psychosis? What about Malden himself – what kind of a personal life did he lead, and was he making or losing money these past few months? There's also that old reliable question – who will benefit most from his death?'

A queue formed at the top of the room when the briefing finally drew to a close. Task sheets were handed out from the jobs book in which details of the evidence would be compiled. Gardai chatted about which would be more tedious, to sit at a desk poring over long lists of phone records, or to be sent on door-to-door expeditions up and down the peninsula. The challenge was not just to endure the boredom – it was to notice the sort of minor deviation from everyday routines that could turn an investigation on its head.

Redmond was handed his own task sheet. He was to assist with witness interviews for the next two days. He tried not to smile too broadly as he turned back to a group of colleagues.

'Well, look at the trouble you've gone and landed us in!' A young woman from Bantry station laughed as she lobbed the remark at him. 'Sure we'd all be better off if you'd only stuck to the script and found a dead sheep on the mountainside.'

A male garda snatched Redmond's sheet to see his assignment. 'Fair feckin' play to you, all the same,' he said. 'The super hasn't dumped a lowly job on you, for sure, now that you've served him up such a juicy stiff!'

Redmond's smile died. He wished fervently that he had the gift of repartee, to answer mockery in kind.

'Oh, you're a right buckshee, Garda Redmond Joyce, there's no doubt about it at all!' The second garda sported a grin, as if he spoke in casual jest. 'You're always ready to please the bosses, but take it from me that you can worm your way up the super's backside and it'll do you no fuckin' good at all. Because at the end of the day, no matter how much sweat and blood we all pour for him and his like, if there are shiny medals to be handed out for solving this crime, they won't be coming to us lowly joe soaps. By Jaysus they won't, for the simple reason that the credit will be appropriated for themselves by the aforesaid Superintendent Tim Devane and our fine lordships seated with him at the top table.'

EIGHT

After two nights of little sleep, Nessa felt a hammer beating insistently inside her skull. She read back over the email she had received. She understood each word, but they seemed as unreal as a fairytale.

'It's good to think of you taking it easy, my love, now that our guests have said their goodbyes to Cnoc Meala. I can picture you out at Rosnacallee headland, watching the waves rise and break on the rocks.'

Her husband's affectionate words from afar, sent from Malawi the previous evening. Patrick made no mention of her repeated messages to him; instead, he explained that his mobile phone had been stolen or mislaid en route. And bad news had awaited him on arrival in Blantyre city.

'Esther's illness is much worse than I'd expected. She's on her deathbed, that's the reality, and I'm so glad I made it to Mwaiwathu hospital before she's carried out in her coffin. It's really hard to take it in, and it's not made any easier by constant comings and goings at her bedside. There's no such thing as visiting time here, of course, and relatives and friends of all the patients camp out in the ward overnight, chatting and keeping themselves busy. It's the same as ever in Malawi – the western world's idea of "private space" is unknown to most people.'

Nessa scrolled up and down. Patrick's new phone number was staring back at her from the screen, but the words she would have to use made her pause. Murder. Strangulation. Postmortem results. Forensic evidence. Cold, cruel words, whether she spoke them aloud or put them in an email. Patrick would want to return home immediately, but how could she ask him to abandon his beloved aunt in her final days?

'I keep thinking of the conversations I never had with Esther, and whether it's too late to ask the questions I've carried with me all these years. I'd love to get some time with her alone, but even if I do, I'm worried that she's too weak for a proper conversation. I should have come months ago, but what's the point in saying that now?'

Patrick had grown up in Malawi in an era of iron dictatorship that his father tried to oppose. Police threats had forced Patrick's parents to leave the country with him when he was a teenager, but then his father had returned home for a secret political meeting and was never seen again. Rumours reached the family that he was tortured and his body thrown to the crocodiles in Lake Malawi. That was how it was in those days, but of course, nobody could prove anything. And like thousands of others, Patrick's mother remained silent for the rest of her days, resisting her son's questions and making it clear that he should not pick at Esther's wounds either.

Arguments pounded back and forth in Nessa's head. Of course she would tell Patrick about Oscar's death. She wanted so badly to talk to him, and in any case, he might chance on the news on the internet. One look at the Sunday newspapers online would confront him with his own name amid the grim details. The murder was the lead story in the Irish media, and photographs of Cnoc Meala accompanied those of Oscar on several front pages, along with predictably alliterative headlines: 'Holiday Murder Horror'; 'Brutal End To Beara Idyll'; 'Businessman's Body Lay by Lonely Bridge'.

She had been plagued by media phone calls since the story broke the night before. Some requested an interview with her, while former colleagues begged her to put them in touch with Oscar's fellow guests. She found several of them difficult to ignore, but flattering messages were also left on her phone by hacks she would cross the street to avoid. A few mentioned her success as a journalist and asked whether she had begun her own investigation into Oscar's murder.

She did not answer any of the requests, apart from writing brief texts to close friends and regular guests who sent their sympathies to her. She was afraid to switch off the phone in case Patrick tried to get through, but she knew she would be stepping into a minefield if she made even off-the-record comments on the situation. She wished she could be out and about, hearing every rumour and whisper and looking for glimmers of new information herself. But she was on the other side of the fence now and had to act accordingly. A throwaway remark by her could become tomorrow's tabloid flurry, just as her silence was already being turned against her by Jack Talbot.

She opened a link to his paper, which had eight full pages of the story. 'Oscar Killer Crux' was one of the lyrical headlines on offer, and another was 'Hellish Scenes in Holiday Heaven'. Jack's name adorned several of the articles, of course, including one in which he insinuated softly that Patrick's trip to Africa gave cause for suspicion: 'Family Silence on Sudden Departure'. Police sources were unable to confirm Patrick Latif's whereabouts, according to Talbot, but they were pursuing the precise circumstances of what was described as his 'last-minute flight to faraway Africa'. Detectives were keen to interview him as a matter of urgency, he said, but Latif's wife Nessa was unwilling to say when exactly he intended to return to Ireland.

Damn and blast Jack Talbot, she said to herself. It was such an old trick, to place unrelated events in the same paragraph in order to imply a causal connection between them. She knew perfectly well that if she complained to him or to his editor, they would just ramp up their insinuations the very next day. There was nothing for it but to hold her nose as the contents of the sewer flowed past her.

Talbot's first approach had been to entice her to give him an exclusive interview. He had arrived at Cnoc Meala on Saturday night, and persuaded the young garda at the gate that he was a welcome friend. Persistent knocking on doors and windows yielded no results, so he left her a string of messages. At first, he sounded concerned for her and she was briefly tempted to believe in his sincerity. Then he suggested that he could share information from garda briefings with her, in return for confirmation of a few details of the holiday group. Finally, he added a lightly veiled threat to his blandishments: 'You must be suffering terribly in the face of this appalling tragedy, my dear. I'm still hoping very sincerely for your cooperation and can promise you'll be treated on the most favourable terms. Indeed, I really fear for you if you leave yourself open to negative interpretations.'

She picked up the phone. She would tell Patrick that Oscar had been killed but suggest that he had left Beara before it happened. She would also omit Dominic's attack altogether, and play down the media invasion of the peninsula. Her husband would want to talk about Esther, and in a day or two, she could tell him more of what was happening at home.

By then, the gardai could well be making an arrest. Or if the murder investigation dragged on, she would have time to think properly about Oscar's time in Beara, and what she could do to help to identify the perpetrator.

'There's a man . . .' Her son Ronan hovered at the door of Nessa's small office upstairs. He was slightly built and brimful of nervous energy. 'He has a camera.'

'I don't bloody well believe it!' Nessa knew that the job of the garda at the gate was not so much to protect the family as to keep the site secure until Oscar's bedroom was examined in the afternoon, so there was little point complaining to him.

'He was at the window. I was playing *FIFA* on the Playstation, Barca against Man U., and Messi got a fantastic goal just after Rooney put one in. But when I looked up I saw a man staring in at me.'

Nessa closed the media pages on her computer. Ronan had asked nonstop questions about the murder after his return from his friend's house the previous evening. What colour was Oscar's skin when his body was found? Was he strangled by hand or with a rope? Would the gardai shoot the killer when they found him? Nessa's fear was that her son's curiosity would soon turn to anxiety. Ronan would ponder everything he heard and then lie awake at night as his worries festered in silence.

She hugged him tightly, something he rarely permitted at his grown-up age of twelve. 'I'm really glad you told me,' she said. 'You stay here for a minute while I look.'

'Maybe he's a police cameraman, and he thinks the murderer is still in our house?'

'We locked the doors last night, love, and the neighbours are helping us too, so I'm sure we're as safe as can be.'

But as she hurried downstairs to close the curtains on every window, Nessa felt anything but safe. They should probably abandon Cnoc Meala until things settled down, instead of pretending they could lead a normal life. For example, Ronan and Sal could hardly go to school next morning – there were very few black youngsters living in Beara, so they would be spotted all too easily by lurking photographers.

She could just imagine the kind of snake who would slither under the garden hedge to snap exclusive images of Oscar's holiday hideaway. And once they had their pictures, the papers could make them say whatever they liked. Ronan innocently playing his screen games could reappear as 'Life Goes On after Holiday Horror'. Or much worse, 'Murder Hunt Dad Abandons Lonely Son'.

Nessa almost fell over the man standing at the bottom of the back staircase. He was calling out to someone upstairs. She panicked as she tried to think which door into the house had been left unlocked.

'Get out! Get the hell out of here now!'

'Hey, chill!' The man had a mellifluous, laid-back voice. 'Chillax, take it easy.'

'We gave no permission to anyone . . .' Nessa was surprised not to see a camera in the man's hands. Then she noticed his sleek hair falling onto his cheeks, in a style reminiscent of seventies' rock musicians.

'Pleased to meet you too,' he said, smirking as he gestured towards the staircase. 'I do promise you I got permission to clamber up to the lovely Rapunzel in her bedchamber.'

It was Marcus O'Sullivan, the young man Sal had fallen for, his eyes dancing under long silky lashes. How many hours had he been in the house? Had he just come in, or had Ronan seen someone else at the window?

'I'd like you to leave now, this minute. Things are difficult enough, as you must realise.'

'So long, so.' Nessa thought she got a whiff of cannabis as he passed her. She watched him go out the back door and up the garden steps. Presumably he arrived without a car and was now taking a shortcut across the hillside.

She found Sal sitting on her bed, dressed in a long T-shirt

which allowed her to display her shapely legs to best effect, and humming quietly as she listened to music on her earphones.

'Are you soft in the head, or what?' Nessa felt like tearing off the headphones. 'The whole country is watching us and you decide it's the right time for a smutty romance!'

'Thanks for your vote of confidence,' said Sal. 'Glad to hear you care so much about my feelings.'

'Give it up, Sal, you're just trying to imitate him and his smart remarks.'

'His name is Marcus.' Sal's eyes lit up as she spoke his name with slow pleasure. 'He is so amazingly handsome, isn't he? Or were you too busy making a fuss to look at him properly?'

'I can't believe what I'm hearing. Surely you understand the trouble we're in, Sal? We have to beware of every move we make and every single person we allow into the house.'

'Listen, I know something horrible's happened. But I don't agree we have to be so totally paranoid about it.' Sal gave a faint smile and Nessa noticed the shiny gloss on her lips. 'If we turn ourselves into, like, prisoners in our own home, people will assume we've something to hide, right? Plus, I think you're forgetting that I'm eighteen now and can make my own choices.'

'I'm not forgetting that you live under this roof, where we've certain rules and standards, or that you're preparing for some very important exams this year.' Nessa felt the hammer blows getting louder in her head. 'What time did he come to the house, might I ask?'

'Why? Would you like to hear a full and frank account of what we've been up to?'

'I'm warning you to keep control of your tongue, Sal. I was already angry with you for staying overnight at a party without a word in advance, and now you think it's OK to let your new pal Marcus sneak in here in the middle of the night or some such time, grinning all over his face from whatever he smokes.' Nessa gesticulated with frustration. She wanted to shake her daughter, to make her see sense. 'Besides which, throwing yourself at anyone is a bad start to a relationship, you know.'

'Oh my God, if you could hear yourself!' Sal plugged her earphones back in and rearranged her pillow. 'You are just so clueless. Number one, you're plain wrong about drugs, because Marcus says we should only allow what's natural into our bodies, which means that smoking is a no-no. Number two, it so happens that he left the party before the crack of dawn because he had to sort some dreary work problem. And Number three, you are *way* mistaken to accuse me of spiriting him into the house last night so we could bunk up in bed together. In fact, you're doing exactly what slimy Jack Talbot does, inventing the kind of story that suits your own prejudices!'

Nessa felt hollow inside. Both she and Sal were too quick to fling sharp words at each other. Patrick would have said some of the same things without a row.

'I expect you to study all afternoon,' she said as firmly as she could manage. 'You should have asked me about Marcus coming over, considering the state we're in today. If you want to see him regularly, you'll have to prove that you can be responsible.'

'What's the mission?'

'What do you mean, the mission?'

'I told you, the secret mission we've to finish before the assassination.'

Ronan was crouched behind the wall that ran along the upper boundary of the back garden. Nessa closed the gate and crouched down beside him. She had felt suffocated sitting indoors with the curtains drawn, and while she longed for a solitary walk to soothe her nerves, leaving Ronan in the house was not an option. Unsurprisingly, his planned game involved murder.

'We're spies, you see, so we've to follow people to find out if they leave secret messages for each other. Then once we've decided who the enemies are, we can kill them. I've done it before, and now that I know about strangling . . .'

'OK, I get it,' Nessa whispered. In a way she found it quite touching that Ronan still invented these childish games, so she tried to get into the spirit of it by adding her own ideas.

'Let's say that the enemies have taken over Derryowen village,'
she said. 'They've just started to move out into the countryside,
so part of the mission is to check which areas they control.
That's before we kill them, of course.'

The game might help her to find out how much of the
neighbourhood was being trawled by the media. But she was
still taken aback at the image she had created for her son.
News journalists were now her enemies in spite of her own
years in the same profession. Of course, she had always
believed that certain individuals, suspected of abuse of power
or position, had to be pursued by the media and if necessary,
slowly speared with sharply pointed questions. But it was a
different matter when a whole community was targeted simply
because a tragedy took place in their midst.

She followed Ronan as he moved swiftly along by the stone
wall. The day was bright, the occasional shadow of a passing
cloud adding to the graceful curves of the landscape. Open
hillside rose above them to the left, while the fields below
were dotted with a variety of scrub and wooded thickets. They
soon arrived at a gate that brought them onto a steep road.
Down the hill lay the village of Derryowen, and beyond it,
the waters of the Atlantic. Cnoc Meala, the village itself and
the surrounding hills were on a tongue of land just a few miles
long, splayed out like so many others along the fringes of the
Beara Peninsula.

Nessa had no intention of approaching the village, however.
She and Ronan would stay inland, following tracks and boreens
on the slopes of the hillside. They crossed the steep road, went
quickly to a gap in the hedge and onto a track which widened
into another road, known locally as the Briary. On Thursday
evening, Sal had made her way from Cnoc Meala's front gate
to this same gap, and along the Briary to meet Darina near
the spot where she had found Maureen. The shortcut was too
narrow for a car, however, and Nessa had driven a longer way
around to the Briary.

She felt her stomach tighten as she and Ronan approached
the place. She looked down the cul-de-sac on which Maureen
had lain, peaceful now in clear autumn sunlight, a profusion
of blackberries and dark red fuchsia bells glistening with the

sheen of a recent shower. Had Maureen just ambled along the boreen to enjoy its pastoral delights – or to swig alcohol on her own, as Sal had suggested? Thank goodness she had been found in time, unlike Oscar. One funeral was more than enough to bear.

There were a few isolated houses further along the Briary. Nessa could see a curl of smoke from one of the chimneys, where an elderly couple lived. A white garda car was parked at their gate. She hurried Ronan past the house to a T-junction at the far end of the Briary.

'Watch out!' Ronan gestured to join him behind a tree. 'I can hear people.'

They both listened carefully. Voices were approaching from uphill.

'Should we retreat? Or crouch down here by the tree?'

'No, we can't stay here,' said Ronan. 'We'll be surrounded if the garda car comes from behind. Let's get over the wall!'

Before Nessa had time to argue, he darted across the road and hauled himself up onto a drystone wall, nimble as a goat. She followed him as he jumped down into the long wet grass on the other side, glad they both had solid footwear on. She thought first that they would have to kneel low on the ground to avoid being seen, but then she understood what Ronan's idea was. There was a standing stone only a few metres from the wall, an impressive monolith as tall as herself, which her son had skipped behind. Nessa joined him and when they peered out, they saw a man and a woman walking along the little road, carrying a camera and tripod.

Nessa understood immediately what they had been doing. A wooden bench had been installed a bit higher up, where walkers could sit and admire vistas of land and sea. Further up still, past the bench, the road became an untarred track, with a gateway and yellow fingerpost marking the start of Coomgarriff Walk, leading to a distinctive hill about twenty minutes walk inland. So the news crew had picked their spot well. Not only could they shoot panoramic views of Beara from the bench, but they could also show the place Oscar Malden had planned to walk on the day he was murdered. Before he left Derryowen Hotel on Thursday morning, he mentioned Coomgarriff to the young barman. But Nessa did not know if there was any evidence that he had actually accomplished his walk.

'I'll run up to the bench,' said Ronan. He peered out again, getting ready to dash away. 'I could find out—'

Nessa caught hold of him just in time. 'Not now, love. For all we know, there's another news crew up there.'

'I'll be really careful, I promise, especially if they look like enemies. But maybe somebody has hidden secret notes up at the bench, and I told you it's part of the mission to find them.'

She managed to persuade him to postpone that part of the game until another time. The crew might come back to nab a few scenic shots of Beara's archaeology, only to find herself and her son lurking in their hiding place. The whole region had hundreds of standing stones, megalithic tombs, boulder burials, and stone circles, and compared to well-known sites such as those at Ardgroom and Cashelkeelty, this solitary stone was not particularly notable; but nevertheless, it could make a nice evocative picture.

Nessa steered Ronan downhill towards a house at a corner, where the Coomgarriff hill road met the main coast road into Derryowen. They could call in to an old man called Ambrose who lived there. His main pastime was to stand at his gate watching the world go by, so he would know how many media people were nosing around, and how much ground had been covered by the gardai.

They made their way down the hill warily. As they reached the last bend before Ambrose's house, Ronan went ahead to check for enemies. Nessa crossed the roadway and watched from beside a rocky outcrop. She saw him stop suddenly, as if rooted to the spot. Then she heard a shout and saw two figures step out from Ambrose's gateway. One of them, a stocky bearded man, pointed a camera.

Nessa tried to signal to Ronan without drawing attention to herself. If she ran down to snatch her son from their gaze, she would be trapped too, and she did not want to provide the photographer with a dramatic image of mother and son fleeing uphill.

She scrambled onto the rocky hillock behind her just as

Ronan took flight. She called out to him, and then found herself tumbling into a damp field for a second time. She cursed herself for not staying safely away from all public roads. Ronan soon landed beside her and they knelt in the undergrowth, almost crying out when they got stung by a swathe of nettles.

They could hear voices on the roadway.

'Damn, I'm sure that was the Latif boy from Cnoc Meala. I tried to shoot him but I'll have to check the pics.'

'I didn't see who called out to him.'

'I think we should head over to the Latif property and suss it out. We've had enough of the old geezer at the gate, and with any luck, we'll catch the boy on his way back. We could do with something meaty . . .'

Nessa wished she could cover Ronan's ears as they stayed hidden in the field. She did not know how to explain to him why they had to run away. But she was sure of one thing – she would have to arrange for him to leave Beara and stay with friends elsewhere for a few days at least. She had seen the mix of excitement and genuine fear in his expression when he scrambled to join her in the undergrowth. Whether she and Sal could leave too was a different decision, and she even wondered about hiring a private security firm to protect Cnoc Meala from intruders. But it would be a relief to get Ronan out of harm's way. Then she could find time to think properly about the hurricane that had brought havoc to their lives since Thursday.

She stood up when the voices nearby died away. Her jeans were soaked below the knees, as were Ronan's. She whispered to him that they could get out of the field at a gate further along, onto a minor road that ran parallel to the coast road. Darina's house and studio were only five minutes along that byroad, and their best chance was to ask her for a lift home, out of sight in the back of her van. Otherwise, they would have to pick their way across fields and thickets, like fugitives wrongly accused of a crime they had not committed.

'Oh, I'm sorry, you startled me!' Darina's face appeared out of the gloom of the henhouse at the back of her place. Nessa had put her head around the door when there was no response at the house or the barn she used as a studio.

'No, it's my fault, Darina, I'm so jumpy myself that I forgot you might be the same. Have you been hassled by the media crowd yet?'

Darina shood away a hen pecking at Nessa's feet. 'Not here at the house, no, but I was down in the village earlier and I was stopped by somebody who wanted to know whether I knew you, and had ever met Oscar, and what I had to say about it all.'

Nessa looked around to check on Ronan, who had been very quiet on the way to Darina's. He was pulling flowers from the long fuchsia hedge that separated the studio and henhouse, and trying to suck the sweet juice from the purple-red bells.

'To be honest, I said I didn't really know you,' said Darina. 'I was afraid I'd be pestered with questions, you see, and it seemed the best way.'

'I think you were absolutely right to say as little as possible.'

'It all seems unreal, doesn't it? Have you been to Derryowen today and seen those monster trucks with satellite equipment on top? The place looks like a film set or something.'

'So it's true that there's a big media presence?'

'The place is swarming, Nessa, and I've heard that some of our neighbours are even refusing to open their doors. I'd just never imagined this sort of thing in Beara.' Darina glanced over at Ronan, who was losing interest in the fuchsia. She handed him a hosepipe and told him to continue what she had been doing, spraying water into the henhouse to clean it. 'I was talking to my cousin Marcus yesterday evening and he said he saw gawkers just driving up and down, satisfying their curiosity—'

'Marcus O'Sullivan, did you say? He's your cousin? The same lad Sal is so keen on?'

'Did you not realise, Nessa?' Darina chewed on her lips as she regarded her. 'But of course that was the reason . . . The party we went to the other night, Sal wanted me to get us both invited, that's how it came about, you see. I mean, I wouldn't have bothered on my own account, because I'm not into his crowd.'

Nessa felt a splash of water on her feet as Ronan whirled the hosepipe towards the hens scratching on the open ground. She tried to steady her own thoughts as she steered him away. She could see that Darina was wired up about the media invasion of the area, and she did not want to pressurise her to tell tales on Sal.

'You were very good to go to the party as a favour to Sal,' she said gently. 'I hope she appreciates it.'

'Oh, I'm sure, yes . . .' Darina looked uncomfortable, pulling on a lock of hair that fell onto her face. 'Sal is mad about him, Nessa, but I don't know . . .'

'I hope she hasn't been underhand, Darina, or given you any reason to be angry?'

'Oh no, I'm not angry at her, it's nothing like that.' Darina paused again and glanced over at Ronan, who was still slopping water in all directions. She led him down the path firmly and told him he could fill an empty wheelie bin which she pulled out from beside the hedge. When she returned, she had clearly decided to say her piece.

'I'm fond of Marcus, Nessa, or at least, I used to be fond of him when we were younger. But ever since he came home from Spain, I don't know . . .' She spoke rapidly, her eyes avoiding Nessa's. 'I think Marcus just suits himself, do you know what I mean? And the thing that gets me is, I saw him with another woman recently, that's what I'm trying to tell you. I was going for a swim and his car was parked by the sea, and there he was, draped over a woman is the only way I can describe it.'

'That was before the party, I presume?'

'Yes, but the same kind of thing happened another time recently – and I'm not even sure it was the same woman each time. So I wouldn't like to bet that he'll devote himself one hundred per cent to Sal, that's what worries me. But please, Nessa, don't tell her that I said so.'

NINE

Monday 21 September, 3.00 p.m.

Fergus Malden was nervous, his eyes flitting from Redmond to Inspector O'Kelleher. As several witnesses had already agreed, Oscar Malden had passed little of his self-belief on to Fergus – if anything, Oscar's surfeit of confidence might have overwhelmed his son.

The gardai were on their fourth interview with him. Superintendent Devane had spoken to him the first time, soon after Oscar's body was found, and O'Kelleher had gone over the same painful material twice on Sunday, along with another senior colleague. This was Redmond's first opportunity to see him close up. It was hard on Fergus to be scrutinised so often, of course, but he must have known Oscar better than almost anyone else, and in addition, a heavy shadow of suspicion inevitably fell on the next of kin of a murder victim. The gardai had to check whether he varied his story from one interview to the next, as well as digging for new details.

O'Kelleher spoke in his quiet, unhurried way. 'How would you describe your father as a person, then?'

Fergus examined his hands, another of his nervous habits, before he put together his answer.

'I suppose he was . . .' His eyes shifted around the room. 'My father was . . . He was friendly and cheerful, just as the newspapers have been saying. He was a strong person, as I'm sure you know, and he believed he could . . .' Fergus looked at his hands again and eventually settled on an answer. 'He always believed he could achieve whatever he set out to do, that's what I mean.'

'That was certainly his reputation in business.' O'Kelleher's voice sounded softer than ever. 'But on a personal level, is it possible that he antagonised other people in his zeal to get what he wanted?'

'Antagonised? Well, no, that's not the word . . . No, it's not true that he antagonised me, but if you're asking . . .' Fergus stopped and looked over at the small camera recording each interview. 'But certainly in business matters, he wasn't afraid to antagonise people, if he felt he needed to.'

'A few of the guests at Cnoc Meala told us they sensed some tension between you and your father.' This was Redmond's first attempt at a question. 'If so, what was the cause of that tension?'

'I'm not sure . . . That is, I couldn't say there was anything like that, except maybe . . .'

'Except what?'

'I don't mean anything big, just that . . .' As Redmond watched Fergus, he hoped he hadn't interjected his supplementary question too quickly. It was important to allow witnesses enough time to add to their initial response, without leading them on. Redmond was very conscious of the inspector listening to him.

'I'm sure you understand,' Fergus continued with more assurance, 'that it's not always easy to talk to your parent when you're grown up. That's all I meant.'

'Well, perhaps that was the reason you needed to escape from your father's company on occasions? Fellow guests have also said you went out for a solitary walk on a few of the evenings at Cnoc Meala, is that so?'

'Yes, but . . . I didn't go out that much, and anyway I wasn't trying to escape, as you put it. I just like to be on my own now and then, that's all.'

'Did you meet up with anyone else while you were out on these walks? Another guest from the house, for example?'

'I'm sure I talked to whoever I met on my way, but . . .' Fergus started fidgeting again, picking at the cuffs of his shirtsleeves. 'I can't remember exactly . . . I met a few people when I went out, but I'd no arrangement to meet anyone, if that's what you mean.'

'And suppose it's true that Oscar was attracted to a woman he met on holiday here?' Redmond tried hard to hold onto Fergus's eyes. It was difficult to listen fully to his answers while thinking of the most productive follow-up questions. 'I wonder did you feel obliged to stay out of his way for that reason?'

'What do you mean, obliged . . .?'

'Did your father make it clear that he wanted some private space too?'

'No, that wouldn't be . . . My father and I didn't really talk about things like that.'

'I think it's fair to say that he had a certain reputation, all the same? A reputation for attracting women, that is to say? It's been reported over the years that he had a series of relationships since his separation from your mother?'

Fergus looked out the window and Redmond tried not to step into the silence as he had earlier. This must be the art of questioning, he thought, to recognize when to make a reluctant witness sweat, or to give him just enough breathing space to utter the unsayable sentences.

After a long moment, he decided to add to the pressure on Fergus. 'We've heard from colleagues of Oscar's that at least two of his women employees left their jobs without notice, following rumours of a sexual relationship in each case. So anything you can tell us about his patterns of behaviour, or about particular relationships, could be crucial to the investigation.'

'We understand this is difficult for you,' said O'Kelleher after another pause. 'But we need to know who had cause to be angry with Oscar, or jealous of him, or to have some other motive to kill him.'

Fergus looked from one to the other. 'I know all that and I'm trying to think of what I can tell you. Really, it's just that . . . I never asked him about, you know, other women in his life. I preferred not to know the details, can't you understand that?'

Redmond tried not to feel impatient. However difficult it was for Fergus, at least he had not insisted on the presence of a solicitor throughout his interviews. But the gardai had a difficult job to do too.

'As you know,' he continued, 'some people believe Oscar became involved with Maureen Scurlock during the week, even though she was on holiday with her husband Dominic.

Do you believe it's true that they became involved? And if so, would your father have set out to get what he wanted, in that determined way you described earlier?'

'That wasn't what I said exactly.' Fergus reddened but then he spoke more firmly than before. 'No, you see I don't believe my father was attracted to her at all. I think he played a sort of game with some women . . . Women like Maureen, for example.'

'What game was that? And what do you mean, women like Maureen?'

'She wasn't the sort of person . . .' Fergus was still blushing. 'I'm sure Maureen Scurlock is a fine person. But I think my father preferred a different type of woman . . . I suppose I mean a more sophisticated woman, and probably younger too.'

'OK. And the game?'

'Maybe game is the wrong word. All I'm saying is that my father liked to flirt. He liked the fact . . . He liked to be reminded that he was attractive to women, but that doesn't mean he had a relationship with every woman he looked at twice.'

'Was Dominic wrong, then, when he claimed that Oscar had assaulted Maureen?'

'I don't know.' Fergus hesitated and then found his firm voice again. 'No, it just doesn't fit, I don't believe it was my father who attacked her. Dominic must be wrong about that.'

'How can you be sure?'

'I can't be completely sure, but . . . My father wouldn't do something like that, down a country laneway, losing control of himself. No, I just can't believe it.'

O'Kelleher spoke softly, but with a steely undertone. 'Or maybe Dominic knows his wife rather better than you knew your father? Maybe you're the person who's wrong about what happened?'

The afternoon wore on amid further questions and faltering answers. The air in the room grew heavier. Redmond began to wonder whether Fergus was putting on an act, hoping that the more he hesitated and fidgeted, the less the screws would be turned in the interview. On the other hand, Fergus had every reason to be dazed – he was young, shy and dealing with a traumatic shock all on his own. There was also a kind of stiffness or formality about him, as shown by his constant use of the word 'father' rather than 'dad'. Redmond could not decide what to make of him.

He jotted notes and questions on his laptop as the interview proceeded. How come Fergus was so sure about Maureen, if he had always kept his distance from Oscar's relationships with women? When he was questioned about his solitary walks, had he reacted uneasily? And earlier in the interview, why the assertion that his father had not antagonised him, when he had actually been asked about other people?

Fergus told them that he was very disappointed when Oscar decided on Wednesday night to return home to Tipperary the next day. Fergus had booked the holiday in Beara in the first place, as a surprise present for his father. But he repeated several times that they did not have a row about Oscar's decision. When he made up his mind, he rarely changed it. Indeed, Fergus said that his father was prone to impatience, and could suddenly lose interest in a place or in a group of people.

O'Kelleher pushed him to explain why he had chosen Beara in particular. Had he or Oscar any previous link to the area, or with others in the Cnoc Meala group? Were there any concerns in advance about the likely success of the holiday? But Fergus stuck doggedly to the answers he had given to the same questions already. He found the Cnoc Meala website by chance. They knew none of the other guests in advance. He had been hopeful that they would both enjoy the week.

He explained that he had just got a job in Australia, and booked the holiday as a leaving present, which he told his father about just a few weeks beforehand. It seemed a good idea to spend some time together before he, Fergus, departed to the far side of the world. Oscar liked to keep fit, and he thought he would enjoy a walking holiday. And being in a group would be easier for the two of them.

He relaxed a fraction while answering such general questions. He had never planned to work in his father's business, he said, but there was no conflict between them as a result. He had qualified as an engineer, but he was not particularly interested in electronic gates or communication systems that showed you who was ringing your doorbell. His new job in Australia was in solar energy research, developing giant mirrors placed strategically in desert locations.

'I worked with him. I spent a few months working with my father. That was the year before last.' Fergus examined his thumbnail for a moment. 'But I couldn't . . .'

'You couldn't what?' Another half-sentence left dangling in the air.

'My father had a strong personality, as you know by now. I couldn't . . . I wanted to stand on my own feet, so I was really looking forward to the new job in Australia. But now I don't know . . .'

It was impossible to follow up on every unfinished sentence.

There was a shortage of solar gain in Derryowen that afternoon, Redmond thought, as he looked out the window at a low sky over a grey sea. Plenty of energy in the waves, no doubt, as they beat incessantly on the shore, but he would go out of his mind if he stared at them too long. The gardai had been given the use of an empty house for some of the Derryowen interviews, while others continued in Castletownbere and Bantry stations.

Redmond had noted the times of various events on the day of Oscar's disappearance, and Inspector O'Kelleher went over the details with Fergus.

10.00 a.m.: Oscar left Cnoc Meala; bought a newspaper in O'Donovan's shop; had a conversation outside the shop with Darina O'Sullivan and said he might call in to her studio a while later, but did not do so.

10.20 a.m.: Oscar went for a walk along a coastal path near Derryowen Hotel, where he was seen by two other tourists.

10.30 a.m.: Oscar texted Fergus to ask him to book a taxi for him for 2.00 p.m., from the car park at Scannive Strand, a few miles from Derryowen. Fergus texted back soon afterwards to confirm that he had done so.

11.30 a.m.: Oscar had a coffee at the hotel; he mentioned to the barman that he planned to try the Coomgarriff Walk;

he had a conversation with Maureen Scurlock, as seen through the hotel window by the two sisters and fellow guests, Stella and Zoe.

11.50 a.m.: Oscar left the hotel to go walking; he had a conversation with an old man, Ambrose, outside his house on the road out of Derryowen, and mentioned that he was on his way to Coomgarriff Walk; Ambrose also gave evidence that Oscar's phone rang and that he spoke to someone for a few minutes. Gardai did not know yet who had phoned him.

1.40 p.m.: Phone text from Oscar to Fergus asking him to cancel the taxi booking.

Mid-afternoon, perhaps 3.00 p.m.: Oscar was seen walking at a location about three miles from Coomgarriff, according to an English tourist who contacted gardai. No confirmation of this sighting by other witnesses.

Fergus agreed with the times noted, in so far as his own involvement was concerned. His mobile had already been taken away for forensic examination of the texts he had received from his father. Gardai were particularly interested in the 1.40 p.m. text, and whether the style or wording could suggest that Oscar wrote it under duress or threat of violence.

Redmond had the wording off by heart. It was brief and to the point: 'Change of plan, work reasons, have lift, cancel taxi.' Fergus had no idea who or what gave rise to the change of plan. But he had already discussed the text with gardai on Friday, when they were trying to contact Oscar about Maureen's incident, and he said that he was not at all surprised at it. Oscar generally did as he pleased, and felt no need to justify doing so.

'Did your father have a car at home in Tipperary?'

'No, he didn't. But I thought I told you already . . .?' Fergus seemed more weary than impatient. His face was pale and haggard, as if he had not slept for a week. 'My father didn't like driving and gave it up years ago. He often worked while he was travelling, so he employed a driver for business trips.'

'And you drove him to Beara last Sunday? But you didn't offer to drive him home when he had to leave early?'

'Yes, we came here in my car. But no, he didn't ask or

expect me to leave early along with him. It was no problem to him to pay for a taxi.' Fergus sighed and looked out at the grey rolling waves. 'As well as that . . . I don't know this for sure, but I think he quite liked to have other people at his beck and call, if you know what I mean.'

'What about baggage? What did Oscar carry with him on Thursday morning?'

'Surely I answered these questions yesterday? He had a small rucksack with him when he left Cnoc Meala. The rest of his stuff was in his room and I'd agreed to bring it home this weekend. But I thought his rucksack . . .? Your colleagues told me yesterday that you haven't found it yet?'

O'Kelleher eventually suggested a short break. Supplies had been provided on a side-table and he went over to put the kettle on. Fergus had brought his own mint tea, as he was still having stomach trouble, and just asked for hot water. Redmond watched the young man standing by the window. Slightly built, with unremarkable looks and light-coloured hair cut very short. But there was something missing too, Redmond decided. It was as if his blood ran too thinly, or the light in his eyes had gone out.

'OK, let's go back over last Thursday one more time,' said O'Kelleher when they resumed their places. 'You've told us you stayed in bed all morning, Fergus, because you were feeling ill. Around midday, you got up and sat around in the guests' living room, as Nessa McDermott has verified. At half past one, she offered to drive you to Castletownbere to buy some medicine from a pharmacy. You both returned to the house shortly after three o'clock, and you stayed in the living room for the rest of the afternoon, along with two Dutch visitors.'

Redmond took a gulp of black coffee as he listened. He hoped the bolt of caffeine would help him to concentrate.

'Let's suppose you'd set out to guarantee yourself a good alibi, Fergus,' said the inspector. 'You knew that your father was in danger, maybe, because his business enemies had pressurised you to help them?'

'I don't understand what you mean.'

'What I mean, my friend, is that you made a very good job of your alibi for Thursday, isn't that so? You spent most of the day in company, in spite of your claims that you enjoy time alone. When you and Nessa McDermott returned from Castletown, you didn't try a spell of fresh air on your own to improve your health, did you? Instead, you stayed nicy and cosy in Cnoc Meala where other people were sure to see you?'

Fergus shook his head in silence. O'Kelleher sipped his tea for a moment, his mild blue eyes regarding him steadily. When he spoke again, his voice had taken on a razor-sharp edge.

'It seems very strange altogether,' he said, 'that you knew so little about your own father's business affairs, or who phoned him or why he might have altered his plans, either when he decided to leave Beara on Thursday morning or when he changed tack again that lunchtime. For God's sake, son, you lived with him in Tipperary, you worked with him for a while, and you came on holidays with him. But yet after all that, you still haven't a notion in the world who might have wanted to kill him or why?'

'I'm sorry, I'm doing my best . . .' Fergus shoved his hands into his armpits. 'I've answered every question as well as I can.'

'Well, so you say, but let me tell you now that if you're keeping information to yourself, or protecting somebody else, you'll be more than sorry when we find out about it!'

Fergus made no attempt to answer this time. Redmond glanced out at the wide waters of the bay. The tide itself was at a standstill, it seemed to him, as they tried to dredge answers from the young man sitting across the table.

'We're here to help you unravel what happened,' said O'Kelleher then. His voice was still sharp, but he sounded tired too. 'You told us previously that Oscar was in a good humour when you saw him for the last time on Thursday morning, even though he had just been confronted with some major business problem – something so pressing that he had to leave Beara that day in order to deal with it?'

'I've tried to explain to you.' Fergus became more animated, making a real effort to answer decisively. 'My father was never happier than when he had a work problem to sort out. He wasn't like other people, that's what you have to understand. It always seemed to me that . . . You see, an easy life was the last thing he wanted.' His voice became stronger. 'I used to worry about it, to be honest, that he took too many risks and maybe even . . . Sometimes I was afraid he actually courted danger, just for the sake of it.'

'What kind of danger?'

'I don't know, not in detail. I mean, if I knew that, I'd have told you all about it. But I picked up earlier in the week that he was expecting a phone call, and that it was about a business problem abroad. So when he told me on Wednesday night about leaving early, I assumed that was the reason. But I've no evidence, so it's just an impression . . .'

Fergus paused as he had many times previously, and then spoke in his firmest tone yet. 'On Thursday, when I got word that he'd arranged a lift home, I thought the person who was supposed to phone him had arrived in Ireland and that they had arranged to meet. And now . . . Now I think my father was in terrible danger from that person, and didn't pull back from the brink in time.'

TEN

Redmond was glad to leave the interview room. His head was exploding after two long days of questioning. Images and words popped in his mind like fireflies: Nessa McDermott, for example, who gave him a poisoned look every time he asked her a question; one of the sisters, Zoe, who made political speeches instead of answering simple questions; and the other sister, Stella, who said she had met Oscar Malden once before at a conference in the Middle East, while she was doing academic research in the Gulf States. Wrestling with taciturn interviewees took up a lot of time too – not just Fergus Malden but also the likes of the young lad who worked in Derryowen Hotel, who was so absorbed in a silly mobile phone game that he had no idea what time Maureen Scurlock had left the place.

Redmond inhaled the evening air as he walked westwards out of Derryowen. The interviews were hard work but they were satisfying in their own way. He should not allow Nessa or anybody else get to him. He noticed how shafts of sunshine were breaking through the clouds, making the colours of the hills so much sharper as they alighted here and there.

He was surprised to feel his mood lift unexpectedly, as if a breeze had caught him. The joy of doing really challenging work, that was the sensation bubbling up in him. His heart was pumping with the adrenaline he craved.

The day's work was not yet over, which pleased him all of a sudden. He and Sergeant Fitzmaurice were to question the young taxi driver, Marcus O'Sullivan, whose previous interviews did not add up. O'Sullivan had been parked at a well-known beauty spot, Scannive Strand, awaiting Oscar's arrival as instructed, but claimed he returned home as soon as the booking was cancelled, at about quarter to two. Nessa

McDermott and Fergus Malden drove past the same parking spot shortly after two o'clock, and said it was deserted. But according to a further witness, there were at least three cars at the Strand at half past two, and Marcus was in his taxi with another person.

Scannive Strand was less than two miles from Derryowen, on the road between the village and the main Beara routes. If Oscar had walked from Derryowen up to Coomgarriff, he could have taken a different route back towards the sea, looping around the hill and down to join the main road near Scannive Strand. It was a two hour walk, for a fit, active man like Oscar.

Redmond had arranged to meet the sergeant on the road towards Scannive, to give him a chance to stretch his legs after spending the day indoors. He paused for a few moments to watch three television crews prepare for their evening bulletins, at a layby with enticing views of the coastline. He remembered a remark made by O'Kelleher at lunchtime, that the media crowd were like dogs gnawing at the decomposing meat of the dead, but it gave Redmond quite a buzz to watch them at work. The reporters were pacing to and fro, each memorising a little script while their camera people adjusted equipment and looked anxiously at the changing sky. One reporter made several false starts, speaking confidently to camera and then cursing loudly when he stumbled on a word. Clearly, it was a job that required its own brand of patience.

Sergeant Fitzmaurice was outside a house at a crossroads, with an elderly man whose hair was like a thatch of decayed straw. Redmond realised that this must be Ambrose. He was probably a little deaf, because when the sergeant tried to introduce them, Ambrose paid no attention and gabbled on.

'What that poor man intended, God rest him, was to go off looking at the old stones lying about on the slopes of Coomgarriff, that's what he told me anyway, and he seemed a very genuine man, and keen to know all about the wonderful memorials we have in this area to remind us of our ancestors long ago. Well indeed, I says to him, if that's what you're looking for, you'll find a lifetime's worth of ancient slabs in every corner of the peninsula—'

'Ambrose is telling me about the conversation he had with Oscar Malden,' said Conor Fitzmaurice quickly. Redmond looked around as the old man chattered on. The house was perfectly situated for somebody who liked to observe the comings and goings of his neighbours. It was on a rise, looking east down a gentle incline towards the sea and the village, and west in the direction of Scannive Strand and the mountains of the main Beara peninsula. There were two small roads leading inland from the crossroads too: the first, the route taken by Oscar, dipped and rose towards the pointed summit of Coomgarriff; and the second, almost parallel to the coast road, twisted out of sight among trees.

A flow of words continued to pour from Ambrose. 'As I was telling you a short while ago, sergeant, I was standing here by my own little gate, keeping an eye on the road the same as I do every blessed day, when Oscar Malden came by, holding a map in his hand. Well, may God and his Holy Mother protect us, but I had no idea then what tragedy lay in store for him, the poor man! So I'd certainly like to help your inquiries to the very best of my abilities.'

'If everyone was as alert to the world as you are,' said Fitzmaurice to him, 'there'd be little or no work left for the guards, that's the truth of it. So tell me about the phone call Oscar got, just before he set off on his way?'

'All I heard was a few sentences, sergeant, and maybe it's a pity I didn't listen more carefully but of course I knew the man was having a private conversation. He turned away from me for the first few minutes, but then he turned back and spoke plain and clear on this very spot. "We'd better talk it over", that was the first bit I heard, and then he mentioned that it would be just as well to avoid trouble.' Ambrose leaned in to Fitzmaurice, happy to recite every detail. 'Yes, and he ended the call by saying: "I'll be with you shortly". Now, I've been thinking over this ever since, and wishing I could tell you I witnessed his meeting with the other person. But Oscar bid me goodbye after another minute, and that was the last I saw of him, Lord rest his eternal soul.'

'And who else walked past your house after Oscar? I know you've been through all this yesterday . . .'

'It's no trouble, sergeant, but the only people I saw soon after were the same neighbours and friends I see every day. The postman stopped by for our usual chat, and then my friend Darina came by. The Egg-girl, that's what I like to call her, and I can tell you she had a fine clutch of eggs to deliver to me that day. What's that radio advertisement they had – "an egg a day is OK", isn't that it?' Ambrose allowed himself a little chuckle as he looked up at the sergeant. 'Well, it was time for my egg of the day, because it was coming up to one o'clock by then and I was getting hungry for a bite to eat.'

'I'm sure you were, my friend, but I wonder whether you also saw another woman who was walking around Derryowen the same day? She was wearing a silky blouse and a short skirt, and had been staying above in Cnoc Meala.'

'Well, she sounds like someone who'd make an impression alright. But was that before dinnertime, or a while later?'

'We're not sure, Ambrose, and of course, you might have gone indoors to get your food ready and missed her at that very moment.'

'I might, but as you know, sergeant, I don't miss much. I eat my dinner at one o'clock exactly, the same minute the national news comes on the radio, sitting at my little table by the window so's I can keep an eye on the road, up and down the whole time.' Ambrose raised a hand in greeting to a passing driver. 'That means I could swear on the holy book that no such woman as you mention came this way, wearing a short skirt or a long dress either. Nor did I see poor Oscar again, in case you were about to ask me that selfsame question I was asked yesterday. No, indeed, I did not, which leads me to the conclusion that he didn't return from Coomgarriff by the same route he took up the hill.'

Redmond gave a quiet sigh of relief when Fitzmaurice finally said goodbye to the old man. Trying to follow his rigmarole was more of a challenge than the formal interviews.

'Honestly, isn't he a great lad altogether?' said the sergeant, as he turned the ignition in his car. Redmond folded the empty crisp packets he had picked up from the passenger seat. He could see signs of his colleague's family life on all sides – a pile of football magazines at his feet and a broken doll in the car door pocket.

'But is Ambrose's evidence reliable?' he asked. 'If it is, Oscar must have been murdered somewhere between the crossroads and the top of Coomgarriff, which leaves a big question about how his body came to be found fifteen or twenty miles away. Or else he went to Coomgarriff and returned to Scannive Strand via the far side of the hill? And then he met his killer later that day?'

'Well, now, I'd say that Ambrose's evidence is sound enough as it goes, fair play to him. But I wouldn't push him into a witness box in court, all the same. We can believe what Ambrose says he saw, but that doesn't mean he saw everything and everyone who passed his house all day long.'

'You mean he's not as observant as he thinks? So his evidence proves nothing about where Oscar or Maureen were at specific times?'

'That's the gist of it alright. After all, Ambrose has to turn his back on the outside world a few times a day, if only to attend to his natural functions. Added to which, I'm of the opinion that his advanced years are getting the better of him, poor divil. When he's grand and comfy by the window, and well fed on those tasty eggs of his, I think he dozes off to sleep in spite of himself. A few times recently, I've noticed gaps in his accounts of the afternoon comings and goings around Derryowen.'

Sergeant Fitzmaurice slowed as they approached Scannive Strand's parking place. Beyond the shingly beach, the sea glinted under broken skies and Beara's dramatic contours rose against the sky. They turned right just before the beach, and when Redmond checked the map, he saw that they were at the Scannive end of a stretch of land jutting out to sea between Derryowen Hotel and the strand.

'It wouldn't surprise me one bit,' said Fitzmaurice suddenly, 'if this whole case was solved by the end of the week.'

Redmond hid his surprise by saying nothing. His opinion of his colleague had changed in the past few days. Rather than smug self-importance, what he saw now was an easy unselfconscious manner. He did not hanker after the kind of lifestyle Fitzmaurice had: chatting to lonely people at their rural gateways and driving his children to afterschool activities. But it was obvious that Fitzmaurice was master of his own domain – a person and a place suited to each other.

They passed small tourist signposts to holiday accommodation and fishing spots, and Fitzmaurice pointed ahead as the coastline came into view again.

'Pooka Rock is not far up the coast from here,' he said. 'That's where Dominic Scurlock whiled away his time last Thursday, just pondering and plotting how to entice a few innocent fish to bite, if we're to believe his statements. But it so happens that the coastal path from Derryowen Hotel passes near the rock, the very same route walked by Oscar that morning, before he made his way back to the bar for a refreshing coffee. So let's suppose the two of them met by the sea, and that they exchanged words, to put it at its mildest?'

'But there's no evidence of that, is there? Dominic denies that he set eyes on Oscar at any time on Thursday.'

'Hold the pony a minute, and I'll explain how I see it. Dominic had it in for his rival, as he believed. We're all agreed on that, so it's highly plausible that if he saw Oscar sauntering along on his own, he challenged him to keep his hands off his wife, following which one of them threatened or even took a clatter at the other. Oscar returned to the hotel and met Maureen, who made known her willingness for action, and to hell with her husband's scruples. So they arranged an intimate rendezvous for themselves up in the hills, either on the boreen where Maureen was found, or maybe at the start of the Coomgarriff Walk.'

'Fergus Malden says that his father was not in the least attracted by Maureen.'

'Indeed, and maybe Fergus is telling the truth, and that Oscar didn't care two damns for her. But he could have led her on just to get his own back at Dominic, couldn't he, because my guess is that Oscar wouldn't like to be told what to do by anybody? Then Dominic follows the pair of them, and when he sees them tearing the clothes off each other . . .'

'But there's a serious flaw in your theory, surely? Nobody saw Dominic make his way from the coast to the Coomgarriff Walk, either on foot or in that old BMW he drives? Ambrose certainly didn't see him.'

'Maybe he didn't, but let's not forget that Dominic knows these parts very well, because his mother is from the area. There are byroads and tracks around here that you won't find on a map.'

'But how would Dominic have known that Maureen went to meet Oscar? And even if it happened, how could it be proven? Do you think Maureen is going to give evidence against her own husband?'

'Yerra, never mind poor Maureen, won't the evidence come from Dominic himself? The man is in a bad state already, as we saw when he frightened Nessa McDermott the other night. He's below in Cork city now, dutifully visiting his wife in hospital once a day. But I've been talking to some of our lads in the city, and what I hear is that he's also busy drinking himself into a near-stupor every day. The burden of his guilt lies heavily on his conscience, I promise you, and sooner or later, he'll blurt out the truth and give us enough to put him on trial.'

Fitzmaurice pulled up at a large ornate gateway. A sign proclaimed it as the entrance to 'Carraig Álainn – Luxury holiday homes available for rent, beautifully appointed throughout. Private and serene setting, mature landscaping.'

'Maybe you're right,' said Redmond. But the sergeant's theory did not really convince him. Things might change, of course, when the forensic results came in: Dominic's car was being examined for any evidence that a body had been transported in it, and a full report was also awaited on the scene of the laneway itself. In the meantime, Redmond's own fervent hope was that the investigation would continue for several more days at least.

'I don't think Inspector O'Kelleher believes that Dominic is the murderer,' he said then. 'My impression is that he suspects Fergus Malden quite strongly, in spite of the alibi evidence.'

'Well, if you can figure out what goes on in the *cig*'s mind, you deserve to be promoted, boy. But what's the point of looking for a complicated solution to the murder, when a plain answer is staring us in the face?'

A large van was parked near the first of Carraig Álainn's houses. Its rear doors were slammed shut as Redmond and

Fitzmaurice approached and a young man hurried into the front seat, turning on the ignition as they spoke to him.

'Is Marcus O'Sullivan around, or you could tell us . . .?'

Redmond recognised the driver. His name was on the tip of his tongue. He had been up in court in a case Redmond had worked on the previous year. He was in his twenties, with long straggly hair and a goatee beard.

'He's here somewhere alright,' the man replied. Then he smirked and Redmond remembered his case in an instant. He was accused of speeding at a 150 kilometres an hour on a wide stretch of road outside Bantry, but escaped conviction because of a stupid mistake made in the paperwork by another garda.

A slogan on the side of the van advertised a furniture removal business. 'See ya, so,' the driver said cheerily as he drove off. Two fingers to authority, and the same sly grin on his face as when he walked out of the courthouse. Carl, that was his name, Carl O'Sullivan.

Heavy blinds shuttered the windows at the first house. Redmond went ahead to the second house, and as he rounded a copse of trees, he saw another young man holding a phone to his ear. Redmond called down the slope to him and the man gave a startled glance in his direction.

But then he turned and took off towards the cliffs, disappearing along a wooded path. He was carrying something under his arm, perhaps a large package or box. Redmond was sure the young man had seen him but then pretended otherwise.

A raised patio, furnished with table and chairs, adjoined the third house at Carraig Álainn. Redmond bounded up steps to a wooden rail at the far side of the patio. The rocky fringes of the coastline suddenly came into view, and down by the sea, he saw a boat at a concrete slipway.

After a few minutes, the same young man he had seen a minute earlier appeared on the slipway. Redmond called to him loudly and this time the man looked up and acknowledged him with a wave. But there was no sign of whatever package he had been carrying. He stepped onto the boat and into the cabin.

In the fading light, the sea was a deep navy blue. The holiday enclave of three houses was peaceful and secluded, but Redmond felt like hurling stones at the boat, to let its insolent owner know what he thought of him. Conor Fitzmaurice joined him at the rail just as the man reappeared from the boat.

'That's young Marcus, right enough,' said Fitzmaurice. 'And as you've probably guessed, the gentle soul who drove off in the van is his brother, Carl, who has his own collection of holiday properties over in Clonakilty.' The sergeant allowed a shade of sarcasm in his voice. 'The family is a fount of enterprise, to be sure.'

Marcus O'Sullivan came up to the patio a few minutes later, apologising for any delay he had caused them. He had been cleaning out one of the houses, he explained.

'Hard times, eh?' he said lightly. 'Work is an incurable affliction, there's no doubt about it.'

'You made a statement to Sergeant Fitzmaurice yesterday,' said Redmond, his own tone as curt and authoritative as he could make it. 'A false statement, as it appears now, so we're here to get an accurate account of your movements last Thursday, and the identity of the person seen with you in your car at half-past two that afternoon.'

Marcus leaned against the rail and shut his eyes for a moment. Unlike Fergus Malden, he was not in the least nervous in the presence of gardai.

'Look, I'm sorry if there was a misunderstanding,' he ventured then. 'But I'm sure you can both remember the follies of youth?'

'Listen to me carefully, son, because I'll say this much just the once.' Fitzmaurice had no problem asserting his authority. 'You can forget your shameless blather because we're not here about a misunderstanding. It's an offence to give false information to a garda, and if we hear any more fables from you—'

'OK, cool, no worries.' Marcus assumed a serious air and looked directly at the sergeant. 'The point is, the person I was with last Thursday . . . Well, I was trying to avoid getting her into trouble, you see. She's not Irish, she's Slovakian, and the situation is a bit tricky.'

'Keep talking. The plain facts, that's all we need.'

'The plain facts are that her name is Katya and she lives in

Clonakilty. She became friendly with my brother Carl a few months ago, but very recently, herself and myself, you see, let's say—'

'Let's say you've been shagging her, is that it? She's your brother's girlfriend but she's happy to keep another stallion in the stable?'

'Hold on, sergeant, I don't think you should insult a woman you've never met, *por favor*. What happened was that I drove straight back here last Thursday when I got word that the Tipperary gig was off.' Marcus picked a bit of brushwood off his shirt and then looked back at Fitzmaurice. He had long elegant hands, and in spite of the dirt he could see under his fingernails, Redmond figured he had no love of manual work.

'But then I phoned Katya,' he continued, 'because I happened to know that she was over in Castletown on business, and she told me she was free for the afternoon.'

'And then, *por favor* yourself? Did you pick her up in town or what?'

'No, we met at Scannive, which is why I was seen there with her at the time you said. After a while I suggested we take a little scenic tour, and lucky me, she was gameball so off we went.'

'Off where, or do we have to extract your story like rotten teeth?'

Marcus winked man-to-man at his interviewers. 'We went over to Ardgroom, and then up the valley to Glenbeg Lake, to a grand quiet spot where we could admire the view. Then one thing led to another, you see, the way these things sometimes do.' He flicked a lock of dark hair off his forehead and resumed a more serious look. 'But maybe you understand now what my problem was when you quizzed me first. So if you could possibly not mention this episode to my brother, I'd appreciate it, and there's also a young lady living in this area—'

'If you could possibly keep your trousers zipped, we'd all be better off.' Fitzmaurice glared at Marcus. 'We don't give a tuppenny curse about your sleazy love life, but your play-acting is a waste of our precious time, and I promise you we'll check out everything you said, if we need to.' He spoke briskly. 'Now, would you mind telling us whether you laid eyes on

Oscar Malden at Scannive Strand, while you were warming up for your scenic tour, *mar dhea*?'

Redmond took note of the negative response. He found it hard to believe a word Marcus O'Sullivan had said. He thought he was a waster, just like his brother. They all got up, but then Redmond asked Marcus a final question as he made to saunter off.

'You were carrying a box or a package when I arrived. You seemed to be in a hurry to get rid of it, so perhaps you'd like to tell us what was in it?'

'A box, guard?' Marcus seemed surprised at the question. 'Oh, you mean . . .? Sure that was just a few old shrubs I cleared from the front of the house above, and tipped over the cliffside to get rid of them.'

ELEVEN

Wednesday 23 September, 6.30 a.m.

Nessa checked her travel bag, packed since the weekend. Her friend Caitlín had urged her to leave Beara for a few days if the pressure became too much. On Sunday afternoon, Ronan had been collected by family friends who lived on the far side of Bantry. The only option now was for her and Sal to join him.

Monday and Tuesday had been relatively quiet, but just before midnight on Tuesday, she received a text from a sub-editor on Jack Talbot's newspaper, a woman Nessa knew since their time in college decades earlier, who was doing her a favour by giving her advance warning of a hostile story.

'Bware JT,' the text said. 'Going big on OM & ur husb, alleg secret mtg, Russ consp theory no less. Take care out there.'

An hour later, the paper's online edition was leading with Talbot's story. 'Surprise new evidence,' it said, 'confirms a phone call at midday on Thursday last between Oscar Malden and Patrick Latif, co-owner of Cnoc Meala guesthouse where murder victim Malden spent the last night of his life. It is also believed that the two men actually met after their call, and if so, Patrick Latif may have been the last witness to Malden's movements before the brutal killing that has stunned the nation.' Then he added: 'But that same evening, Latif took a last-minute flight to faraway southern Africa, and has been uncontactable since that time.'

The words swirled in front of Nessa's eyes as she read on. Talbot was careful, of course, not to fling around murder accusations against Patrick. Instead, in a typical piece of word-play, he stated that, 'No evidence has emerged to implicate Latif in Malden's shocking murder. But gardai refuse to rule out the possibility that he could hold vital clues to the case. They admit that they wish to interview Latif urgently, not only about Thursday's events, but about new information revealed exclusively by your correspondent today.'

'Oscar Malden's successful business empire included a number of companies in Russia. Following extensive research, we have established that Patrick Latif also had long-established connections in that part of the world, having spent his student days in Soviet Moscow. Latif maintained close links with both business and security figures in the Russian capital, and took part in a controversial trip there only last year, during which two extremist agitators in his group were arrested. We can also confirm that Oscar Malden visited Moscow in the same month as Latif.'

Nessa managed a faint smile at the last sentence. So what if the two men had visited Moscow, Madrid or Madagascar in the same month, when thousands of others had achieved the same feat too? But the story was damaging, she knew that only too well, whatever sources Talbot had for it. And trying to get to sleep was futile. Every time she closed her eyes, his insinuating phrases echoed in her head: 'may have been the last witness'; 'no evidence has emerged to implicate'; 'could hold vital clues to the case'; 'a last-minute flight to faraway Africa'. She got up to look at the internet several times, and saw the same lines spread to more papers, chatrooms and tweets. Before they had eaten their breakfast cereal, the whole western world would have heard enough to make Patrick a prime suspect. And the media would be camped out in Cnoc Meala's front garden.

It was still dark when she dressed herself. She had already agreed with Caitlín how to organise a hurried departure, and by twenty to seven, she forced herself to dial her friend's number.

'I'm really sorry to wake you up so early.'

'Never mind sorry, tell me what's happened overnight?'

'Are you still OK to drive me?'

'I'll be with you as soon as I can. You can explain things on our way.'

Nessa made a second call to her friends Mary and Tom in Dunmanus, on the other side of Bantry. Only the night before,

Ronan had told her on the phone that it was fun to go to school with their two boys. He would probably be quite happy to see his mother and sister join his unplanned holiday – but as for Sal, Nessa was not surprised to hear a torrent of complaint as soon as she woke her daughter.

'No way, I'm not going anywhere. You can't make me.'

'I'm really sorry, Sal, but I've no choice.'

Sal held on to her duvet, pushing her hair out of her eyes with the back of her hand. '*You've* no choice, you say? Well, why don't you think of me for a change? I've been stuck in this room studying every blasted evening, and now I won't be able to meet Marcus on Friday night. You're doing it deliberately . . .'

'Sal, listen to me, please, because we have to hurry. Caitlín will leave you with her next-door neighbour, who'll drive you to school, while Caitlín and I go on to her cousin's house in Adrigole. You'll be brought there later, and at teatime, Mary will drive over from Dunmanus.'

'So we're going to slink around in other people's cars in the dark, like criminals or something? And this is to stop Sky News spying on us from a helicopter? Jesus, get real!'

'Give it up, Sal, in the name of goodness. Maybe it seems ridiculous to you, but we have to deal with a very nasty reality just now.' Nessa could hardly think straight after her sleepless night, but she did her best to soften her tone. 'And Sal, make sure you don't say a word to your friends at school, love, because it's so horribly easy for innocent words to be twisted out of all recognition.'

Derryowen was almost deserted at seven in the morning. The enormous satellite trucks had retreated to Bantry the previous day, along with the main assault line of news troops. But there were a few cars in the village that Nessa did not recognise, and she kept her head down while Caitlín ran into the shop for a few minutes. She felt as if she had been stripped naked and had to hide from the world.

She thought back over the conversation she had finally had with Patrick on Monday morning. He was very upset, having just left his aunt's bedside. Esther was slipping away, he told her, and preparations were already being discussed for her funeral, to bring her to her home village almost two hundred miles from the city. Patrick was also involved in financial and legal arrangements for four of her grandchildren, whom Esther had looked after since their parents died from AIDS years earlier.

When he finally got around to asking Nessa how she was, she kept to a very limited version of the turmoil at home, having decided to tell him the full story if Esther rallied, or as soon as the funeral was over. She explained that Oscar Malden had died suddenly and tragically after his departure from Beara, and that the circumstances were being investigated. Gardai had taken statements from herself and others, and would have to speak to Patrick in due course. He commiserated with her on the phone, but it was clear to Nessa that his mind was elsewhere.

The next morning, on Tuesday, she got a text from him announcing Esther's death and plans for the funeral on Thursday. Nessa sent him all her love and condolences, and then phoned Superintendent Devane. She had told him at the weekend that Patrick lost his mobile phone en route to Malawi and as a result, that it was difficult to contact him; now she said apologetically that her husband had to go to a remote part of the country for a family funeral, and that it would be best if gardai could wait until Friday to speak to him. Devane was very sympathetic and, contrary to the impression given by Jack Talbot, simply added that gardai would be very glad to talk to him as soon as that could be arranged.

As she hunched in the car on Wednesday morning, Nessa decided to phone Superintendent Devane again, to check whether Talbot's story had changed things. She wished, of course, that she had been able to share the whole story with Patrick as soon as she knew of Oscar's murder, but there was no point in going back over that ground again. What's more, currying sympathy from Talbot by telling him about Esther would probably have made no difference. He was out to make life hard for Cnoc Meala's owners, and to cast a malicious cloak on any version of the truth.

Caitlín turned on the car radio as they headed out of Derryowen. Before long, they heard Jack's smooth voice gliding through an interview on a leading current affairs' programme. He was clearly enjoying himself to the full.

'As we understand only too well,' he said, 'the Garda Síochána are doing their utmost to solve this heinous crime. Indeed, Interpol and police forces in several countries are also cooperating fully with those efforts.'

'Have you reason to believe, then, that Interpol or Russian police officers are investigating the kinds of links you make in your story today?'

'I regret that I cannot disclose the precise lines of enquiry being followed, but I am certainly confident that my own researches are of relevance, yes, and that the authorities will pursue every possible avenue in their search for this cold-blooded killer.'

'You're so sly!' said Nessa under her breath. 'Saying everything and nothing in one breath.'

'And the witness you name in your story today, how might he be able to assist the investigation?' asked the interviewer.

'As we know,' Talbot intoned solemnly, 'Oscar Malden had several companies in Russia. We also know that a Russian ship has been stranded in Castletownbere harbour for some weeks, amid competing claims of responsibility for the welfare of its crew. What I have now established is that Patrick Latif, who is normally resident in Beara, also has close links with Russia, and appears to have been in contact with the abandoned ship's crew. Indeed, he travelled to Moscow less than a year ago with a group of people from Ireland whose mission was shadowy to say the least.'

'And you say he met with Malden on the day of the murder?'

'He is believed to have spoken to him on the phone, yes, and may well have met him shortly afterwards. But I would like to assure your listeners that there is no suggestion that such a meeting was anything but lawful and innocent.'

'Christ Almighty!' said Caitlín, turning down the sound as the interview came to an end. 'What is all that about, tell me? Jack makes it sound like a James Bond film, doesn't he?'

Nessa looked out the window. Streaks of light were breaking through the eastern sky, the colour of blood oranges. She tried to assemble her fragmented thoughts.

'I've no idea where this stuff came from,' she said, 'about Patrick meeting Oscar on Thursday. He was in a fluster getting ready to leave, but for all I know, the pair of them just passed each other on the road and were seen having a friendly chat.'

'Fair enough, that sounds plausible, but what about Russia? Are these so-called shadowy connections a figment of Jack's fevered imagination?'

'Well, not completely, but it's the way he describes it.'

'I remember Patrick going off on that trip last year, and I know he speaks Russian fluently, but that hardly counts as a crime, does it?'

'I think it's a case of putting a few unrelated facts on the same page and hoping they look like cause and effect, as if Patrick being in Moscow proves he plotted with Oscar's enemies to kill him. But having said that, there was some trouble during the trip, so there's material there to exploit. As for the Russian ship, it's also true that Patrick met with two of the crew last Wednesday. It wasn't his idea, he did it because a trade unionist he knows in Cork asked him to help out with translation, and naturally enough, Patrick didn't like to say no.'

Nessa felt exhausted. If she could rewind her life just one week, there were so many details she would change. But self-pity made her cross too, and she tried to remind herself that her biggest regret should be for Oscar Malden's sake.

Caitlín's tone was careful when she next spoke. 'So even if the facts are being totally manipulated, you're saying there's something in Talbot's story? If that's the case, it doesn't look good for Patrick, does it, as far as explaining himself goes?'

'It looks grim at this moment.' Nessa looked at her friend anxiously. 'And I'd imagine there's a lot of talk around the area already – for example, that Patrick and I are outsiders to Derryowen who've brought a whole lot of trouble to the place?'

Caitlín's voice was very gentle when she replied, after paying great attention to the next bend in the road.

'Don't torment yourself, Nessa, about that sort of idle back-chat. You've enough to worry about, especially while Patrick's not here to defend himself.'

Nessa held her face in her hands. Her skin felt as brittle as her feelings. 'After that night with Dominic . . . It's hard to describe, but half the time I'm just boiling mad, like a pressure cooker without a vent, and then all of a sudden I feel helpless, as if I've no say anymore over what happens in my life, which makes me angry too.'

'Shush now, it's terribly hard on you.' Caitlín fiddled with the radio again. 'Why don't you take a rest and we'll listen to a bit of music for a while? We could pull in at the Healy Pass, how about that? And if you feel like telling me more about Patrick's Russian adventures, I promise to keep my mouth shut and let you talk.'

Caitlín had decided not to drive through Castletownbere on their way to her cousin's house, but instead to take the longer Kenmare road on the north side of Beara, and to cross the mountain road in the middle of the peninsula. That way, they would be less likely to meet roving journalists. Nessa looked out the window at the wide waters of the bay to her left. She felt as if her teeth had been clenched tightly all night long, but as the notes of a piano sonata rippled from the radio, she allowed her eyelids to drop and her breathing to ease. When the car jolted on a pothole a while later, she was surprised to see that they were on a steep road above a valley, surrounded by purple-grey mountains.

It took her a few minutes to remember where they were going and why. Then she became aware of a sharp new realisation. She had to stop simply reacting to events, and to channel her frustration and anger instead of being overcome by them. She was only as helpless as she would allow herself to be.

It was bad enough that a man she and Patrick had welcomed into their house was dead, and that Cnoc Meala's reputation would suffer in the aftermath. Local gossip and stares were unpleasant too, and now the whole family would have to bear up to Talbot's smearing insinuations, and the possibility that gardai might take them seriously enough to suspect him of murder. But the dart that pierced Nessa most deeply was the hint of doubt she heard in Caitlín's voice. How could Patrick hold up his head if their closest friends wondered whether his actions had been honest and totally innocent of all violent intent?

His reputation and his liberty were both at risk. Meanwhile, the garda investigation seemed to be grinding on without a breakthrough. Waiting passively for good news was no longer enough, and Nessa would have to figure out what on earth she could do to help unearth the truth.

'I haven't been up here for years!' Caitlín manouevred the car into a parking space by the roadside. 'I should be ashamed of myself, forever spouting to our tourists in the pub about the fantastic views they'll get from the Healy Pass and not bothering to make the trip myself. I even give the tourists a bit of history, you know, about the pass being named after Beara's own Tim Healy, the first governor of the Irish Free State.'

Nessa was happy to let her friend chatter on for a while. Things were stressful for Caitlín too. Her shop and pub got plenty of new business during the media invasion, but many locals stayed away, avoiding the glare of public attention. Indeed, some of her older customers were now afraid to go out at night, in case the killer was lying in wait for more victims. Others talked about the case all the time, elbows propped on the bar while they grumbled about the gardai's ceaseless questions. Where did you spend last Thursday and Friday? How can you be sure you remember the time you saw this person or that? If you met Oscar Malden, how did he look? What did you eat for breakfast the day before yesterday?

The women clambered over a low wall to a patch of grass and heather. Behind them, Beara's great backbone of the Caha mountains stretched along the peninsula. Ahead of them, they gazed out at an enticing vista: the dark waters of Lake Glanmore in the embrace of shapely hills; beyond it, a soft quilted blanket of fertile farmland and abundant hedges; and on neighbouring Iveragh peninsula across the slender rim of the bay, the tip of Carrantouhil, the country's highest mountain, rising up to the clouds above the muscular shoulders of the Reeks.

'Here we are,' said Caitlín quietly, 'saluting the sunrise in this earthly paradise, while the shadows of death pursue us.'

Nessa listened to the silence of the place before she spoke in her turn. 'It's terrible to remember too that Oscar's murderer drove along at least a part of this road, to leave his body by the little bridge on the far side of the pass.'

'Did you ever hear about the funeral processions up here long ago, where the ridge marks the boundary of the two counties?' Caitlín gestured in both directions. 'Cork is behind us and Kerry is on this side of the Healy Pass, as you know. So let's say that two people from Beara got married, a Corkman and a Kerrywoman, and they lived on his patch but had no children. Well, when the woman died, it seems that the man's people would carry the coffin up to the mountain pass, and leave it on a slab of rock right at the boundary; and her people had to come from the Kerry side to take it away and bury it in their own graveyard.'

'What was the reason for that?'

'I presume it had something to do with the fact that she hadn't produced children, which meant that she was useless in the eyes of some.'

'So you mean she hadn't earned the privilege of burial with her husband? And maybe it was also a show of rivalry between the two counties?'

'It was probably both. I suppose the rituals of death express a lot about the culture we live in.'

Nessa pulled a woollen cap down over her ears. She could feel a chill wind ascending from the valley, but the image that came to her was of a funeral in a warmer country. Esther's coffin would be carried to her native place on the back of a truck, accompanied by relatives singing hymns and songs of lament as they made the journey along the shore of Lake Malawi. Nessa could remember vividly making the same long journey for Patrick's mother's funeral, when Ronan was still a toddler, and the crowds greeting them outside the thatched huts of the village as they arrived in the sweltering heat. She wished she could be there with Patrick this time, slipping her hand into his.

Caitlín sat on a low rock to read a printout of Jack Talbot's articles and Nessa looked over her shoulder, imagining thousands of people around the country reading them too. When she looked up again, she saw that large clouds had gathered in the distance, smothering the Reeks in a dense white fog.

'So explain to me,' said Caitlín in a light voice. She swept her long hair back into the collar of her jacket. 'How did Patrick come to be a commie-loving student who has maintained close links with business and security types in Russia for the past few decades?'

'He got a scholarship to Moscow when he was aged about twenty, that was how it started. He was living in Mozambique then, after his family had fled from Malawi, and a lot of students from Africa and Asia went to university in the Soviet Union on scholarships of the same kind. I suppose it was all part of the Cold War battle for hearts and minds.'

'And then?'

'And then he moved elsewhere, and ended up working as a tour guide and translator in a number of countries. But he returned to Moscow around the time of the collapse of the Soviet Union in the early nineties, mainly out of curiosity.'

'You must have met him for the first time soon after that?'

Nessa smiled. 'Yes, the following autumn – but far away from Moscow, in the mountains of Mallorca. Later, though, Patrick got some work translating and organising for Irish companies that were keen to dip their toes in Russian waters, and he was invited back a few times, which accounts for his alleged familiarity with business figures. Mind you, we're not talking shady billionaires here, or even Oscar's kind of millionaire either.'

'But Jack also claims that Patrick's in with some sinister security types over there?'

'For which you should read that Patrick knows one individual who worked in Russian intelligence for about five years, in a desk job that involved no spying. I've been racking my brains about this, as you can imagine, and I think he also knows someone else who works as a security guard for a private company.'

'But even so, how did Jack Talbot come up with that information? Has he been hacking Patrick's emails, or learning Russian in his spare time?'

Nessa sat on the cold rock beside Caitlín, hugging her hands in her sleeves. 'I'd say it's simpler than that. Someone has been whispering in his ear about last year's trip to Moscow.

A few of the group fell out with each other afterwards, so for all I know, one of them is sniping at the others by dragging the story into the news now.'

Caitlín fingered the paper, and Nessa noticed how she chose her words carefully. 'So these supposed extremists are not Patrick's bosom pals, is that it? I mean, I have to say it doesn't sound like him, because I didn't even know he was a member of a political grouping?'

'He isn't,' said Nessa firmly. 'He's always shied away from joining any campaign, no matter how much he supports the cause. I think his family history made him nervous of political involvement, so it's pretty ironic to see him painted as a dangerous militant now.'

'What was the trip to Moscow for, in that case? I don't suppose he was promoting a band of jolly musicians, or Ireland's cottage cheese industry?'

'Not quite, no. He went because a friend of his in Bandon, James, asked him to do a favour to someone else – and while I said that Patrick doesn't join things, he's also quite a sucker for helping people on a personal basis. The trip was organised by a number of activists campaigning on ethical standards in international business, which is a pretty major issue, as you can imagine. They got hold of some money to investigate employment abuses in Russia but unfortunately, the trip turned into a bit of a fiasco.'

'You mentioned earlier that people fell out with each other?'

'Yes, they couldn't agree on priorities for a start. And in any case, two or three of the group were prima donna attention-seekers. They were the ones who got arrested, not for taking part in a legitimate protest, but just for rowdy behaviour at an event. Some of the others tried to disown them, which led to a split in the group. A familiar story for some fringe groups, I'm afraid.'

'But whatever happened, it makes Patrick look untrustworthy, doesn't it?'

Nessa did not answer, as she watched great coils of cloud furling from the horizon. The view they had admired a short while earlier was changing by the moment. Curtains of mist swept over the steep slopes of Knockatee and Knockanoughanish,

and dazzling rays of light fissured the sky. In another few minutes
the ocean's vapours would smother the rocky mountain pass they
stood on. She had a brief sensation of vertigo as she thought
about the volatility of everything.

'Patrick was really upset at the whole thing,' she said after
a few minutes. 'But at the same time, Jack could be on to
something. I don't mean his insinuations about Patrick, but
what if there's a link between Oscar and the abandoned Russian
ship, say?'

'You mean Oscar could be one of the owners of the ship,
and caused it to be abandoned?'

'Anything is possible, that's all I'm saying. His murder may
have very little to do with Beara, except that a deep and
dangerous current from across the seas made its way into our
sheltered bays.'

They returned to the car and drove through a cragged mountain gap. The road plunged into a wide and striking valley,
twisting around one hairpin bend after another. Nessa remembered the story Caitlín had told her about funerals in past
times. It reminded her of something but she could not figure
out what. An image of a corpse, perhaps, or an insight into
the rituals of death.

Another idea struck her as she was grappling with it.

'I wonder if you'd mind . . . I'd like to stop at the bridge,
Caitlín, if you can spare a little more time?'

She paused as she realised that Caitlín had her eye on a car
in the rear-view mirror, and another approaching from below.
The road was too narrow for anyone to pass, but after a few
minutes, the car behind her drew into a small layby.

'It's just a little theory I'd like to try out,' Nessa continued
then. 'But if you'd prefer not to bother, we'll go directly to
your cousin's house in Adrigole.'

TWELVE

Redmond refocussed his camera lens but he was too late. The people he was trying to photograph had moved out of frame, and getting a close-up would be impossible now. He had taken one shot but he was fairly sure it was fuzzy. There was nothing for it but confrontation.

When he saw something being thrown from the bridge, his first wild thought was that he was hallucinating. Then he wondered whether a fly had buzzed past the camera. But when it happened a second time, he could have no doubt about it. He jumped into his car and drove around the hairpin bends as quickly as possible. He knew very well who was down at the bridge.

He'd seen them outside the shop in Derryowen early that morning. Caitlín O'Donovan hurrying out of her car, and someone else in the passenger seat, head bent low. He guessed it was Nessa McDermott, even before he identified her reddish hair through the long lens on his camera. Redmond had already seen the news online about her husband. Patrick Latif's actions since the day of Malden's murder certainly gave cause for suspicion, especially as McDermott seemed to be unwilling to help gardai to contact him.

Redmond decided to follow the two women as they drove out of Derryowen. He wanted to do something, anything, to play a fuller part in the investigation. The morning's briefing session in Bantry had been cancelled and he had driven to Derryowen on a whim, having two hours to spare before meeting a colleague in Castletownbere for a door-to-door assignment. Of course, the women could be off on a shopping trip to Killarney or Cork. But suppose Latif had returned to Ireland and was lying low to see how the wind shifted? McDermott could be on her way to meet him secretly, and if so, the super would be very grateful for that information.

Luckily, Redmond was driving his own Renault and not a marked police car, which Caitlín O'Donovan would have spotted instantly in her rear-view mirror. Even so, it was quite difficult to tail her unnoticed. When she pulled in just before the Healy Pass, he had to drive past her, sunglasses in place, to park on the far side of the gap. Then the two women delayed interminably as they chatted and gazed at the view, while he froze to the marrow behind a hillock fifty metres away.

When they finally set off again, he followed them at a cautious distance and pulled into a layby when they drove down to the bridge. He could watch them from his car window, using the long lens on the camera as binoculars. At first, he had no idea what they were up to, but he almost dropped the camera when he saw them fling a large black item from the parapet of the bridge.

As he drove down the hill at speed, his memory of finding Oscar Malden's body rose up like bile. According to the pathologist, one or two animals had been on the scene before the birds of prey arrived. The double plastic bag might have torn on stones when it was thrown, and as the morning grew warmer, the ripe smell of flesh had attracted a fox or a badger. Redmond knew he would never forget the image of a human hand protruding pitifully from the ragged heap by the stream.

The women's car was still parked by the bridge but there was no sign of them. He tried to keep his footing as he ran down the uneven slope. 'Stay where you are!' he shouted. 'I saw you throw a bag, and then something else.'

Drops of rain spat on his face. He hoped the women were not playing a game of hide-and-seek, hiding under the arched bridge and hoping to reach their car by dashing up the slope on the far side.

He glanced upstream. A lone tree was crouched against the wind and black clouds had obliterated the mountain tops. He turned back towards the bridge and called out again just as Nessa McDermott stepped out from under it, carrying a long navy-blue sports bag in one hand, and a torn black binliner in the other.

'I can explain what we're doing. We just wanted to understand—'

'You can keep your explanations until we're at the station. A murder investigation is underway, as you know full well, and as a member of the Garda Síochána, I have the authority to request . . .'

Nessa opened the bag's zip brusquely and removed an old towel. Several large stones lay underneath. 'We wanted to find out how much strength it took to get Oscar's body over the parapet, and whether a woman could do it, for example.'

'As I've just said, you may explain your little games to Inspector O'Kelleher at the station.' Redmond was getting angry. These women were making a fool of him.

'We're really sorry about this, Garda Joyce, but we didn't realise we had an audience.' Caitlín O'Donovan's voice was friendlier than McDermott's. 'I'm sure your technical people have carried out these tests already, but we've worked out a few useful points.'

'Whatever your intentions, I will be obliged to inform the inspector that I encountered you here in suspicious circumstances.'

'And will you inform him that you followed us for miles, as I presume you did? What was your garda authority for that particular decision?' McDermott's eyes were glinting like bullets. 'Or alternatively, instead of wasting Inspector O'Kelleher's time, maybe we could try helping each other?'

'It is a garda matter to decide what constitutes time-wasting, Mrs McDermott.'

The women regarded him silently. The rain was getting heavier, and Redmond was afraid they would walk past him in disdain. He was also burning with curiosity to know what they had found out.

He tried for a more conciliatory tone. 'Of course, we welcome the cooperation of the public in our investigations, and I can accept that your intentions were good. I may have to mention this incident to the inspector, but nevertheless . . .'

He was rewarded with a hint of a smile from Caitlín O'Donovan.

'We're all out of sorts, Garda Joyce, on account of this

business,' she said. 'But for what it's worth, we've confirmed that only a very strong person could have dumped poor Oscar's body where it was found.'

Redmond nodded at her encouragingly, relieved not to feel intimidated by at least one of the women.

'If the bag was dropped from the centre of the bridge,' Caitlín continued, 'it should have landed directly in the water and not up on the bank. So it's more likely that the person stood further along, by the lower part of the wall. The snag is that there's a level patch of ground just below that, and therefore only a really strong person could have thrown the body in such a way that it would have rolled down the slope.'

Nessa McDermott did not bother to smile as she added her own observation. 'An alternative scenario is that the bag was carried down the slope to where it was found, but again, that would require strong muscles, and would be pretty difficult in the dark. However, it's always possible that two people were involved, either in the murder itself or in the act of disposing of the body.'

Redmond did not get an opportunity to speak to Inspector O'Kelleher until teatime. He spent the day calling to all the guesthouses and B&Bs in the Castletownbere area. Superintendent Devane was hoping to collect phone numbers for everyone who had visited Beara during the week of the murder, in order to check whether any of them had been in contact with Oscar. A garda team was still combing the lists of numbers provided by the phone companies, showing every single call made in the area that week: the young barman in Derryowen Hotel calling his girlfriend in Glengarriff on Thursday evening; Nessa McDermott on the phone on Friday to Derreen Gardens over in Lauragh; Sal texting friends about the party that night. A snapshot compilation of community life, along with tantalising evidence of Oscar Malden's final hours.

Redmond had a copy of the calls involving Oscar, and in particular those for which gardai did not have a satisfactory explanation:

12.02 p.m.: Call from Patrick Latif to Oscar, answered, duration three minutes.

01.05 p.m.: Call from unknown phone to Oscar, not answered, voice message left.

01.20 p.m.: Call from Maureen Scurlock to Oscar, not answered, voice message left.

01.35 p.m.: Oscar listened to his voice messages.

01.37 p.m.: Call from Oscar to the same unknown phone as above, answered, call duration four minutes.

01.43 p.m.: Text from Oscar to Fergus, telling him to cancel the taxi booking because of a change of plan. Ten minutes later, Fergus phoned Marcus O'Sullivan's hackney company.

Clearly, Oscar Malden had been busy around the time he disappeared from sight. But while phone records showed which calls had been made, they could not reveal what was said. And at a quarter past two on Thursday, the telecommunication signal from his mobile phone had ceased, suggesting that the SIM card had been removed or damaged. No further record of his phone or his movements had been identified. On the second day of the investigation, an English tourist had come forward to say he saw Malden around mid-afternoon on Thursday, in the hills east of Coomgarriff. But when he was questioned again, he apologised and withdrew his statement, saying he had mixed up the days, and had seen Malden on Tuesday. It was difficult to remember one day from another while on holidays, he said.

Superintendent Devane had not told the garda team whether he was confident of speaking to Patrick Latif soon, to hear his explanation of the call to Oscar. However, Latif's own movements on Thursday were being tracked via other calls he had made, as well as his mobile phone signals. Maureen Scurlock had been interviewed several times – she now admitted phoning Oscar after leaving the hotel, but stuck to the line that she had failed to speak to him.

There was also the mystery of the unknown phone. It was a prepaid rather than a bill-paid mobile phone, and therefore no owner's name had been registered for the number. Gardai had found out that it was purchased in France, and they were trying to pinpoint the exact date and place of purchase. The purpose of Redmond's door-to-door work was to establish whether the phone belonged to someone who had stayed in a local hotel, guesthouse or rented accommodation in Beara that week.

It was repetitive work, asking the same questions time after time. There was no problem getting B&B proprietors to open the door – the majority of them were women who loved to talk, and had ample opinions on the case. Some had clearly prepared their answers in advance, so Redmond and his colleague came to the conclusion that a chain of neighbourly phone calls preceded their every move from one B&B to another. Of course, the proprietors were also professionals when it came to offering tea and apple tart, not to mention a nice warm spot by the fire 'to toast your feet after being out in that terrible rain', as several of them put it.

After refusing all such offers, Redmond found himself ravenously hungry by midday. He had decided a few weeks earlier to tackle his thickening waistline, and was on breakfast rations of a half litre of water plus a piece of crispbread. In order to prevent himself succumbing to the comfort food on offer, he allowed himself a lunch of two bananas, an apple and a litre of water, followed by oat biscuits at four o'clock.

By that time, he and his colleague had visited at least twenty B&Bs and two hotels. They had been told about visitors who had changed plans at short notice, or washed their car on the Friday night or Saturday morning, or done anything else remotely akin to suspicious behaviour. But they had nothing new on the unknown phone; and the word on the grapevine was that their colleagues had drawn a blank in other parts of Beara too.

'I wonder if I could have a word with you privately?'

Redmond felt nervous as he put his question to Inspector O'Kelleher in Castletownbere station. He was not at all sure how best to explain the incident at the bridge, but he felt equally nervous of not mentioning it. But O'Kelleher countered with another question.

'Have you ever been to the the Buddhist Centre a few miles from here?' When Redmond looked at him in surprise, O'Kelleher continued. 'It's called the Dzogchen Beara, and there's a fine hostel there, as it happens. They also rent out a few houses to their visitors, so we could check out this business of the phone numbers with them, and have a quiet chat ourselves. It's some place, I promise you that, and now that the sky has cleared at last, we'll see it at its best.'

They drove southwest of Castletownbere on the Allihies road, and eventually took a minor turning towards the sea. The inspector talked about the pathologist's report, which was to be discussed at the following morning's briefing. Unfortunately, he said, the report gave no new indication of the time or place of death. Nor was it possible to identify precisely the material used to strangle Malden. The nearest the pathologist could suggest was a smooth cable, or perhaps a thin scarf of silk or other cloth that did not leave telltale marks, as a rope would, for example. It was confirmed, however, that Malden had been seated and his killer standing at his shoulder, as indicated by the angle of the injury on his throat; it was also clear that Malden had offered no resistance when approached from behind.

'Why do you think the pathologist was unable to determine clearly the time of death?' O'Kelleher spoke in his usual soft voice, but Redmond realised that his senior officer was testing him, and he was glad he could answer promptly.

'If a body is found within a day of death, its temperature indicates the number of hours since death, plus or minus two to three hours. But once twenty-four hours have elapsed, the temperature is so low that it's irrelevant as a factor. The evidence of rigor mortis also ceases to be useful, I believe, because after a day or two, depending on the air temperature and so on, the muscles loosen again.'

Redmond tried not to sound as if he was reciting from a book. 'I presume, inspector, that as a result of these difficulties the Patrickhologist can only say that Oscar was killed on Thursday, some time between lunchtime and late that night.'

'Very good, Redmond. You can move on from beginners to the intermediate class.' O'Kelleher was clearly enjoying his role as examiner. 'Now, what might the pathologist have searched for, in order to determine where Malden was killed?'

'The type of soil on his clothes, perhaps, if he had been lying on the ground outdoors for a period? But if Malden was seated, as you said . . .'

Redmond paused, worried that he did not have a pat reply this time. He knew that seeds and other such material could be very important, but O'Kelleher might expect him to be able to name the likely plants. Just in time, however, he remembered that insect evidence was crucial too.

'It would be very helpful to determine whether death took place indoors or outdoors, inspector,' he said carefully. 'So if Malden's body was placed in the plastic bag indoors, it's possible that a housefly got into the bag at the same time, and laids its eggs on the body. And in that case, the number of eggs or maggots could give some indication of the time period too.'

'So it could. But unfortunately, our helpful fly didn't make it into the bag, and we're left wondering whether it would have been a housefly or one of its hardy country cousins.'

They parked in a large carpark and walked through woodland to the Buddhist Centre. Redmond half-wondered whether they would see barefoot monks in prayerful chant. But when they emerged on the far side of the trees, he gasped at the view that lay ahead: a series of green and russet slopes tumbling and curving down to the sea along Bantry Bay, whose wide waters glistened in the pink evening light. Other than the centre's neat buildings on the cliffside, no human habitation could be seen.

O'Kelleher led him to a tranquil garden high above the rocks. Redmond felt as if they were perched on the edge of the known world. He vowed silently that he would return on his own to absorb the utter peace of the place, which he found seductive and terrifying all at once.

O'Kelleher said nothing for a while, and it occurred to Redmond that perhaps he practised meditation regularly at this very spot. If so, that would explain the unusual calm of his working methods.

'We'll have a word with someone in the centre's office

shortly,' said O'Kelleher then. 'But our precious phone evidence may not really amount to much.'

'Is that because one person could have two or three mobile phones, for example? So the unknown phone may belong to someone we've already questioned?'

'That's entirely possible, Redmond. And it's also difficult to rely on telecom evidence in a place like Beara, where masts are sparse and inconvenient mountains get in the way of straight lines. In an urban area, we might be able to pin down Oscar's location at a particular time by checking how his phone had tuned in to the nearest or most powerful mast in the area. But really, he could have been anywhere within a few miles of either Derryowen or Coomgarriff when he was in contact with our mystery caller.'

Redmond found it strange to discuss the mechanics of murder in a lovely garden by the sea. He finally made himself recount the incident with the two women, giving the impression that he had chanced upon them by the bridge.

'I'm grateful to you for telling me this, Redmond,' was O'Kelleher's bald comment when he had finished. The inspector pondered in silence for several long minutes, while Redmond glanced anxiously at his lean profile. 'Tell me something else,' the inspector said then. 'I sensed a particular tension between yourself and Nessa McDermott when we interviewed her, and I wondered why that might be?'

'I'm sorry, I don't understand what you're getting at.'

'My own impression is that she's a shrewd woman, and very alert to the world around her. But she certainly has a rather direct manner, and maybe you found that difficult?'

'Well, no, but I thought—'

'In our job, as you know, it's important not to make instant judgements about people, whether we like them or not.'

'I thought you were wary of her yourself, inspector, and didn't trust her?'

'What gave you that idea?'

'You said something last week about expecting trouble from her . . .'

'Did I? Well, maybe I didn't mean it quite as literally as you assumed at that instant.' O'Kelleher smiled gently, to take the sting out of his words. He interlocked his long thin fingers, and hunched his shoulders in a way that reminded Redmond of his father.

'One of the great challenges of garda work,' he continued, 'is how to be wary of people and still win their trust. Without that mutual trust and respect, they won't tell us anything, but of course we can't be such fools as to believe every word we hear.'

Redmond nodded, to avoid saying the wrong thing again.

'I'd like to mention another little thing, Redmond, now that I have this opportunity. We've been in each other's company quite a lot recently, and yet you still call me by my fine official title, as if we'd only met the day before yesterday.' Redmond looked quickly at his companion and saw the kindness in his eyes. 'For goodness sake, just call me Trevor, the same as everyone else does!' He laughed lightly. 'Or cig, if you prefer the Conor Fitz way of doing things.'

'I'm sorry, I didn't intend—'

'What's more, you shouldn't watch me like a hawk, in case you might displease me. You've plenty of ability, son, but you need to stand on your own two feet and make judgements for yourself. Not instant ones, mind you, but the sort that will teach you when to take the initiative and when to hold back.'

Redmond stared out at a darkening sky over the sea's silky expanse. He wished the conversation would end, so that he could sit alone in the garden instead of listening to kind words from a man of his father's generation. He didn't want to be reminded of his father or mother, whom he would never see again.

His companion was speaking as if from a distance. 'It's up to you how you live your life, Redmond, but it might be good for you to go out with the lads from time to time, do you understand what I'm saying? If you keep yourself apart from them, there's always a risk of resentment and backbiting, instead of enjoying yourself and relaxing for a while in their company.'

THIRTEEN

Saturday 26 September, 9.40 a.m.

Drimoleague and Dunmanway, Enniskeane and Inishannon. Nessa recited place names to herself as she studied the route eastwards to Cork city. She had always loved Ordnance Survey maps, not just for the way they evoked the landscape, but for the names of villages, valleys, rivers and hills, that echoed like songs full of memories of lives long ago. Ballineen came from the original Béal Átha Fhinín in Irish, which she figured meant the Mouth of the Ford of Finín, whoever he may have been; and Inishannon was Inis Eonáin, the island or water meadow of Eonán, who could have lived a millennium or two earlier. The Irish 'cnoc' for hill was dotted across her map: Knockgorm, the blue hill; Knocknagarrane, the hill of the groves; Cappaknockane, the tillage field on the hillock. Those same words were familiar to her from Beara, where she had compiled a trove of local information for Cnoc Meala's guided walks.

But as she and Sal travelled towards the city in Darina's van, she knew well that gazing at a map was just a way of distracting herself from the challenges of the day ahead: a visit to Maureen's hospital bed in Cork, and then an hour's journey to Oscar's home area in County Tipperary, to attend his funeral. His remains had been released by the authorities, and as was usual in Ireland, his family arranged to bury him as soon as possible. Nessa knew she would have to attend – that was customary for everyone connected with the deceased, but after three days of seclusion at her friends' house in Dunmanus, she felt unsure of the outside world.

She was relieved, however, that Ronan had clamoured to stay on in Dunmanus, very happy to have two other boys to play with all day long. Their games featured variations on the theme of murder, as Ronan suggested more and more ways to act out their fears and fantasies, but the adults allowed them to get on with it, on the grounds that play-acting in daylight was better than struggling with nightmares. They drew the line, however, at a vociferous competition in which the boys thought up new and unusual methods of strangulation.

Nessa was also greatly relieved to have had a long phone conversation with Patrick the previous evening. This time, she did not hold back on the details of Oscar's violent death, and she told him to expect a phone call from Superintendent Devane. Her husband was shocked to realise that Oscar had been murdered, and so soon after he himself had left Cnoc Meala, and immediately said he would return home to Ireland on the next available flight. Meanwhile, he explained all he could to Nessa about his contacts with Oscar on the day of the murder.

'I don't get the logic. I mean, it was bad enough . . .'

Nessa put aside her map. Their stay in Dunmanus had been marred by Sal's constant grumbling. Even her style of speech was driving her mother mad.

'I think you should, like, make up your mind what you want,' Sal continued. 'There we were three days ago, getting the hell out of Beara as if an actual war had started, but today, it's all "let's make it happen, people, the world is waiting to welcome us". Honestly, I could just about take this dreary funeral in Tipperary, but visiting Maureen in hospital is *way* too much. I mean, what's the plan? A cheery bedside chat with Dominic? I *don't* think so.'

Nessa looked out at the lush greenery streaking past the windows. She could think of ten good reasons not to visit Maureen, most of them involving Dominic, but she felt strongly that it was a courtesy owed to her former guest. That much she could explain to Sal with no difficulty – it was rather trickier, however, to admit that she was also on tenterhooks to hear Maureen's version of Thursday's events.

Sal grimaced when her complaints were met with silence, and after a few minutes, she tried a different tack. 'Well, here's an idea,' she said brightly. 'How about Darina does the hospital thing with you, while I whizz into the nearest shops? I mean to say, I didn't get a chance to pack my funeral outfit before we left home, did I, so I'm not looking my best?'

'Please, Sal, that's enough for now. It may not be your idea of fun, but you know very well that I can't see Maureen on my own in case Dominic is around, and Darina has other things to do.'

'I'd offer to go in with you, Nessa,' said Darina hesitantly, 'but I've arranged to meet an old family friend who lives only five minutes from the hospital. You know it's Mam's second anniversary next month, and we're organising a little commemoration, you see.'

'I wouldn't dream of asking any more of your time, Darina, and anyway, Sal and I had this discussion already—'

'Discussion? As in, *you* gave me my orders for the day,' Sal interrupted. 'You haven't even explained why Maureen is still in hospital, considering she wasn't badly hurt in the first place?'

'I understand she's having more tests, to check why she's still getting dizzy spells. Today is definitely our best chance to see her.'

'Your best chance, you mean.'

'Well, maybe I could make time to go in,' said Darina. 'We'll get to Tipperary quickly enough on the motorway and the funeral is on quite late, isn't it?'

'Yes, it's not until half twelve,' said Nessa, 'which is handy for all of us who have a long journey to get there. But really, we've discommoded you enough already so there's no question of it.'

Darina seemed about to disagree. 'I nearly feel I've a responsibility for Maureen, after finding her last week. But at the same time, I'd feel a bit awkward because I hardly knew her, really.'

'You hardly knew Oscar,' said Sal, 'and, what's more, neither did we, but look at us barrelling off to his funeral as if he was our favourite uncle. I seriously don't get this fixation we have in Ireland, so-called paying our respects to people we've only met once or twice in our lives.'

'Give over, Sal, and please think of other people for a while.' Nessa felt worn down by three days of guerilla sniping. She could understand why Sal felt resentful at leaving Beara, but she found herself longing for the diligent and helpful girl her daughter used to be. Sal used to try to prevent arguments in the past, rather than fomenting them as she did now.

'When I was on the phone to Marcus last night, we got onto this same subject.' Sal's voice softened when she mentioned her new boyfriend. 'The whole Irish funeral thing, you know. It amazes him, he says, that any work ever gets done in this country, considering how much time people spend at funerals. Needless to say there'll be a mass exodus from Beara to Tipperary today.'

'So is he coming himself?'

'No, he's far too busy, that's the point he was making.'

'I can't imagine that the hackney service takes all his time,' said Darina. Nessa noticed a barb in her voice. 'And wouldn't you think he'd want to see you, Sal?'

'Yeah, sure, and I *so* want to have a romantic rendezvous with him at a funeral. Anyway, he's working on the holiday homes, because his latest idea is to rent them out over the winter to a group of teleworkers from India, which is a pretty neat scheme, if you ask me. He says he can set up a satellite connection, or something.'

'Marcus is a great man for schemes, alright. Did he mention whether they'll be male or female teleworkers?'

Nessa thought she should steer them back to a more neutral topic. 'I do understand what you said about funerals, Sal. When I was your age, I remember telling my parents that funerals should be small family events, as they are in some countries. Once I'm dead, I said to them, I wouldn't care who'd be looking at my coffin.'

'That's just exactly what I said to Marcus.'

'But don't you realise, Sal,' said Darina fervently, 'that the reason the whole community turns out for a funeral in Ireland is not only to show respect for the person who's died, but to honour the grieving relatives? I really didn't understand it until my mother's death. It's hard to put in words, but I remember someone saying that it's like being wrapped in a warm blanket, and I can tell you it helped me hugely to walk into a church full of people, after all the months I'd spent caring for her.'

Sal blushed at their neighbour's outburst, and Nessa told herself that she could not expect them to become close friends so easily. Their age gap of five years was still significant, and Sal had not really grasped what hard times Darina had had.

'OK, right,' said Sal after a pause. 'But when we get to Tipperary today, I promise you both that I'll have my shades clamped over my eyes. I wouldn't like anyone to think I was there just to gawp or to get my mug on the TV news, like some of the hangers-on in the crowd.'

Sunlight flashed through the leaves. Nessa had always enjoyed the changing vistas on the road from Bantry to Bandon, where the wild beauty of the west gave way to abundant fertility and great tunnels of stately trees along the river valley. She tried to relax for a while, but found she could not stop thinking of the murder investigation.

The senior gardai on the case would be present at Oscar's funeral, of course, and she planned to steer clear of them. Trevor O'Kelleher had phoned her on Thursday, and while he did not refer directly to the incident at the bridge the previous day, he let her know that he was aware of it. It was imperative, he told her, to tell the gardai of any new evidence she came across, or any stray details she might remember. He spoke as pleasantly as before, but when the call ended, Nessa's feeling was that Redmond Joyce had made a fool of her in the inspector's eyes. From now on, she decided she would stay out of the gardai's way unless she had solid new information to offer.

'I wanted to tell you, Nessa, that I called in to see Ambrose yesterday, and he's in a bit of a state, poor man, because of the stuff that's appeared in the papers. As a matter of fact, he's worried that he's responsible for the garbage Jack Talbot wrote about the phone calls Oscar got.'

Nessa waited patiently for Darina to come to the point. She had a habit, quite common in Ireland, of approaching a story in a roundabout manner.

'The thing is that Ambrose had two or three conversations with Jack Talbot, who encouraged him by turning up at his gate with a nice bottle of whiskey. But now Ambrose says he can't swear by every jot of information he gave him. And the problem is, he was the source of this whole notion about Oscar getting a call from Patrick.'

'You mean, Ambrose heard Oscar getting a phone call, but he can't actually confirm who was on the other end?'

'That's it, yes, and worse still, Ambrose also told Jack that Oscar and Patrick met up shortly afterwards, even though he didn't set eyes on them together. Then ten minutes later, while he was chatting to the postman at the gate, he saw Patrick's car passing by, something he only remembered a few days ago.'

'At which point I'm sure Jack asked him if there was anybody in the car with Patrick?'

'Exactly, and Ambrose couldn't say one way or another, but Jack pressed him until he said that Patrick could well have had a passenger. At that stage, I think Ambrose was so bamboozled that he said whatever Jack wanted to hear.'

'You should tell him not to worry,' said Nessa. 'I'll call in to see him myself when I'm back in Beara.' Her husband's explanations on the phone were fresh in her mind. 'You see, the fact is that Jack's story was true – Patrick did phone Oscar at midday on the Thursday, and what's more, they met at the junction of the Briary, up the hill road from Ambrose's house.'

Sal raised her head from her mobile phone. She had been listening to new ringtones, and one of them continued to jingle when she removed her earphone.

'So what's the big hoo-ha about it? Is Dad supposed to have strangled Oscar at the side of the road because he suddenly felt like it? Or the idea is that he drove off with Oscar and then strangled him a while later, because they had a little argument about some walking route?'

'I know it seems ridiculous to us,' said Nessa. She gazed at her daughter's phone, willing it to stop so that she wouldn't have to complain once again. Sal glanced at her and sighed, clicking off the sound. To Nessa's relief, she seemed to have cheered up.

'Anyway, even if Dad had been on the spot to do the dirty deed, what happened next, according to Slimy Jack's theory? Did he hump the body into the boot of his car so that he could feed it to the foxes at just about the same time as his plane landed on the far side of the world? I mean, *hello*?'

'It is ridiculous, Nessa. The gardai couldn't possibly suspect Patrick of being involved, could they?'

'They've been quite formal with me, Darina, so it's hard to work out what they suspect.'

'There must be other evidence to show that Patrick had nothing to do with it.' Darina chewed on her lip for a moment. 'The gardai asked me loads of questions about everyone I saw in the area between about one o'clock and two o'clock on the day, and if that's the crucial period of time, you should have nothing to worry about. As far as I remember, you said that Patrick left the house a lot earlier than that?'

'Yes, he left around a quarter to twelve, and he should have been in Bantry by one o'clock, even after stopping briefly to meet Oscar.'

'So that's alright then, surely? Plus, there must be people who saw him driving through Castletownbere or Adrigole or wherever?'

'I don't know about that, but gardai have certainly examined Patrick's car. He left it in Bandon, because he has a friend there, James, who was on an afternoon shift at Cork airport and gave Patrick a lift the rest of the way.'

'That means they can ask James what time Dad arrived in Bandon, and therefore work out that he'd no time to hide a body or whatever?'

'Yes, but suppose the gardai claimed that Oscar got into Patrick's car at the Briary, and they went off to meet someone else, who killed Oscar later in the day? And maybe that James was in on the plot too? How could we prove that it didn't happen? It may sound farfetched, but sometimes the craziest scenarios turn out to be true.'

'Well, it can't be true,' said Darina anxiously. 'And we wouldn't even bother discussing it if Jack Talbot hadn't stirred things up. I hope you don't really think his lies will come to anything, Nessa?'

'The longer the investigation goes on, the more dangerous these stories are. But yes, of course we have to be hopeful.'

Nessa tried to keep her voice upbeat, but she was very

worried about Talbot's continuing researches. His Russian theory had tailed off during the week, but his latest find was a photo of two of the people who had been on the trip Patrick made to Moscow taking part in a human rights protest in Dublin against a visiting delegation from Saudi Arabia, because of that country's unyielding embrace of the death penalty. Talbot had paired it with a second photo, showing Oscar at a business event with Saudi government officials. Needless to say, he made no direct link between the two, but his conspiratorial hints kept a shadow of suspicion over Patrick. Any day soon, Nessa expected to read in the paper that one of her husband's grandfathers was a Muslim – another entirely innocent fact that Talbot would twist and taint for impressionable readers in search of a readymade culprit.

Sal had returned to her ringtones, and busied herself with two options from a well-known television series, seemingly immune to serious concern about her father.

'You haven't enlightened us on why Dad met Oscar,' she said after a while. 'I know he wouldn't be able to prove in court what they talked about, but still . . .'

'The reason he met him was quite simple,' said Nessa. 'As you remember, Jack was very keen to get an interview with Oscar earlier in the week, and pestered Patrick about it until he promised to ask Oscar once more. But then Patrick was up to his eyes changing his flight arrangements and so on, and it slipped his mind until the very moment he was driving out Cnoc Meala's gate.'

'Typical Dad, always too concerned about doing things for other people.'

'Yes, it would have been a lot better for him now if he'd forgotten all about it. But instead, he phoned Oscar, and when they realised they were both close to the Briary, they met for a few minutes and had an amicable chat. According to Patrick, Oscar undertook to phone Jack on Thursday afternoon, to sort out the interview issue once and for all.'

'But Oscar was killed before he made that phone call?'

'I guess so – which would explain why Jack turned up at our front door on Friday, annoyed that he'd heard nothing from Oscar and all set to make trouble for myself and Patrick if he didn't get a precious exclusive feature for his paper.'

'So what's your own opinion, Nessa? I mean, who do you think is the killer?'

Nessa contemplated the horizon, where the city suburbs could now be seen. Her thoughts had been on Maureen, and her growing dread of the visit ahead. If Dominic turned up, she and Sal would have to leave immediately.

'I really don't know, Darina,' she replied slowly. 'I change my mind about it every second day. The easiest thing to believe is that Dominic did it, but that doesn't seem to fit some of the facts, does it?'

'How about Maureen herself?' Sal shifted her earphone to join in the discussion. 'Let's say she killed Oscar because he tried to force himself on her – or more likely, because he refused her desperate offers of hanky-panky? And then she got into a state and rang Dominic, who came hotfoot to the boreen to help her out, at which point they concocted a plan that Dominic would knock *her* out, to throw the gardai off the scent?'

'If that happened, Dominic had a lot of work on his hands, hiding Oscar's body in some ditch until Friday night, and then returning in his car to carry it off to the mountains. And that had to have happened either before or after . . .' Nessa became agitated as she remembered her own experience. She still had to decide whether to make a formal complaint against Dominic. 'That was the same night he assaulted me in our house, so maybe it would explain why he was so aggressive with me, but on the other hand . . . I don't know, I can't really imagine it. He and Maureen are not the most well-organised pair, are they?'

'It doesn't look as if it was a cold-blooded plan, though? And dumping the body in full view of the road shows that the killer wasn't thinking very clearly.'

'Well, maybe so. And maybe nobody saw Dominic driving to and fro on Friday night because the roads were quiet then. But I don't really see it.'

'Let's not forget another possible factor – the Lotto loot, as

Marcus calls it.' Sal was clearly keen to mention Marcus at
every opportunity. 'His pet theory is that Dominic attacked
Maureen up on the hillside during a row about the money, but
that Oscar was nearby and heard them shouting. So he rushed
to defend Maureen, say, at which point Dominic killed him to
keep him quiet.' She glanced from Nessa to Darina and smiled.
'Pretty cool theory, really, wouldn't you both agree?'

Darina smiled slightly in return, but remained serious when
she spoke. 'The rumour going around Derryowen is that
Dominic has given the gardai an alibi for Thursday lunchtime,
but that they don't believe it. It's something about a boat that
was anchored on the water near Pooka Rock, where he was
fishing.'

'Why do the gardai not believe him?'

'I'm not sure, but maybe they haven't tracked down the
boat. I went for my usual swim that day down at the hotel
pier, soon after I'd called in to Ambrose, and the gardai asked
me a few times whether I noticed any passing boats. They
quizzed me about Dominic and Oscar too, of course, and
whether I saw either of them on my way to the sea, or on my
way home, or at any other time.'

'And what did you tell them?'

'Very little, really.' Darina paused as they drew up at a busy
roundabout, and Nessa reflected that she'd missed out on a
lot of the rumours wafting around Derryowen. She would have
to sit down with Caitlín at the weekend, to try to separate
solid facts from speculation.

'I wish I could come up with something really useful,' said
Darina then. 'But, after a while, they'd asked me so many
questions that I couldn't remember who I saw on which day.
They must think we all keep little notes by the hour, accounting
for our comings and goings.'

'That is so totally true. Marcus says he hasn't got a clue
anymore what he did on Thursday.'

'It would be very different during the winter,' said Darina.
'I definitely notice each and every stranger then, because there
are so few of them around the place. But Derryowen is still
quite busy at this time of the year, ever since we got tourist
facilities like the walking trail and the hotel's golf course.'

'Yes, you're right,' said Nessa. 'And of course, we're all hoping that the murder was carried out by a stranger, and not by someone we've met.' She grimaced. 'Even if that someone was Dominic.'

'Isn't it terrible that we think like that? I suppose it's a kind of self-protection, to keep the thing at a distance from ourselves? But I also keep wondering whether Oscar was just in the wrong place at the wrong time, or whether someone was going to get him, regardless of his own actions on the day?'

Nessa and her two young companions lapsed into silence as they drove into the western suburbs of Cork city. They had no answer to Darina's question, and another dilemma nagged at Nessa's mind instead. Some of her guests had solid alibis for the day of Oscar's death – but the absence of an alibi was not in itself a useful indicator of guilt.

At least five of her guests seemed to have been excluded from garda inquiries as a result of their alibis. The French couple, Sébastien and Béatrice, had taken the ferry from Castletownbere to Bere Island on Thursday morning, and had plenty of witnesses to say that they had not returned until teatime. Similarly, the three Dutch people staying in Cnoc Meala's lodge had been shopping in Kenmare until mid-afternoon that day. As for Fergus Malden, gardai had interviewed him at great length, but Nessa herself could vouch that he had had no opportunity to kill his father up until at least seven o'clock in the evening.

If Oscar was killed between one and two o'clock, those who had difficulty proving their whereabouts at the crucial period included Dominic as well as Maureen. Two others in the same category were Zoe and Stella, the sisters who had been sitting on the hotel terrace when Oscar arrived at eleven thirty. A short while later, they drove some distance to the centre of Beara's main peninsula, where they spent the day walking in the Caha Mountains. Nessa remembered well two of the peaks Zoe had talked about that evening: Tooth Mountain and nearby Knocknaveacal, an anglicised spelling of the Irish words for the same image, literally, 'the toothed hill'. It was quite an isolated area, and Zoe and Stella had met no other walkers who could verify their account of the afternoon.

But Nessa reminded herself again that a lack of such witnesses could not in itself be construed as a cause for suspicion. As far as she knew, there were no connections between the two of them and Oscar before they found themselves in the same holiday group at Cnoc Meala: following her adoption, Stella had grown up in England and had only met her half-sister Zoe for the first time the previous Easter; and while Zoe had had a few vociferous political arguments with Oscar during the week, they had hardly caused her to murder him.

Nessa had remembered a conversation with Zoe as she racked her brains about Oscar's business, and what likely enemies he may have had. His company provided security installations in a number of countries, including alarms and electronic spyholes. But Nessa knew that such useful civilian equipment could also have more sinister uses, for example, in military or intelligence operations. She had written an article a few years previously on dual use manufacturing, and how certain companies in Ireland were suspected of circumventing the country's avowed policy of military neutrality by claiming civilian use for products that could equally be sold to groups or countries intent on war. Zoe had reminded her of the article on her second evening in Cnoc Meala, when she told Nessa that she was a longtime admirer of her journalism, and was thrilled to meet her. She added effusively that as a result of that particular piece, she had joined an international campaign against the arms trade and met some amazing people taking on that massive issue.

Nessa decided in Dunmanus that she would do some digging about Oscar's company, making use of her former journalistic contacts. But as she reflected again on her conversation with Zoe, a new idea occurred to her, and when Darina drew in at a service station near Cork Regional Hospital, she took the opportunity to phone Zoe.

'Great to hear from you, Nessa. Yes, we're on the road now. A friend from Tipperary is giving me a lift to the funeral.'

'I'll look out for you after the Mass then, in case we're a bit late arriving. Text me if I don't spot you in the crowd, because I'd love to talk to you about some info I'm trying to check out.'

'Is it about Oscar, Nessa? I absolutely knew you'd get to

work on him as soon as you could. In fact I was thinking of talking to you about it myself, because when I saw Jack Talbot's photo showing him with the Saudi officials, I felt really sick. There I was being all cheery with someone who'd filled his pockets by cosying up to such an oppressive regime. So yes, I'll do anything I can for you.'

'I'm sure the gardai are working on his business links already,' said Nessa carefully. She wanted to tap Zoe's enthusiasm, but was wary of being cast in a heroic role by her.

'Yeah, sure. But I'll bet our PC Plods won't ask too many hard questions about bribery or corruption, will they? And actually, Stella could help us out too, Nessa, because she goes to all these conferences in the Middle East, and watches Al Jazeera, and probably knows a few people in Russia too, which is another nasty regime that Oscar got pally with.'

Nessa smiled ruefully. She hoped her energy levels would be up to Zoe's that afternoon. 'You mentioned a campaign group on the arms trade that you're involved with. So I wondered—'

'Fantastic idea! They're based in London and I'm actually going over to stay with Stella in a few days, so I could call in to them on Monday. I'm at a bit of a loose end, as you may remember, because my advice worker job in the inner city was axed this summer, which is just typical of the kind of cuts this shoddy government is making to services for the most vulnerable people. So yes, that's exactly the sort of thing I'd like to be doing, and I'm raging mad at the way Jack Talbot is picking on Patrick . . .'

Nessa signalled to Darina that she would pay for the fuel. 'Great, let's talk about it later then, Zoe. But I'd appreciate it if you could keep this to ourselves. We have to remember that Jack Talbot and his ilk will be sniffing around at the funeral, hoping for any scrap of info that can be turned into a front page story.'

FOURTEEN

Saturday 26 September, 10.30 a.m.

'I'm so jealous of you, I wish I could go too. I mean, it's sure to be the funeral of the year!'

Maureen was sitting up in bed, supported by a heap of pillows. Her soft bedjacket was festooned with pink rabbits, with a matching pattern on her hairband.

'I hope the staff won't mind us coming in so early in the day?' Nessa looked around, trying to decide where to sit. There were two chairs by the bed, but one was piled high with gossip and fashion magazines, and the other was strewn with discarded underwear, sweet wrappings and other detritus.

'Don't you pay any attention to the nurses, I've to outwit them every time I go out for a smoke. Just make yourselves at home, if that's humanly possible here.' Maureen beamed at her visitors. 'Oh, and look what you've brought me, a lovely box of chocolates. Mind you now, I hope they're low fat, low sugar, the way we all have to eat these days?'

Sal removed the pile of magazines and pulled up a chair close to Maureen. Nessa perched on the opposite side of the bed, to give herself a good view of the door. But as Maureen was in a single room, sidling out unseen was not an option if Dominic arrived.

'Hand me over my little mirror, there's a good girl.' Maureen gestured to Sal, who found the mirror behind an enormous Get Well card on the bedside table. Maureen fished in a pocket for her lipstick and applied a generous pink smear. 'It's important to keep up appearances, you know,' she said conspiratorially. 'After all, the gardai are watching me day and night. I wouldn't be surprised to find out they've put a camera right here in my room.'

Nessa smiled, pretending not to notice Maureen's last comment. She was unsure how to begin her own questioning.

'I suppose the gardai have interviewed you a few times?' she asked cautiously. 'It must be hard to remember everything that happened.'

'Oh, you can say that again! I've tried my very best for them but I still don't know what answers they really want from me.' Maureen sighed loudly. 'I should have stuck to the motto my poor mother had long ago. "Whatever you say, say nothing"; that's what she recommended.' She turned and searched under the pillows until she found a large album, bound in red leather. 'But just wait till you see what I've been up to. I haven't been idle, anyway.'

She turned over the pages of the album, showing her visitors a collection of cuttings from newspaper coverage of Oscar's murder. They included a large photograph of herself, published several times since the story broke and showing a sleek and rather younger Maureen, smiling attractively and holding a large lottery cheque in her hand.

'I thought I was dreaming when I saw the papers the first time. It's like a film you'd see at the cinema, isn't it, except that myself and Dominic are in the lead roles?' She continued to turn the pages, emotions flickering on her face like swift cloud shadows on a hillside. 'So here we are, fame at last, as they say!'

'Do you remember what happened to you that day?' Nessa asked, hiding her surprise at Maureen's tone of voice, and at her album.

'Do I remember? How many times have I been asked that same question – do I remember this and do I remember that?' She threw her head back on the pillow, closing her eyes tightly as if she had been seized by a sharp pain. She looked so much older than she had a week earlier, and sounded exhausted when she resumed. 'It's just horrible and unbelievable, isn't it? Poor Oscar dead, and me lying injured on a lonely laneway.' Maureen opened her eyes and looked from Nessa to Sal. 'God help me, I might have died that same night, and never even been found.'

Nessa nodded quietly, trying to keep up with Maureen's unpredictable moods, which seemed more extreme now than they had been in Cnoc Meala. She wondered what was coming next.

'When I think back over it, I wish I'd stayed put in that nice hotel down by the sea. I was safe enough there, wasn't I?'

Sal regarded her sympathetically. 'You had a chat with Oscar at the hotel, I believe? Everybody said you got on really well together.'

'Oh, that's right, we got on like a house on fire all week – and why wouldn't we, considering we both came from the same part of the country?' A gleam of energy reappeared in Maureen's face. 'You know the old saying, that it takes one to know one? Well, that was very true about myself and Oscar. You see, he was a man who knew how to get a kick out of life, unlike poor Dominic.'

'I suppose Dominic was jealous of Oscar, then?'

'Of course he was jealous, and who could blame him, but I told him to have sense and not to nag me about it.' Maureen met Sal's eyes and seemed to take encouragement from them. 'I mean, I was doing very nicely having an admirer like Oscar Malden, but really, it was just a bit of sport – a little flirtation between friends, that's what I called it.' She stroked her wedding ring gently as she warmed to her account, her finger-nails a deep purple-black that matched her hair. 'It wasn't easy, though, because I realised that Oscar was just as jealous as my poor husband. So I tried to explain the situation to him in the hotel. It's not meant to be, I said to Oscar, but he didn't take it too well, I regret to say.'

'And he left the hotel then, or what?'

'Exactly. He walked out on me and I was worried that I'd hurt him, which I'd honestly hate to do to anyone. Live and let live, I always say.' Maureen glanced quickly at Sal and then Nessa, as if to check that they approved of her account. 'So then I wanted to tell him that I was sorry, and I left a message on his mobile asking him to phone me back. But he never did.'

Maureen stared into space for a moment, and Nessa watched the door, hoping they would not be interrupted. She was so glad that Sal had agreed to come along, however reluctantly.

'That's why I decided to follow Oscar, you see, so that he wouldn't think I was a heartless bitch. But I must have got lost on those little roads in the hills. My shoes got so tight that they cut into me, and I couldn't see a single sign-post anywhere, or anybody to help me. I wish I could blot out that whole day, I really do. God help us, I never saw so many stones in my life, I felt they were coming alive on the hillsides and closing in on me from those ugly high walls along the byroads! Surely it would be better to get rid of the whole lot of them and build some neat little fences in their place?'

Sal laid her hand gently on Maureen's arm, to comfort her.

'If only I could turn the clock back! But how could I know then what was in store for us?' Maureen gazed at Sal and spoke forcefully. 'I have to tell you it scares the hell out of me, wondering what will happen to Dominic and how I'll manage when I leave this hospital.'

Sal held Maureen's hand, taken aback at the fear showing in the older woman's eyes. But after a few minutes, Maureen looked down again at her album and turned back a few pages. She seemed to have arrived at a new understanding.

'I'll have to accept it sooner or later, won't I? The only explanation that makes sense is that he attacked me brutally because I refused to abandon my husband for his sake.'

'Oscar attacked you?' Sal almost whispered it.

'It's so hard for me to face up to it, that a man like him would be capable of it, but that's how it is. And then Dominic must have arrived on the scene and defended me in the only way he could.' Maureen smiled nervously. 'It's an awful situation but maybe some good will come of it in the end. Why would I be afraid of anything, tell me, when I'm married to a man who was prepared to do that for my sake?'

Maureen lay back again and Sal leafed through the album, turning it towards her mother from time to time. Each photo was captioned carefully with the name and date of the newspaper in which it had appeared.

Nessa was preoccupied with what they had just heard. Even if Maureen was telling the truth, it was not enough to stand up in court without corroboration. She was clearly a very unreliable witness, and was also very unlikely to condemn her husband in front of judge and jury. But if Dominic thought she might do so, she had good reason to be scared. Nessa wondered whether the gardai were biding their time, awaiting Dominic's own confession.

'Where's my bag?' said Maureen suddenly. 'I hope those nurses haven't taken it away. They're so nosy, I've to hide everything from them.'

She rummaged under her pillows and among the bedclothes. She was agitated, like a child who had lost a favourite toy. 'Has anyone seen my bag? I had it a while ago, I know I did.'

Nessa and Sal both stood up and scrutinised the mess around the bed. They found the bag under Sal's chair, and handed it to Maureen, who pulled a plastic bottle out of it. She opened it and sucked thirstily at the orange-coloured liquid it contained. 'Oh yes, I promise you, Maureen will get the better of those nurses yet, with their silly rules. It's a free country, after all.'

Sal's hand was on her mouth as she watched her. Nessa kept her own eyes on the bedclothes, afraid her daughter was about to giggle. Clearly, Maureen was not savouring a fruit drink for the sake of its vitamins.

'I'll tell you what worries me,' she said presently. She sat up and arranged the pillows to her satisfaction. 'It's taking the gardai a long time to catch the person who killed poor Oscar Malden, that's what. I don't know what's going on, but I've passed on my suspicions about a few individuals.'

Nessa almost exclaimed aloud. Maureen seemed to have erased everything she had said five minutes earlier, and was off on a new tack, fortified by continuing sups from her bottle. The events of the past week were taking a heavier toll on her than Nessa had anticipated.

'Look at Oscar's son, for example. Far too quiet if you ask me, and not a bit fond of his father, was he? It's the quiet ones you have to watch, that's a well-known fact.'

'You mean Fergus? It's hard to imagine—'

'Listen to me a minute, I saw how things were between the pair of them. We went on some trip or other, to Killarney I think it was, across those big scraggy mountains.' Maureen's eyes were brimming with enthusiasm again. 'Myself and Oscar were trying to have a nice friendly chat as we walked along by the lake, but his son followed us every footstep, like a shadow. It was like something you'd see in a horror movie, the way he kept stalking us.'

'But Fergus is the sort of person who wouldn't, like, kill a fly.'

'Don't depend on it. Oscar told me he was very concerned about his son. He gave him every advantage money could buy, he said, and got no thanks for his trouble.'

'But they came on holidays together, all the same?'

'True enough, but I believe Oscar decided to go home early because they'd had a row.' Maureen took a final gulp before screwing the top back on her bottle. 'Take it or leave it now, but that's my opinion of the matter.'

'And what was your opinion of the others in the holiday group?' Sal asked the question while Maureen fussed with her bag, pushing the bottle under a pile of tissues.

'The others? Well, I can't say they bothered me either way. I do my best to get on with people – rich or poor, old or young, they're all the same to me. Mind you, there was one young woman I didn't take to. She had one of those new names – Zelda, was it?'

'I think you mean Zoe,' said Nessa. 'And her sister's name is Stella.'

'OK, Zoe then, if you say so. Well, I'd a pain in my ear listening to some of the ridiculous things she said. Do you remember that place we visited, the great big mansion with a view of the sea?'

'You mean Bantry House? The weather was beautiful while we walked around the gardens.'

'That's the one, and a fine place it is indeed. Well, we were all enjoying ourselves nicely until Zelda started pronouncing about the moneyed classes of Ireland, as she put it – which means anyone who ever made a decent few bob for themselves, like Oscar Malden or indeed myself. Her idea was that nobody should be allowed to get rich while we've poor people in the world. Honestly, as if that would work in a million years!'

'What did you think of her sister Stella?' Nessa asked slowly. She was afraid that their visit had become undignified, but her curiosity was keeping her in the room.

'I don't remember much about her, except that she was

quiet. Too quiet, actually, just like the son, Fergus. Two of a kind, when you think of it, and my guess is that there was something going on there – eyes across the table and what have you. Yes indeed, it wouldn't surprise me one bit.'

'Stella must be at least seven or eight years older than Fergus,' Sal interjected.

'What's that got to do with it? I think he's the type of fellow who'd be led on by an older woman.' Maureen yawned conspicuously. 'But God only knows, I'd a lot on my mind that week and it wasn't my business to worry about other people.'

She dropped her head back on the pillows and Nessa nodded to Sal that they would leave as soon as possible. But after a minute, Maureen sat bolt upright again and looked at Nessa as if she saw her properly for the first time. She opened her album and turned the pages urgently.

'Oh, Christ almighty, I've just remembered what Dominic told me about you! You're the owner of the guesthouse, of course, and you're married to that foreigner, the dark suntanned one like this girl here.' She looked from Nessa to Sal and back to her album. 'Dominic is going to kill me if he hears I let you in the door! I must be going gaga in this godawful hospital.' Her voice grew louder. 'So just get out right now, will you? He told me how you attacked him and that he hasn't had a minute's peace from the gardai ever since.'

Nessa murmured some bland reply but Maureen turned her back to her, pulling the bedclothes over her shoulders.

'I'll have a little sleep now and everything will settle down. Then Dominic will come in with another bottle of orange for me.' She seemed to be talking to herself. 'And didn't he say he'd bring me a nice visitor today? A friend of his from the papers,who wants to help us, that's what he was on about.'

Nessa and Sal slipped out the door. Neither spoke a word until they were halfway down the main hospital stairs.

'Oh my God, I *so* can't believe how sad she is!'

'She's much worse than I'd imagined. And I'm sorry you got to see her like that, Sal, but I really appreciate that you came here with me.'

'I thought she was OTT when she was with us at Cnoc

Meala, but now she is seriously losing it. I thought I'd choke when I saw the album!'

Nessa put a protective hand on her daughter's back as she steered her towards the main door. 'It's frightening to see how the whole episode has affected her. She really can't handle it, and she needs somebody to look after her, poor woman.'

'Do you believe what she told us about her conversation with Oscar down at the hotel? That he was heartbroken and jealous over her?'

'I believed her, just about, while she was saying it, because she seemed so convinced of it herself.'

'But it doesn't add up, does it? Oscar was hardly that utterly desperate, considering he'd women all over the country panting to get into bed with him.'

'Maybe he led her along, all the same, and Maureen added on her own fantasies,' said Nessa. She took a deep breath as they stepped outdoors. 'What took me aback most, though, was how she changed her story completely, as if she'd said nothing at all about Dominic being guilty.'

'Yeah, and then blaming Fergus instead.'

Nessa paused as she tried to straighten her thoughts. 'Well, what I'm wondering now is whether she realised that she'd said too much about Dominic, and wanted to send us off in a different direction? She could be more manipulative than we've given her credit for.'

'She's a total drama queen, no question. But I can't believe she's capable of acting a part from beginning to end?'

'Maybe not. But if she did let a bit of the truth slip out early on, she might have decided to cover it up by acting as if she'd lost her marbles?'

'I don't think she can tell the difference between truth and lies, Mam. Can you just imagine being some poor garda sap, taking down reams of interview notes from her and trying to make sense of them?'

FIFTEEN

Saturday 26 September, 11.10 a.m.

Dominic stood at the bar and ordered a drink. The place was quiet, as most of Cork's Saturday shoppers had not yet earned a break from their labours. Two men dressed in dark suits came in from the street, and nodded to each other when they saw Dominic.

In the mirror along the back of the bar, his eye caught their movement. He spoke hurriedly to the barman, took another quick look in the mirror and walked off. He almost knocked over a low stool in his haste to reach the double doors at the end of the bar, which led further into the hotel.

'So what's burning your heels then, you blaggard?' Conor Fitzmaurice muttered curses under his breath while he and Redmond Joyce followed Dominic through the inner doors. They found themselves in a wide corridor, adorned with small windows in which local craft and cosmetic products were displayed for the benefit of tourists. They spotted Dominic heading for the main stairway at the end of the corridor, and the lifts to the upper floors of the hotel.

Sergeant Fitzmaurice called out to Dominic just as a group of people exited one of the two lifts, laughing boisterously. It took a few minutes for the gardai to get past the group, by which time the lift door had shut and their quarry had eluded them.

Redmond signalled that he would take the stairs while Conor awaited the second lift. They had glimpsed Dominic pressing the up button, but there was no sign of him at the first- or second-floor landings, and Redmond was almost out of breath as he paused at the next set of stairs. As well as several floors of bedrooms, he remembered that the hotel had a basement car park. There was nothing to stop Dominic changing course midway, and driving off into the city streets in his car.

Redmond turned back quickly and saw that the lights over the lift doors showed Dominic's lift arriving at the floor above him. He hurried up the stairs two steps at a time, reminding himself that he had not been to the gym in the previous week. As he rounded the corner of the third landing, he heard his colleague's unmistakeable Kerry voice.

'Now, my buckeroo, you'd better *whisht* awhile and listen to me.' Redmond guessed that Dominic had tried to confuse his pursuers by changing lifts, only to be confronted by Conor when he stepped into the second one. The sergeant was holding the door open with his foot, while blocking Dominic's retreat back on to the landing.

'Get away from me, you bastard, you're way out of line. I've already complained to my solicitor about your harassment!'

Redmond decided to play the soft cop. They had no arrest warrant and Dominic was entirely within his rights to refuse to cooperate.

'Take it easy, Dominic,' he said quietly. 'We'd just like your assistance with a small detail. We tried to phone you last night, and when we got no reply, we figured we could drop by at your hotel, on our way to Malden's funeral.'

'My head is done in with your stupid questions, and you still don't believe a fuckin' single word I've told you.'

'You've nothing to fear from us, boy,' said Conor, 'if you've kept your nose clean these past nine days.' He drew Redmond into the lift and pressed the button with his elbow. 'Let's head back downstairs, Dominic, in case your friend the barman is worried that you've had a seizure on your way to the loo.'

'The detail we'd like to clarify,' said Redmond, 'is whether you met anyone while you were fishing at Pooka Rock on Thursday the 17th September, or spoke to anyone who passed you on your way there that same morning? Maybe there's something you've remembered since your last garda interview?'

'There's nothing I could've remembered because I've been telling you the bloody truth all along. I didn't follow Oscar Malden anywhere, I didn't strangle him to death and I want to be left in peace.'

'Let me ask the question once again, Dominic. All we'd like to know for now is what happened when you went to Pooka Rock. You parked near the hotel and walked along the coastal path to your fishing spot, is that right? So it's possible that Oscar strolled past you in the opposite direction?'

Dominic looked sulkily from one to the other. 'Don't try to corner me with your clever words, guard. I'd no wish to see smarmy-face Malden that morning or any other morning.'

'Suppose Oscar threatened you, or said something that started a row between the two of you, what happened then?' The lift had arrived on the ground floor but Conor pressed the button to carry them upwards again. 'We're trying to help you here, Dominic, if only you'd listen to us.'

'You're trying to pin a murder on me, you bollocks, and you know it. So give up your pretence of being nice to me.' Dominic spat the words angrily. 'A few of the news people have given me a fair hearing, but as for you guards . . .'

'We gave a fair hearing to your story about the boat near Pooka Rock, supposedly occupied by tourists watching seals or some such.' Conor had no difficulty remaining calm under provocation. 'But as you didn't pay attention to the name of the boat, it's proving a bit tricky to identify it.'

'The boat was flying a French flag, as I told your bullyboy colleagues. But maybe they're so stupid they forgot to write that down? Surely you can send out a radio call or something?'

'We'd like to know what time you met Oscar that Thursday,' Redmond repeated. 'Telling us the truth will work out for the best, you know.'

'I refuse to say another single solitary word. I'm sick to my back teeth of the lot of you.' Dominic pushed Conor's hand away from the lift's control panel. 'I've an appointment in the bar just now at midday, and if I see the two of you spying on me, I promise you my solicitor will be onto the garda complaints outfit straightaway.'

'Please think carefully about our questions, Dominic, for your own sake. We'll be happy to meet you again – here in Cork or in your own homeplace, whatever suits you when you're ready to talk.'

Redmond and Conor did not follow Dominic when he lumbered out of the lift. They took a quick look into the bar five minutes later, however, and saw him seated with a man who was dressed in a blue pinstriped suit, complete with canary yellow handkerchief in his top pocket. Jack Talbot, eyes glinting with anticipation, had a small recorder in his hand.

Redmond had a good view of the crowd as he stood inside the church, arms folded respectfully. He estimated that the seats held four hundred people, and many others were crowded at the back and along the pillared side aisles. Coughs and whispers broke out as they watched the local bishop walk solemnly to the lectern to deliver the funeral mass sermon.

Only a week had passed since the investigation into Oscar's murder had begun, but new forensic evidence pointing to Dominic's involvement could bring it to an end quite soon, Redmond thought. Two tiny shreds of wool had been found snagged on the front zip fastener of Oscar's jacket, and appeared to match the fibres in the multicoloured jersey worn by Dominic on the day of the murder. They would hardly be enough to convict him of the crime, but his failure to verify any contact with Oscar that day seemed to make his guilt more, rather than less, likely. However, further tests were taking place on all clothing samples taken by gardai – to check, for example, whether Dominic's jersey had left similar shreds on Maureen's clothing, a few of which might then have transferred from her to Oscar. Meanwhile, gardai were on full alert at the funeral, to watch for any gesture or conversational slip that could betray the murderer's presence in their midst.

'We have heard the same phrase time and again in the past week,' said the bishop in a sonorous voice, 'to describe Oscar Malden as we all knew him, before his soul departed to the heavenly reward we hope and pray he has now attained. The phrase on everybody's lips is that Oscar Malden was a gentleman; and we have also been reminded that he was a true patriot whose tireless efforts contributed greatly to the betterment of many lives, in this country and beyond our shores.'

A bishop, no less. Redmond counted five priests on the altar too, but it seemed that they alone would not suffice when a person of Oscar's status was to be buried. The country's big guns were well represented in the congregation, including cabinet ministers and politicians of every hue, leading industrialists and media personalities, along with embassy staff from countries in which Malden had operated. Artists and musicians who had enjoyed his patronage were also sprinkled among them. No doubt a bishop's presence added the necessary religious gravitas to the prestige of the occasion.

'We understand only too well that our words are inadequate to express our heartfelt sympathy to Fergus Malden and to his mother Louise. The best we can do is to trust in our prayers and our faith.'

Redmond hated funerals. He accepted that they were a great social institution in Ireland, open to all who had ever known or cared about the bereaved. He knew many people who attended perhaps ten funerals a year, gladly proclaiming them to be part of the glue that bound communities together. He appreciated such genuine sentiments, and wished he could share them. But when he walked into the church in Tipperary, he knew that his eyes would be immediately drawn to the altar, and that he would see two coffins instead of the single one that was there.

Two coffins, his mother and father side by side. And himself, their only child not yet twenty years old, seated a little apart from his aunts in the front row and unable to draw consolation from the crowd gathered behind them. That was the memory that confronted him at every funeral he had to go to in the past twelve years: his parents in two wooden boxes, their cold lifeless bodies encased inside. They had been killed in a car crash and their injuries were so horrific that only Redmond and his aunts had been allowed to glimpse their bodies before the coffins had been closed.

Seeing Oscar Malden's ravaged body had been difficult, but it had been nothing compared to the shock and violent horror he had experienced then. And his parents' deaths had had a cruel poignancy of their own: on the night they were killed, they had been on their way home from their first ever marriage counselling session. His father had stopped drinking alcohol

six weeks earlier, after half a lifetime of addiction and frac-
tious quarrels at home. Fragile hope had fluttered briefly, only
to be spattered with their bodies on the tarmac.

No bishop had offered to speak at his parents' funeral. In the
eyes of the wide world, their deaths were sad and regrettable,
but nevertheless just one of the humdrum tragedies piled on the
roadsides each year. His mother and father were ordinary people,
who had never looked for attention beyond their own small
circles, and two priests had been considered quite sufficient for
them. His relatives and neighbours had done everything possible
to help Redmond through those nightmare days, and the local
priest had been considerate too; but Redmond could never forget
how the second priest got his mother's name wrong when he
shook his hand after the funeral.

People meant well, he understood that alright, but he could
make no sense of their attempts to console him. It's the will
of God, many had said, as if he was supposed to think that
was a good thing, and that having his parents chanting prayers
for him in some faraway invisible ether was somehow better
than having their company at home at the kitchen table. Others
said sagely that when your number was up, that was that –
which meant, to Redmond's mind, that the speeding driver
who had ended two people's lives had no responsibility for
his actions.

Because that's what a belief in either blind fate or God's
will implied, as far as he could make out. If everything was
predetermined, and his parents had to die that day, then the
offending driver had no choice but to hurtle along a small
country road at eighty miles an hour. In which case rapists,
abusers and murderers also had no choice but to carry out
their vicious crimes in order to bring about predetermined
outcomes. Fate and free will could not co exist, nor could
people pick and choose which particular tragedies were part
of God's greater plan.

Redmond had eventually decided that it was futile to seek
explanations. All he could do was endure the fact that it had
happened, just as millions of other humans suffered for no
good reason from random earthquakes, wars, fatal diseases
and myriad injustices. The car crash should not have happened,

but it had. And if he could prevent even a few other people from committing crimes, or at the very least, help to bring them to justice, perhaps life would become worth the effort.

'In the name of the Father, the Son and the Holy Spirit. Let us take this opportunity to give each other the sign of peace.'

Redmond realised that people around him were shuffling and turning to each other. A woman offered him her hand in symbolic peace and friendship, just as hundreds of others did the same to those around them. Redmond's lower lip was quivering and he was unable to look her in the eye. She probably thought he was upset about Oscar Malden's death. He forced himself to smile, trying to concentrate once more on the ceremony. Otherwise he might cry out and bawl from the pit of his stomach.

When he examined the crowd, he noticed Nessa McDermott quite close to him. A lock of reddish-brown hair falling on her forehead, and her mouth set defiantly. He blushed as he remembered the dream he had had early that morning. He had seen his mother in the dream, walking away from him as happened so often in the desolate years following her death. Sometimes, she would stop and look back at him, and then speak soundlessly so that he could not hear what she said to him.

In his dream that morning, she had turned to look back as before, but instead of his mother, he found himself staring at Nessa McDermott. Her eyes wide open and her expression closed. He felt angry at her for invading his private world, and then he felt angry at himself too. Nessa McDermott was no mother figure reaching out to him, he was absolutely certain of that, and if she had wormed her way into his sleeping mind, it was because he had allowed himself to become obsessed with her.

Since the incident at the bridge, he had trawled the internet for references to her. He read through many of her newspaper articles – stories on planning scandals, dubious business deals and much else. He wondered why she had cut short such a media career to settle in a quiet place like Beara and he pored over Cnoc Meala's own website as well as reviews of it on tourist forums. He found it described as a model of ecotourism, boasting solar panels and all the latest insulation and heating systems, plus – the usual story – making use of the freshest local ingredients in its highly praised cuisine. Redmond had little interest in such issues, but he read every scrap anyway, no matter that it told him damn all about Oscar Malden.

It was the same old pattern every time a work task got a grip on him. First of all, he became excited at the challenge in hand, but soon enough, his work craving took over. During his years in the computer industry, he used to find himself staring at screens late into the night, unable to let go. And then his father's face would appear, flushed with alcohol, a reminder to Redmond of how readily he too might slip into its tempting embrace.

He tried to focus on the funeral ceremony once again. Nessa McDermott's daughter was seated beside her, fussing with her bag, probably texting Marcus O'Sullivan. Redmond had heard his colleagues discuss their rumoured relationship during the week. They had all agreed that they would happily interview her into the small hours. A good hard interview, one of them said, to make her sweat to my heart's content. She might be idle one of these nights, another garda added, while loverboy Marcus is off making music elsewhere.

Redmond had taken a close look at Marcus two nights earlier. He had decided to drive over to Carraig Álainn after his day's work, without telling Trevor O'Kelleher or anyone else. He could not say exactly why, but something had bothered him the day he saw Marcus walk out of his house, carrying the box he claimed to have thrown over the cliffside.

Redmond had found space to park outside Carraig Álainn's gates, and sat in darkness for a while, trying to invent a likely excuse to knock on Marcus's door. Eventually, he had walked in the gates and stood in a shadowy corner, watching the house and reproaching himself for indecision. The blinds were down in all three houses, but he could see a faint yellow glow from Marcus's living room, in the house closest to the sea.

He had not been there long when the front door was opened. Marcus came out, followed by a blonde woman. Redmond wondered whether she was Katya, the Slovakian mentioned by Marcus during his interview. He shrank into the trees as the pair spoke in low voices and then got into Marcus's car – not the large Toyota he drove for his taxi work, but a Mitsubishi Evo, a typical choice for a well-funded young man intent on fast driving.

Redmond tried to peer in the windows when they were gone, but could see nothing. His conscience was at him, in any case, as he had no authority to trespass on private land. He wished he could be like Conor Fitzmaurice, who would have no problem inviting himself in for a chat with Marcus.

On his way back to his car, he had stopped to look at the middle house. There were thick blinds on the windows, as in all the houses. But when he looked upwards at a Velux window in the roof, he noticed a glimmer along its edge. Marcus had left the lights on upstairs, for whatever reason.

Many of the congregation had formed a queue to receive communion. A woman was singing from the choir balcony – a contemporary song, as Redmond realised with surprise. He remembered the refusal of the senior priest at his parents' funeral to countenance a secular music, and his pronouncement that eulogies by relatives were no longer permitted inside the church. Perhaps it was one law for the rich and another for the rabble; or perhaps each bishop decided on the rules in his own diocese. It was a mystery to him, like so many aspects of other people's lives.

It filled him with amazement, for example, to see grown women and men take a sliver of papery bread in their hands, and put it in their mouths in the sincere belief that it was a piece of divine flesh. He wondered whether Oscar Malden had shared such a belief, or would have chosen a conventional religious funeral for himself. If half of the rumours of his casual sexual relationships were true, he had hardly been a faithful Roman Catholic. Then again, he might have repented everything the instant he felt the tug of a noose on his throat.

Redmond made his way to the back of the church, and saw Conor Fitzmaurice leaning by the door. He looked awkward in his Sunday suit, like a farmer who had just scrubbed grit from under his fingernails. The sergeant was studying his phone when Redmond reached him.

'Well now, here's a surprising development.' Conor wrinkled his brow as he scrolled through a text. 'What do you make of this now?'

Redmond was about to take the phone from him when they saw the crowd craning their necks to look towards the altar. Fergus Malden stood at the lectern, getting ready to speak about his father, and both gardai moved quickly to get a better view.

'A lot has been said since his death . . . Every newspaper I open . . .' Fergus mumbled some of his words, eyes cast downwards. He referred to his father's great reputation, and how he had such determination to achieve his aims. As Fergus stuttered uncertainly, Redmond wondered whether the young man was genuinely praising his father or simply reciting a formula. Strength and ambition were not always praiseworthy traits and Fergus, who was so shy himself, may have disliked rather than admired them.

'I would like to say . . . I have to speak now about . . . the terrible thing that happened.' Fergus lifted his head and looked out at the crowd. 'But I understand I have to be careful about this.'

Total silence enveloped the church. Redmond felt his own breath seize in his throat. It was remarkable, really, that Fergus had taken on the task of speaking in public at such an occasion.

'If the person who carried it out . . . If that person is listening, here in Ireland or wherever else . . .'

For a few seconds, Redmond was afraid that the young man's voice had deserted him. But then Fergus found a new wellspring of courage within himself and released a torrent of words all at once. 'What I want to say is that death solves nothing. No matter why this murder took place, or what it was supposed to achieve, it has harmed us all terribly, and not just my father. It has left a stain on us that I think will go deeper over time. The right thing . . . The right thing must be done, but even so, we will never recover. That's all.'

Fergus stopped short, his hands gripping the lectern. He looked paler and more drained than ever. Silence filled the church for several seconds, and then people began to clap.

The sound of applause echoed up to the roof, as Fergus raised his eyes quickly to acknowledge it.

When he made his way outside, Redmond spotted Conor among the crowd, his arm on someone's shoulder, chatting and smiling. The sergeant had that natural ease and informality that was so common in Ireland, leaning in close with his head inclined to listen, giving a gentle nudge of his elbow to share a joke. He would work his way around the crowd, picking up succulent rumours and solid facts without ever asking a direct question.

Redmond envied his easy manners, but he no longer resented his colleague as he had done at first. Instead, he felt surprised and pleased that Conor was so friendly to himself. It crossed his mind that Trevor O'Kelleher had put a word in Conor's ear to do so, but he pushed the thought away quite quickly. Conor Fitzmaurice needed no guidance on how to get on with others.

Close to the hearse, people awaited their turn to express condolences to Oscar's family. Redmond watched them for a while. Fergus and his mother Louise stood stiffly side by side, a few words passing between them when Fergus introduced someone to her. As they greeted each person in line, their hands moved mechanically and their heads nodded like puppets unable to relate to an audience. Caitlín O'Donovan was making conversation with Louise, who seemed to stare right through her. Similarly, Darina O'Sullivan held Fergus's hand tightly and bent towards him to say something, but his eyes darted away in every direction. He was probably feeling utterly bewildered, doing his public duty with an empty, abandoned heart.

Redmond looked back at Louise and was startled to recognise the look in her eyes. She was a slim woman, with deeply tanned skin and a polished appearance, but there was something withered about her too. Her white teeth showed brightly when she affected a smile but her eyes did not quite focus properly, as if a veil shrouded her view of the world. Too often, Redmond had seen that same alcoholic veil droop over his father's eyes, and now he pictured Louise passing her days in Dubai, high up on the balcony of an expensive apartment, desperately clutching her glass under the white glare of the sun.

He gazed back at Fergus, who had been a young teenager when his parents had separated. Redmond felt a surge of sympathy for him, and wondered whether Fergus had ever been able to talk to anyone about his parents' separation, and his own loneliness, and the random cruelties of life.

He walked around the churchyard to find Conor. The television crews were packing up their gear, after completing their work for the evening news programmes. Near the side gate, he noticed Nessa McDermott in discussion with that young woman, Zoe. He felt sure they got on very well, outdoing each other in stubborn defiance of the world. Zoe reminded him of a girl who had been in his class at school – her mouth set in a cheeky pout that infuriated every teacher they had.

Jack Talbot approached the two women from behind, and put his arm around Nessa before greeting them. Redmond noticed with interest how she backed away from him and vociferously refused his offer of a microphone. She must have learned a hard lesson when his articles about her husband had appeared.

When Redmond caught up with Conor, the sergeant took out his phone and handed it to him without a word. The text message on the screen was full of venom:

> Oscar Malden will be praised to the heavens today. Damn him to hell instead. Rotting in his coffin is too good for him. His own heart rotted long ago. He hurt women till they screamed. Torture was a game

Redmond read it a few times before he met his colleague's eyes. He felt a chill on his back, as if an icy gust of wind had hit him.

'What do you make of it, in the name of God?' said Conor quietly. 'It looks as if whoever wrote it had to stop suddenly.'

'Who sent it to you? I know people post all sorts of poison on the internet, but this seems more personal than that.'

'A friend of mine sent it on to me. She works at a local radio station, and it was texted to one of their numbers. The *cig* and the rest of our bosses know about it, of course, and I've a source in Bandon station who'll keep me updated on whatever they decide.'

Redmond looked around the churchyard. The hearse had just driven away and the crowd was dwindling. 'What about people here at the funeral? Have they heard about it?'

'Oh, I've no doubt the word is spreading like a contagion, and the *cig* will tell the family about it as soon as the burial is over. But the first job is to establish whether it's a vile and malicious prank, or a genuine message from the perpetrator.'

'But if it is genuine, what's the purpose of it? To send us off in the wrong direction, or to help us to understand why Oscar was murdered?'

On their way back to west Cork, Conor talked about his day-to-day life, constantly juggling work and family responsibilities – rushing here and there, he said, to collect one or other of his four children from dance classes, football training, dental appointments and an endless round of their friends' birthday parties. But he admitted that getting to know so many local parents was an advantage to the job, even if they did not necessarily see it that way.

'I always spot the moment,' he laughed, 'when their mouths stiffen in the middle of a friendly chat, because they're seized with anxiety about sharing secrets with a member of the constabulary!'

Redmond eventually took his turn to speak, and by the time they were halfway across County Cork, he had told Conor how his parents had died together. His companion responded gently, without betraying any of the condescending pity that Redmond always feared; and soon enough, to his surprise, he found himself describing feelings of anger and heartbreak that he had rarely voiced aloud. As a flood of words spilled out from him, he was enormously glad that he could gaze at the darkening road ahead and not meet the sergeant's eyes.

His story was finally interrupted by the jingle of Conor's phone. Redmond picked it up and read out a text from Bandon, reporting that the venomous message about Oscar had been sent from a mobile phone, whose signals located it in the same area of County Tipperary in which the funeral had taken place. Gardai would not publicise that information, of course, nor the fact that they had immediately recognised the number.

The phone was a pay-as-you-go mobile, purchased in France about eight months earlier. A message had been left on Oscar's phone from the same number on the day of his murder, and half an hour later, soon after 1.30 p.m., Oscar had called back and left his own message. Unfortunately, gardai had so far failed to find the owner of the phone or the device itself, and they had no idea what those fateful messages had been.

SIXTEEN

Wednesday 30 September, 1.00 p.m.

Nessa was on the move once again, after three days at home in Beara. She and Sal had returned to Cnoc Meala after Oscar's funeral the previous Saturday, and while life there could not be described as normal, Nessa felt able to draw her breath for the first time in a fortnight. She dealt with a backlog of business emails and contacted friends who had sent her messages of concern and sympathy. She drove Sal to school and encouraged her to work out a study timetable for the following month. She was in close contact with Patrick too, helping him to change his plane tickets as cheaply as possible. Then she set about tidying their bedroom with uncharacteristic thoroughness, and she put the finishing touches to it by filling a vase with late-flowering orange and red montbretia from the garden.

The best welcome home for him, however, would be a decisive breakthrough in the garda investigation. There was a constant feeling of tension in the area, a sense that dangerous animals had been let loose and could pounce again at any time. According to Caitlín, most people in Derryowen believed that Dominic's arrest was imminent, but while Jack Talbot and others tried to stoke the headlines, each day passed without a newsflash to announce any such development. Meanwhile, Nessa pursued her own contacts, including a business journalist friend who promised to look for possible links between the abandoned Russian ship and Oscar's companies. She did not quite agree with Zoe's scepticism about the garda investigation: they had probably gone through Oscar's office files in forensic detail already, and sent queries to police forces in several countries. Her own efforts were a long shot by comparison; but doing something felt better than doing nothing.

Now she was on a day trip to London, a plan she had

hatched at the last minute. She was to meet Patrick at Heathrow airport in the late afternoon and make the last leg of the journey back to Ireland with him, rather than await him in the arrivals hall in Cork airport and risk attracting potentially hostile media attention there. Her journey had another purpose too. Zoe had been in London since Sunday, where she got going immediately on her researches. She phoned Nessa early on Tuesday and announced that she had a great new lead – but went on to say that she was afraid of discussing it on the phone for security reasons. She was so excited and yet so coy about her find that Nessa offered to meet her for an hour in London.

In spite of leaving Beara well before sunrise, it was lunchtime by the time she arrived in central London. First, there had been a two-hour drive to Cork airport and the usual wait before boarding; then there were endless corridors to navigate in Heathrow and an irritating delay while she acquired some sterling cash; and finally, there was an interminable journey on the underground to King's Cross station. It was an illusion, she thought to herself, that getting from one country to another could be done in a quick hop.

The café Zoe had nominated was an old-fashioned place on a back street near the station, with formica tables and a heavy smell of fried breakfasts. The menu did not feature such exotica as lattés and cappuccinos, and as Nessa settled on a stodgy-looking muffin with her cup of tea, she wondered whether Zoe's new information would be worth the journey.

'I've been reading the latest garbage on the news websites,' said Zoe, bouncing in the door to greet her. 'That interview Jack Talbot did with Maureen is a disgrace. She's in no state to be exposed to vipers like him.'

Nessa had read through the article several times in a Sunday paper. 'I'd say Jack was happy with what he got,' she said cautiously. She did not mention her own visit to Maureen – the more she thought about it, the more it disturbed her.

'I'm sure he put words in her mouth. Saying she hadn't meant to make Dominic jealous, or to have two men fighting over her. It's so tacky, isn't it?'

'That's one word for it alright.'

'And what was the bit about being proud of Dominic in

spite of everything? She pretty well pointed the finger at him there, surely?'

'Yes, but Jack covered himself by doing a separate piece with Dominic, which emphasised the alibi he claims to have.'

'It's all just a way of selling papers, isn't it, Nessa? Talbot doesn't really give a toss who murdered Oscar, as long as his own name is up there in big block capitals. He did his best to pin it on Patrick, and when that didn't quite work out, he turned his sights on Dominic and Maureen.'

Nessa nodded, pleased to see Stella arrive at the door. Zoe got up to fetch coffee for her sister, explaining at the same time that Stella had some useful names for Nessa, to help her find out more about Oscar's business abroad. 'That stuff in the paper is a sideshow,' she added as she stood up. 'I think Oscar's death has very little to do with Beara.'

Nessa scanned a sheet of paper given to her by Stella, once they had exchanged greetings. It listed a number of academic specialists on Middle Eastern countries, including Saudi Arabia, Bahrain and Egypt – countries whose political history Stella lectured on.

'It's best if you phone these people directly to ask if they've picked up any controversies about Oscar's dealings,' she said to Nessa. 'You can mention that you've spoken to me.' Her manner was quiet and apologetic as usual, and even her soft grey suit was understated in style. Nessa reflected that the two sisters were as different to each other as Oscar and Fergus Malden. Then again, that was common enough in families.

'I've something even better to show you,' Zoe declared. She placed two off-white mugs on the formica table and Nessa got a whiff of instant coffee. 'Or rather, my friend Ben will be here in a minute, and he'll show you what we found. He works for the campaign I told you about, trying to expose the whole horrible arms industry for what it is.'

'You seem to have got a very quick result,' said Nessa, smiling. 'Was that just a stroke of luck?'

'Well, I showed Ben a selection of the coverage since the murder, and believe it or not, it was Jack Talbot who sent us in the right direction. Not one of his articles, but that photo we talked about before, showing Oscar having a love-in with Saudi government officials.'

'The one he linked to Patrick's activist friends, you mean, who were taking part in a protest against executions in Saudi Arabia?'

'Exactly. Our new find has nothing to do with Patrick, of course, but nasty Jack could turn out to have his uses after all. And here comes Ben now.' Zoe looked towards the door as a dark-haired young man came in. Nessa noticed her blush, and it occurred to her that incriminating files might not be the only attraction in his office.

Ben sat down quickly, apologising for being short of time, and after exchanging glances with Zoe, he produced a glossy booklet from a folder and handed it to Nessa.

'This is just the warm-up,' said Zoe. 'It could explain where Oscar's riches really came from.'

The booklet was an advertising brochure for a major weapons fair held in London three years earlier. It was one of the largest trade fairs in the world, according to the blurb, drawing together almost a thousand companies to display everything from tanks to assault rifles to surveillance equipment, and providing a prime opportunity for suppliers and customers to get to know one another and assess trends in 'this vibrant market', as it was described.

'How did you get hold of the brochure?' asked Nessa. 'I'd imagine the local tourist office didn't hand them out?'

'No, indeed. Attendance at the event is by invitation only, and military staff, businesses and civil servants in over fifty countries get the call. The British government spends millions promoting this kind of thing.'

'In other words, it's the hard-pressed taxpayers who fork out the millions,' said Zoe, 'but they're told nothing about it. So we never hear reports on the main evening news highlighting the latest advances in how to kill people more efficiently while making an obscene profit into the bargain.'

'That's true enough,' said Ben, 'but there are a few people in the media trying to publicise the issue. I got into this event three years ago with the help of a small television company who made a documentary on it. They put me down on their paperwork as a researcher so that I could get past the layers of security.'

He spoke in a businesslike manner, and Nessa noticed that he was dressed in a well-cut jacket and sober shirt. He certainly did not conform to the long-haired slogan-bearing stereotype of anti-war activists.

'Ben and the TV people did some secret filming at the so-called fair,' said Zoe admiringly. 'You saw army generals from a number of impoverished countries, didn't you, strutting around in their shiny uniforms and plotting how to spend billions on weapons instead of hospitals or schools? Of course, there are no photos in the brochure of dismembered bodies or children carrying machine guns.'

'It's worth pointing out that Ireland is represented at some of these arms fairs,' said Stella. 'It is a legitimate industry, whether we like it or not, seeing as it supplies the defence forces of peaceful and prosperous countries too. And it also happens to be one of the biggest manufacturing employers in the world, employing people in maybe a hundred countries.'

'That's a total scandal in itself, as you know well.'

'But the documentary did get shown on television.' Stella managed to counter her sister's rhetorical declarations without raising her voice. 'I know it was on late at night, but you can't claim that it was banned.'

'So what about Oscar, where does he come into this?' Nessa had drained her cup but felt she could do with a bigger dose of caffeine to keep her going.

Ben glanced at Zoe again, and Nessa thought he looked rather wary. But after a few seconds, he delved into his folder again and withdrew a photocopied image. It showed Oscar with two other men, standing beside a round black table on which guns were displayed in a glass case.

'This was published in a trade magazine,' said Ben, 'in a feature about the London event. I knew nothing about Oscar Malden at the time, but I'd filed it away because of the other two men in the picture. And when Zoe showed me the press coverage on Oscar, and especially the Saudi link, it rang a bell.' He glanced around the café as if to be sure nobody was paying attention to their table, and then turned the photograph to the light before handing it to Nessa. 'His name is quite distinctive so it must have stuck in my mind.'

'Are you sure your photo was actually taken at the weapons fair?'

'Ninety-nine per cent sure, yes. I might even be able to get an attendance list from my contacts, if you want proof that Oscar was present at it.'

'And who are the others in the photo?'

'The thin Englishman on Oscar's left is someone I've been interested in for years, because he's an arms dealer known to have sold guns to a number of west African countries while they were in the throes of very bloody wars.' Ben's tone was still factual and dispassionate, but he dropped his voice as he continued. 'It has also been alleged that he sells equipment designed to torture prisoners.'

Nessa looked again at the photocopy, but the image that sprang into her mind was of Oscar at Cnoc Meala's dining table, so engagingly attentive that fellow guests felt privileged to be in his company. She forced herself to push away the image, and her growing discomfort at any deference she may have shown him herself.

'What about the other man?' she asked as evenly as she could. 'He looks Middle Eastern to me.'

'Our info is that he's fairly senior in Saudi Arabia's military, but he's in civvies in this photo. The mind boggles at the budget he has at his disposal.'

'Do you know whether Oscar actually did business with these people? Maybe he was selling them perfectly innocent electronic gates, or having a casual chat?'

'He'd hardly have his photo taken with them if he disapproved of them,' said Zoe impatiently. 'But the question is which warmongers did he upset so much that they decided to assassinate him?'

Nessa looked expectantly at her, wondering if she could produce a piece of evidence to link Oscar directly with a likely murderer. But after a pause, she realised that Zoe was awaiting her verdict.

'This material you've found is really interesting,' she said.

'It gives us a completely new perspective on Oscar, and it should definitely be publicised sooner or later—'

'You're not throwing cold water on it, are you? We'll keep digging for more, I promise you.'

'I'd like you to keep working at it, Zoe, of course I would. But we have to remember that however good the material, it may turn out to be unrelated to Oscar's death.'

Stella looked sympathetically at her sister. 'That's the down-side of investigative journalism,' she said, 'or indeed any kind of research. You could dig away for months and not find enough credible facts to prove your story, no matter how true it may be.'

Ben got up from the table, looking at his phone. 'I'm sorry, but I've got to head off to a meeting.' He gave them a wry smile. 'That's the reason for the formal wear today. There's stuff going on about a United Nations arms treaty, and who knows, we may make real progress one of these years.'

Zoe walked over to the door with him and Nessa was left at the table with Stella. She heard familiar Irish accents as she took in her surroundings once again. A group of customers at a nearby table seemed to be wearing the same clothes and hairstyles as they had when they arrived on the emigrant train from Holyhead many decades earlier.

Stella looked indulgently in the direction of her sister. 'She likes these retro places, as she calls them,' she said to Nessa. 'She wouldn't touch a fry-up herself, of course, but she sees cafés like this as part of our cultural heritage.'

'You seem to be really fond of each other. It's such a pity that your holiday in Beara ended with this awful business.'

'Zoe has really changed things for me.' Stella took on a serious expression again. 'She has such determination, as you know. I'd never even imagined having a sister, and now I feel my life has begun all over again.'

Nessa could see Zoe on the phone outside on the street, evidently arguing with someone with her usual passionate indignation. 'It must have been nerve-wracking when you were about to meet each other for the first time? Wondering what she'd be like?'

Stella smiled softly. 'It wasn't just Zoe I got to meet, but my birth mother too, on her first trip to London since she'd come here to have me all those years ago. To be honest, I wanted to run back to my own family and leave things be. The truth isn't always nice, and maybe it was that fear that had stopped me looking for them in the first place.'

'But Zoe wouldn't have settled for that!'

'Not a chance. I suspect she's not capable of running away from the truth, whatever it takes to confront it.' Stella stood up and brushed a few invisible crumbs from her skirt. She had a natural elegance that Nessa reckoned she would never achieve for herself. 'But I agree with what you said earlier,' she added, 'that this new information about Oscar may be completely irrelevant.'

Nessa sighed as she pulled on her jacket, remembering the long trek she had to make back to Heathrow. 'We're wandering around in the dark, that's the problem. We could trip up at any time, or find out that the perpetrator is shining a torch into our eyes to blind us to the truth.'

The arrivals hall at the airport was overflowing, as a ceaseless flow of humanity converged and dispersed in every direction. Nessa studied the information board and saw that Patrick's plane had been delayed by half an hour.

She felt the same ache of impatience she used to experience in the first year of their relationship, when Patrick used to travel to Ireland from Mallorca where he was working as a mountaineering guide and, in turn, she had to juggle her working hours to fly over to him every month or two. Longing for that urgent embrace in the midst of the crowd, oblivious to everything but the caress of his voice and the warmth of his body. She wanted the same anonymous privacy for their embrace this time, which was another reason she had decided to meet him in London. Apart from a possible media audience in Cork, there was always the risk of a passing acquaintance striking up a cheery conversation at the wrong moment.

News coverage of Oscar's murder had grown a lot quieter since the funeral, but in case Patrick's return to Ireland stirred it up again, Caitlín had offered to spread a few false rumours about the date and place he was expected. Might as well play them at their own game, she said, as she put out word through her local radio friends that she had heard he would arrive at Kerry Airport the following day. Nessa checked her phone while she waited at Heathrow, and sure enough, Caitlín had texted to confirm that three journalists so far had been on to her to ask whether the rumour was true, to which she replied that it was plausible but not certain.

Nessa manouevred closer to the barrier in the arrivals hall so that Patrick would spot her as soon as he emerged. Even after his plane had landed, there was that grinding wait while he found his way to the baggage carousel, watched everyone else collect their suitcases ahead of him, and trundled his trolley past bland advertisements and poker-faced security officials. All the ritual frustrations of airline travel, magnified by mutual desire.

'We'll get through these hard times, Nessa, I promise you. I'll do some of the worrying from now on.'

'I'm so sorry that you couldn't stay longer in Malawi, love, and that you've been so stressed yourself.'

She nestled into Patrick's shoulder as he stroked her hair softly. She thought he had lost weight since she had seen him almost a fortnight earlier. He had always had that wiry mountaineer's build, but now he looked as if his skin was stretched thinly on his bones. She held on to him and felt relief wash over her. They had a lot to discuss and catch up on, but for these first moments, she wanted to believe that everything would soon be just fine.

They decided not to talk about Oscar on the plane to Cork, surrounded by fellow passengers who could overhear them. Instead, Patrick told Nessa about the conversations he had had with his aunt in her final days. While others were by the bedside with them, they chatted about Sal and Ronan and their young Malawian relatives, and how life had improved in Malawi in recent years. They also discussed food and the kind of meals that Patrick looked forward to tasting again, such as the cornmeal dish called *nsima* and the highly sought freshwater fish, *chambo*. But when they finally found themselves alone for half an hour, Esther had willingly opened up about the agonising years after his father's disappearance. Her voice was weak, but she had confirmed that a number of fellow activists imprisoned at the same time had sworn he was tortured. Nothing they said could ever be proved, however, and Esther used to get terrible pains in her own arms and legs in those years – stinging, stabbing pains that she believed to be her own haunted imitation of his suffering.

Nessa held his hand in silence when Patrick finished his account. She pictured his aunt's kind eyes, and then remembered what Ben had said at lunchtime, about the arms dealer standing next to Oscar who was alleged to trade in the tools of torture. It was horrifying to contemplate: people losing their minds in excruciating pain, and others making foul profits at their expense. She would like to tell Patrick about her researches, but knew that she would postpone it until they had dealt with their immediate concerns.

As they headed westwards from Cork, they began talking about those concerns. 'I haven't paid serious attention to the news stories about ourselves or even about Oscar,' Patrick began. 'I was quite well aware that they were available online, but it all seemed so unreal to me while I was on another continent.'

Nessa smiled as she noticed how Patrick's speech was tinged with a gentle kind of formality after his return from Africa. It was always the same, and in a few days, he would take on the hues and rhythms of Beara. 'I'm not looking forward to reading my own biographical excerpts,' he added, 'and, in particular, the ancient history of my period in Russia.'

'I'm sorry I wasn't able to handle things better,' said Nessa. 'I thought I'd know how to deal with unwelcome media attention – but it all seems so different when the storm is raging around your own ears.'

'There's no need to apologise to me, Nessa. You're not personally responsible for the media's shortcomings, are you?'

'No, of course not. But I've been thinking back over my own work, and wondering who I might have trampled on blithely and left in a state of torment when I'd moved on to the next story.'

Patrick's face broke into a big smile. 'I had the impression that one of your journalistic purposes was to torment powerful people?'

'Yes, I know. But there's a difference between making life difficult for the rich and powerful who are in the public eye, and harassing innocent bystanders who happen to be caught up in a major news event.'

'You've always been clear about that distinction, Nessa.'

'I may have gone on about it but it's still really easy to get carried away by a good story. And now that I know what it feels like, I'm sure I wasn't always sensitive enough . . .'

'You're very hard on yourself, sweetheart. I appreciate that the stories written about me in my absence have been very upsetting for you. But that hardly means that all journalists are suspect, yourself included.'

'Once you've read those stories, you might have a different view, Patrick.'

'That's true enough. But I would still choose Ireland's media culture any time rather than the conditions I grew up in. They were truly frightening, I promise you – people being kidnapped and put to death in total secrecy, and not a single word written or reported about them.'

'Surely these aren't the only two options? If we had a dictatorship in Ireland, I bet you Talbot and his hack friends would be first in the queue to pump out government propaganda. Their real motivation is having power and influence, not calling governments to account or questioning our values.'

They drove through Inishannon, crossing the Bandon river on their way to the town of the same name. Patrick's friend, James, was on night duty at the airport and had met them there briefly to give them the keys to his house. The plan was that Patrick would stay overnight in Bandon and meet gardai at the district headquarters the following morning, before news of his arrival home became public. His car was also back at James' house, having been returned after gardai examined it for any traces of suspicious activity.

Nessa's intention had been to stay the night in Bandon too. Ronan was still in Dunmanus and Sal had not argued about sleeping over at a school pal's house. But as they neared the town, Nessa suggested to Patrick that she would continue on to Beara after all. Now that she had been with him for a few hours, her mind was greatly eased, and she was also sure that he would welcome that private space he had so lacked in Malawi. What's more, they would probably keep each other awake, on tenterhooks about his morning interview. Nessa had learned on Monday that gardaí had tracked Patrick's mobile phone signals for the day of the murder, to check whether he drove directly to Bandon after his brief meeting with Oscar, as he had claimed; but she did not know what the signals had shown.

Patrick made a token protest at her plan to drive all the way home, but gave in quickly once she agreed to stop for a cuppa at the Bandon house. 'I've been going over my conversation with Oscar that day,' he said, as they stood at the kitchen counter. 'It was very short, probably only three or four minutes. Most of it was about Jack Talbot and his planned newspaper feature.'

'I presume, then, that Oscar didn't confide in you about death threats he might have got that week?'

'You presume correctly.' Patrick smiled warmly, and as they held each other's eyes for a moment, Nessa felt her heart lighten with gladness. 'What I remember most vividly,' Patrick continued then, 'is not what Oscar talked about, but just that he seemed to be in a very happy mood, singing to himself as he went off and certainly not fearful of death threats or anything of the sort.'

'Was he impatient or annoyed at Jack's pursuit of him, do you think?'

'He started laughing about it, actually. Again, I cannot recall his exact words, but he gave me the impression that they knew each other well.'

'That doesn't surprise me one bit. I thought it was pretty odd that Jack didn't phone Oscar directly about his article, and pestered us instead.'

'Well, there was something about that. Yes, I remember now that Oscar mentioned a falling out between himself and Jack in the past. It had something to do with a woman they were both keen on. But really, I was so preoccupied that morning that I was not listening carefully to what he said.'

Nessa stared at him for a moment, trying to interpret the significance of what he had just told her.

'I hope the gardai have checked Jack's movements on the day of the murder,' she said eventually. 'To the best of my knowledge, he has never informed the great Irish public of a personal connection between himself and Oscar, least of all a juicy outbreak of jealousy over a desirable woman.'

'Be careful not to get carried away, Nessa! As you suggested yourself a while ago, hints and rumours should not be confused with evidence.'

'I know, I know. He's quite unlikely to be the murderer, however attractive a theory it might be.' Nessa tried not to sound bitter. 'The more I think about it, the more I believe that Jack knew full well that Oscar would refuse to be profiled by him. But Jack pursued him anyway so that he could write a piece of tittle-tattle about the elusive and desirable rich bachelor who deigned to spend a short holiday among the plebs. The pair of them were getting at each other, and we got caught in the crossfire.'

SEVENTEEN

Wednesday 30 September, 11.20 p.m.

Nessa pulled in by the roadside on her way into Adrigole, halfway along Beara on the shores of Bantry Bay. She needed a few gulps of night air before the final lap home. The rising moon above the looming outline of Hungry Hill appeared very large and when she stepped out of the car, she could hear the sea's low swishing nearby.

Her head was filled with unresolved thoughts about Oscar's murder. Could Jack Talbot possibly be the perpetrator? Somehow, he seemed too smug, too calculating, to allow raw emotion to lead him to such an extreme – but then again, who knew what sort of person lay behind the smooth mask of his public persona? His Friday visit to Cnoc Meala may have been for the purpose she and Patrick had just discussed, but if he had strangled Oscar the previous day, could it be seen instead as part of an elaborate plan to cover his tracks?

Nessa was fairly sure, however, that he had a solid alibi, which he was rumoured to have boasted about in Derryowen Hotel. The fact that she and many others despised him did not amount to evidence against him; and keeping quiet about a personal connection with Oscar was no proof of a motive either. The degrees of connection between people in Ireland was a frequent subject of wonderment among her guests: two complete strangers on holiday in Cnoc Meala who found out that they were second cousins on their mothers' side, or that their sisters had been in the same class in school, or that they had both been on the same plane that was delayed for six hours on a New York runway a month earlier. It was hard to believe, really, that the country had a population of millions.

One of the central puzzles about Oscar's death was why it had taken place in Beara. Would a dangerous business rival from the Middle East or Russia travel all the way to a distant peninsula on an island off the northwest of Europe to eliminate him? Would a rejected lover from Tipperary, Dublin or anywhere else do so? But if the murderer was not a stranger to Beara, there had to be some connection between Oscar and somebody who was in the area that week. Caitlín was probing her extensive network of local sources to see if such a link could be found; and gardai were sure to be working on it too. Or could Fergus have slipped out from Cnoc Meala while Nessa and others were tending to Maureen's fall, and somehow met up with his father late that evening, killed him and disposed of his body the following night?

Nessa looked up at the majestic and forbidding mountain above her, stooped against the sky. She was less than ten minutes away from the little bridge where Oscar's body had been found. His killer drove on the Healy Pass road, and may have approached it from Adrigole, on the County Cork side, where she was now. Dominic had certainly had time to make the journey, either before or after his demented visit to Cnoc Meala. Marcus had a similar opportunity when he left the party in Castletownbere in the early hours of Saturday, claiming to Sal that he had a pressing work task to deal with.

Nessa drove up the valley to the bridge. She was bone-tired, but there was something niggling her about the place, ever since the day she had stopped there with Caitlín. After her long day of travel, another half an hour would make no difference.

The road was empty and lonely. Under the moon's pale lustre, the great boulders on the hillsides looked wan, almost colourless, and Nessa began to imagine them as a multitude of ghosts gathering around her. She felt reluctant to leave the car when she arrived at the bridge. She had always believed that spirits were a manifestation of deeply rooted human fears and fervid imagination, but in such a bleak place, she could not easily keep her own fears in check.

She stood by the parapet wall, listening to the water gurgling below her, its sounds insistent and clamorous in the huge silence of the mountain valley. She looked up and saw the lights of a car in the distance, glittering like an animal's eyes in the darkness. The car was coming towards her on the twisting road from the pass, where Redmond had watched herself and Caitlín throw a stone-filled bag down to the stream.

She crouched quickly behind her own car, not wanting to be caught at a crime scene for a second time, or to confront a predatory driver who might relish an encounter with a lone female. She held her breath as the car slowed on the bridge, but it drove by without stopping.

She remembered again the story Caitlín had told about coffins being carried up to Ballaghscart, or Bealach Scairt, as the Healy Pass was known in the past, returning the corpse of a childless woman to her own people. They had speculated that such a woman had not earned the status required by her community for burial with her husband. To Nessa, the story illustrated starkly how the rituals of death could dishonour rather than honour the deceased, and she realised now what had niggled her about its link with Oscar.

Whoever killed him hated him bitterly – hated him enough not only to end his life, but to dump his body in a public place, where birds and animals could feast on his carcass. His killer wanted to shame him in death, and instead of hiding his remains, had put them on display for passing strangers. It reminded Nessa of something she had read about the ancient Greeks and their belief that a soul could not rest in peace until the person's corpse lay under a decent covering of earth. Oscar would not be left to rest in peace even after his murder.

She stood by the wall and tried to picture the murderer driving around Beara at night, preparing to dump his body – a man more likely that a woman, she thought, because Oscar's dead weight had to be hauled onto the parapet, and indeed dragged into the boot of a car in the first place. But wherever Oscar had been strangled, hiding his body would not have been difficult in Beara. The peninsula was dotted with woodlands, ditches and isolated mountain roads where it would have lain undiscovered for weeks, or indeed forever. In that case, gardai could have believed that Oscar had left Beara with whoever he had met that Thursday lunchtime, and would have had no idea where to search for him.

But if his body was deliberately dumped in the open, and the motive for his murder was a deep personal hatred, surely it was unlikely to be the outcome of business rivalries? Or could Dominic have grown to hate Oscar so viciously over the course of four or five days? It seemed more plausible that the killer had nursed a desire for revenge over a longer period. Caitlín had told Nessa about the message sent to a radio station on the day of his funeral, and she thought again about its insinuations of rape and torture against Oscar. The message, as far as Caitlín knew, did not say whether Oscar was accused of raping a woman once or repeatedly, and what kind of torture was suggested. But anything of that kind could certainly arouse a thirst for revenge.

Nessa shivered in the night air, disappointed that her glimmer of understanding a few minutes earlier had left her with more questions than ever. Why was she digging into Oscar's business history, if personal revenge was a likelier motive? She had encouraged Zoe in that direction, but had Zoe spurred her to do so in the first place? Should she even spend time pursuing Stella's list of contacts, or was she being led up a garden path?

But the two sisters were not the only people who had suggested that Oscar's entrepreneurial activities were key to his violent death. He himself had told Nessa that he was leaving Beara early because of an unexpected work problem. And she recalled somebody else referring to the pressures of his work the same day. Yes, it must have been his son Fergus, while they were on the way to or from the pharmacy in Castletownbere. Fergus mentioned a phone call his father got at lunchtime, about a business quarrel he was trying to sort out. He had added something about the call being from France, she remembered now, and that he was worried about it because of how his father dug his heels in whenever it came to a fight.

She took a last look down at the stream before getting back into her car. In the moonlight, she could see the water's ripples at the edge of the heathery banks. Perhaps she was wrong about the reason for dumping his body in this particular spot. The killer might have searched for a more secluded place, but then panicked in case his car was noticed and later identified. And it was also possible that two people were involved, just as she and Caitlín had concluded from their hurried experiment at the bridge.

Coming up with theories was one thing, but it was quite another to figure out which theory was worthwhile. Appearances and truth did not always coincide. The moon might shine brightly in the sky, making us believe that its radiance was generated from within, instead of being a reflection of the sun's low rays lighting up a cold and dark lump of stone.

Nessa decided to have a warm, comforting bath, to ease away the day's weary tensions. She poured herself a generous glass of wine and carried it upstairs to her bedroom. Now that she had made it all the way home, she did not have to worry about getting up early in the morning. She threw off her sweaty clothes and took a large towel from the ensuite bathroom. She was not going to confine herself to an indoor bath – instead, she would soak in the outdoor hot tub on the flat roof of a single-storey extension built beside the guest bedrooms.

She padded across the house, pausing to take a sip of wine and to notice how quiet the house was. They had had motion sensors installed on the house lights the previous year and it was easy to make her way along the corridors. Nessa was surprised, though, that the hot tub switch beside the door leading on to the roof had its red light on, indicating that the tub was in use. Then she heard sounds from outside.

A gurgling noise and a burst of laughter, amplified when she pushed open the door softly.

She waited, clutching her wineglass tightly. Silence. Several seconds of silence, followed by a gentle murmur of voices, with a backing track of bubbling water. Words drifted across the rooftop air.

'This was a seriously hot idea of yours, clever girl!'

'Totally! I said I'd a surprise for you, didn't I?'

'Mmnn . . .'

'If only we had the place to ourselves regularly, it would be just . . .'

Silence again, and then an unmistakeable moan of pleasure. Nessa was rooted to the floor, as if her limbs had turned to stone.

Marcus and Sal, having a fine time for themselves. Clearly, her daughter had lied about the sleepover arrangement with her school friend. She was taking advantage of the upheaval in all their lives, but Nessa's first reaction was a pang of guilt at her own behaviour. She was allowing herself to be sucked into her old journalistic zeal, convinced that she could unearth truths others would miss, while ignoring Sal's need for quiet study routines and supervision.

'You so have to let me spend more time in your house, Marcus.' Sal's tone was coaxing, even honeyed. 'That's if we want to be together properly . . .'

'I know what you're saying, babe, but it can't happen, I'm afraid. It's not as private as I'd like, see.' Nessa took a step from the doorway to the edge of a low screening wall and saw two heads close together. The water slopped around as Marcus detached himself and sat up a little. 'I'm getting work done on the place, I told you that already.'

'But workmen go home at night, don't they?' Sal turned her head and Nessa missed the next sentence or two. She rested her back against the wall, feeling utterly exhausted. Then she heard Sal's voice rise and become plaintive. 'I didn't believe Darina when she told me that you had other women down there recently, but maybe I should have listened to her. She said you had a blonde visitor last week, from Eastern Europe. And I've heard other rumours . . .'

'Hey, what's with the inquisition, kid? So, I've a business partnership with a woman who happens to favour a nice blonde hair colouring? And I sometimes have to meet with other females of the species? That's what the working life involves, *entiende*?' Marcus sounded more dismissive than angry. 'Anyway, I don't get why you're paying so much attention to what Darina says. What do you think she knows about the outside world, locked up in her crummy barn with her paintbrushes and her hammers all day?'

Nessa told herself she had been eavesdropping long enough. Guilt gave way to anger, which burned in her stomach like vinegar, both at her daughter's lies and at her own naive stupidity. Yes, Sal was eighteen years old and Nessa could not be sure what she got up to at music festivals or friends' parties. But it was quite another thing to abuse her parents' trust at home, and in the midst of all their current troubles.

Marcus laughed as he moved back closer to Sal, his words dripping with casual charm. 'Fact is,' he said, 'I wouldn't ask who else gets to frolic with you in the tub, eh, Salomé? See, I'd sooner have fun with you than waste our precious time arguing.'

The bubbling sounds got louder as the two figures in the water intertwined. Nessa put her glass down on the ground and banged the door loudly. She stepped out towards the tub and heard herself shout hoarsely, ordering Marcus to get the hell out of Cnoc Meala. As for Sal, she had better get ready to account for herself in the morning.

EIGHTEEN

Thursday 1 October, 9.30 a.m.

An urgent search was underway, involving gardai in Cork city, Tipperary and west Cork. On Wednesday afternoon, four days after Oscar Malden's funeral, Maureen had left hospital without a doctor's say-so, and neither she nor Dominic had been seen since then. Redmond and Conor were on their way from Castletownbere station to Derryowen, to play their part in the hunt.

The Garda Forensic Laboratory in Dublin had confirmed earlier on Wednesday that fibres found on Oscar's jacket matched the woollen jersey worn by Dominic, providing strong evidence that both men had physical contact on the day of Oscar's death. But it was three o'clock by the time two Cork city gardai went to Dominic's hotel to request his assistance with their questions, only to find that Dominic had checked out and paid his bill an hour earlier. Maureen's hospital ward was contacted to see if he was with her, but instead, it became clear that Maureen was also missing. According to staff, she walked out the front door of the hospital in her dressing gown shortly after lunch, her cigarette packet in hand, and did not come back. When her room was examined, it was discovered that all her personal belongings had been taken away, presumably by Dominic at the end of his morning visit.

Blame and accusation soon swirled among gardai, hospital authorities, media and others. Superintendent Tim Devane demanded to know why city gardai had not acted more quickly and indeed maintained discreet surveillance of Dominic. In turn, they declared that hospital staff had promised to let them know of any change in Maureen's situation. They did not have enough on Dominic to arrest and charge him, and needed his cooperation, however reluctant, to question him yet again.

Meanwhile, a rumour got out that a garda in Dublin had tipped

off a journalist about the forensic evidence, and that the same
eager journalist had alerted Dominic by phoning him to ask for
a comment. The pressure was already piling on himself and
Maureen since publication of Jack Talbot's exclusive interviews
the previous Sunday. Much hype had ensued: for example, one
tabloid claimed on Wednesday morning that the couple had been
overheard arguing bitterly in a hospital corridor, while a radio
commentator claimed the opposite, that the pair were seen on
Tuesday cuddling affectionately on a bench in the outdoor
smoking area.

'Now, what did I tell you, boy? Our friend knows that he's
facing a guilty verdict and he's done a runner to prove it.'

'A guilty verdict?' Redmond glanced at Conor. 'That
depends on us catching him first. He and Maureen could be
halfway across the continent by now.'

'Yerra, I don't think so. The ports and airports have been
all eyes since last night. They'll be run to ground pretty soon.'

'But the new forensic evidence wouldn't survive a challenge,
would it? Who's to say which day the woollen fibres transferred
from Dominic to Oscar, either directly or via contact with
Maureen? And anyway, Dominic could hardly be convicted
of murder on the basis of a few strands of wool. Reasonable
doubt is all that's needed, as we know.'

'What we also know is that whatever the feck happened to
Maureen on the boreen, it wasn't an assault for the sake of
money, because her handbag was found intact.'

'But the DNA tests on those cigarette butts that were found
nearby showed that they were all hers, isn't that true, even
though Dominic is a smoker too?'

'We should've agreed a bloody good bet on this from the
start, Garda Joyce, with stakes upped every time new evidence
appeared for or against Dominic.'

Redmond smiled, happy to be back in Conor's company
after a few quiet days in Bantry. The investigation had been
crawling along for a while, he felt, but the forensic breakthrough
was not the only new development since the funeral. Malden's
housekeeper had walked into her local garda station on Tuesday
and signed a damning accusation against him.

'What I bet is that you've been pumping your ever-reliable

sources about the housekeeper's statement,' Redmond ventured then. 'So tell me all.'

'Well, what I've been told is that she's Ukrainian and her name is Irina. Her English is very limited, but a friend persuaded her to talk to the gardai in Tipperary this week, and an interpreter was brought in. Her story is that her employer raped her, not just once but on three occasions in the past year.'

Redmond frowned, trying to measure the news against other evidence. 'Can her statement be linked directly to the message sent to the radio programme? Did she come forward because she had heard of other allegations of rape against Malden?'

'That's a fair assumption, except that this woman Irina and her friend were asked about the message and they denied knowing anything about it.'

'So we still have no idea where it came from?'

'No, but the word is that Irina is a credible witness. She says she was terrified to say a word against Malden while he was alive, because he threatened to throw her out of the house and not to renew her work permit, the bastard.'

'The story takes the gloss off Malden, that's for sure. You'd think he was a role model for society, what with a bishop on the altar praising his good deeds.'

The two men fell silent for a while. Their bosses would now decide how much information to release about the rape allegation, to see if any other woman came forward with a similar story. Fergus Malden was being interviewed once again too, to probe whether he had known anything about Irina's trauma.

Conor smiled grimly as they passed a signpost for Derryowen. 'I suppose you'll argue now that this new information makes it even less likely that Dominic was the guilty party?'

'You've said it, not me. If Malden was capable of such violence himself, there could be any number of people who had a motive to kill him.'

'It's an argument based on speculation, my friend. Yes, we've a new insight on Malden's vicious character now, but you hardly think this poor housekeeper travelled all the way to Beara to commit the fatal deed? Motive is not the same as opportunity, as I'm sure the *cig* would remind us.'

'No, but what you're trying to do is to fit the existing suspects to the available evidence, and I'm not convinced that it works.'

'Well, let me put it like this, then.' Conor's easygoing manner was no bar to his enthusiasm for a good argument. 'If Oscar Malden went out that morning with an appetite for sexual gratification, forced or otherwise, wasn't Maureen his most likely target? She's the woman he'd flirted with all week, and my belief is that Dominic arrived on the scene in time to see him pushing up her skirt and getting ready for action, God help us. So Dominic seized yer man by the throat, and the fibres of his woolly gansey got caught on Oscar's zip . . .'

'It seems remarkable that a few fibres can be linked so definitively to the clothes Dominic was wearing. I know it was a multicoloured jersey, or gansey as you call it, but still . . .'

'But still nothing, because you see it wasn't any old item of clothing that Dominic bought off the rail in a shop. My understanding is that it was a gansey knitted by Dominic's auntie many years ago, and if she knitted another one of the same pattern for someone else who happened to wear it in Beara on the same day, well, we might as well go home and eat all the fecking ganseys, jumpers and jerseys that we possess.'

Conor grinned in satisfaction, but after a few minutes, he spoke in a more subdued tone. 'You know, of course, that I'm only making light of this to stop me thinking about the horror of it all. And there was one detail of the housekeeper's statement that really struck me. She said that on the first occasion Oscar attacked her, last Christmas Eve, he was singing to himself when he came into the room. He didn't even pretend to seduce her, he just looked at her for a few minutes, still humming to himself, and then he took hold of her and got on with it in a slow, deliberate kind of way.'

Redmond turned left towards the sea before they reached Derryowen. He and the sergeant had agreed to start their search for Dominic and Maureen at the hotel. A low bank of clouds lay over the water, shrouding the horizon in a grey blur. There were a few cars parked at the side of the hotel, but they did not include the couple's navy-coloured BMW. Conor went into the hotel to check whether they or their car had been seen in the area.

While he waited outside, Redmond tried to analyse why he was unconvinced by his colleague's arguments. The murder seemed premeditated, that was the main reason. If Dominic took a fit of anger against Oscar, he was surely more likely to have strangled him with his bare hands? But instead, some smooth and as yet unidentified material had been used. Conor had also not explained why Oscar put up no resistance, and there was also the issue of where the body lay hidden for a day and a half at least.

Before leaving for Derryowen that morning, Redmond heard that Patrick Latif was being interviewed in Bandon. He wondered whether Latif would be as stubborn and unhelpful as his wife. Clearly, he was associated with fringe political groups and could have provided valuable help to a person or persons intent on assassination. All he had to do was to hand Oscar over to other conspirators, and then continue on his way to Bandon.

But Trevor O'Kelleher had outlined an alternative conspiracy theory, which entailed an unknown individual or group getting help from Fergus Malden. The young man might not have known that his father was to be murdered – it was only necessary for him to provide vital information, such as Oscar's whereabouts at a particular time. This could also account for the son's palpable fear and anxiety, Trevor said, on the basis that the killer or killers may have threatened to shut him up for good if he betrayed the truth to gardai. In his usual enigmatic way, however, Trevor did not add his own view on whether it was a plausible theory.

Redmond was stretching his legs in the car park when Conor appeared at the hotel door.

'They've been here,' he shouted, beckoning to Redmond. 'I spoke to a barman who thinks he saw them pass. Going towards the golf course, ten minutes ago at least.'

Redmond almost banged the car door on his hand as he hurried to drive off. 'Could they get to Pooka Rock from here? Is that what you think?'

'The track by the golf course will bring us close to it. What the barman noticed . . .' Conor pointed out directions as he spoke. 'He thinks the car swerved a couple of times. He couldn't confirm it was a BMW, but it was a large black or navy saloon.'

Conor phoned Superintendent Devane's office and Redmond tried to steer along a narrow track while keeping his eyes peeled on all sides. The golf course was almost deserted. On a chilly day at season's end, tourists were few and far between.

They arrived at a fork in the track. Down to their right, they could see a dark vehicle parked between a clump of large shrubs and the shoreline. Conor said they were still half a mile from Pooka Rock, off to their left.

'Let's check out this side first, though,' he said, indicating right. As they approached the vehicle, they saw that it was a van rather than a car. Redmond was about to reverse, but Conor nudged him forward. A small pier lay beyond the van and a navy-coloured car had stopped on the pier.

Dominic and Maureen. The two of them taking the sea air, admiring the scenery from the comfort of their car.

Redmond realised in an instant that his first impression was deluded. The wheels of the BMW had begun to turn. Dominic and Maureen were heading for the water.

He jammed on the accelerator, but eased off just as quickly. His thoughts were in a ferment. If he rushed at the other car, the pair inside might panic.

He jumped out of the car, throwing off his jacket and signalling to Conor that he would run down the pier. His companion was back on the phone, calling for more gardai, ambulances, the coastguard rescue. 'Get them all down here!' he shouted. 'We haven't a fucking second to spare!'

The navy car reversed suddenly and then lurched forward again. It skidded and hit the pier wall. The driver's door was opened but it was hemmed in by the wall. The passenger door was opened and Maureen's head appeared.

She bent over and seemed about to fall out. She might have been trying to vomit.

She dragged herself out of the car. She was dressed in a cream-coloured silky outfit. It was loose and flowing, and part of it had snagged in the car door. Then Redmond realised that Dominic was trying to pull her back inside by holding on to the material.

She was unsteady on her feet. She looked around like someone awaking from a nightmare. She tried to support herself by leaning on the car, whimpering softly.

Redmond was getting close. He was fifty feet from her at most, driven on by a ferocious surge of energy, body and mind in unison, consumed in a moment of pure action.

The passenger door swung open wide, hitting Maureen hard. She fell on one knee and Dominic tumbled out after her. She pulled herself up and they struggled. Her long white sleeves flapped like sails in a scant wind.

Redmond tried to grab hold of them both. They were shouting at each other but he could make little sense of it. They all teetered to the edge of the pier. The water was streaked black and green.

Dominic bellowed and Redmond hooked his arm around his neck. But the other man jabbed his elbow in his stomach.

Redmond saw Maureen fall into the water. She seemed to flop sideways like a doll. Redmond lunged out to stop her but Dominic kept tugging at him, his face red and puffy. Redmond punched him under the chin. He could not tell whether Dominic had pushed Maureen off the edge.

He saw Conor arrive just behind him. He kicked off his shoes and dived into the cold dark water. Maureen's head was down, her silky clothes billowing from her limbs. A few strokes and he could save her.

But the sea erupted around him as Dominic hit the water and Conor dived in after him. Redmond's ears were filled with the water's tumult. He lifted his head but was unable to see Maureen for a moment. He gulped for air, holding his head up, and saw her pale sleeves drawn away by the current.

He swam strongly, dipping his head under once again. His fingers were numb. He felt his own clothes dragging at him. He was pounding the water but his energy was waning.

Maureen seemed to be moving very fast and he found it hard to catch up. She was almost on the rocks when he realised that someone else was involved. A strong swimmer in wetsuit and goggles was manouevring Maureen over slippery seaweed. He grasped a rock and hauled himself up to help her. When they managed to get Maureen onto a fairly flat slab of rock, the other person pushed her goggles off and he recognised Darina O'Sullivan.

'You'd better . . .' She nodded urgently towards the pier. 'I think they're in trouble over there . . .'

Redmond turned and saw Conor, gasping for air and diving under again. 'Can you manage?' He wished he had realised sooner that his efforts to save Maureen had not been needed. He was in the wrong place, wasting valuable time.

'I can go,' said Darina. 'I'm in the gear.' But Redmond gestured for her goggles. She handed them over wordlessly, holding Maureen's head at the same time to help her dribble out seawater. He could see that she knew what she was doing, so he pulled on the goggles and swam away. He could not bear to sit on the rocks with Maureen while Conor was in danger.

The water near the pier was agitated. Even with goggles on, it was hard for Redmond to make out the shapes underwater. Dominic and Conor close together, moving as if in slow motion, rising towards the surface and sinking again. They seemed to be struggling but he could not make out who had the upper hand.

His eyes got used to the blackness as he neared them. Now he saw one man in a heap on the seabed, and the other doing his utmost to drag him up.

The rest of the day passed in a blur. Emergency services on land and sea, gardai of assorted ranks and roles, a confusion of onlookers, helpers and the media horde who swept back into Beara as soon as the whiff of a big story reached them.

Conor was brought to hospital once he was out of the water. Word came in the afternoon that he would be kept in for a few days, under orders to rest completely and receive no visits except those of his wife and of Trevor O'Kelleher. Maureen was back in Bantry Hospital too, confused and shocked but in no serious danger. Dominic was in a different category, however. The rescue helicopter had landed on the golf course to transport him to intensive care in Cork Regional Hospital, but a rumour seeped out after some hours that he had suffered a heart attack or a stroke on his way there and was on a life-support machine as a result.

Redmond was tired and sore from his own time in the water. Dominic had collapsed onto the seabed by the time he arrived to help Conor, and it took a great effort from both of them to get him to the surface. Redmond had been interviewed at length by senior gardai following a medical examination. Afterwards, he sat around in Derryowen and Castletownbere awaiting news of the people brought to hospital. He was offered a lift home to Bantry a few times, but decided instead to return to the golf course pier to pick up his car. He felt restless, unsure how he wanted to pass the evening.

'I suppose you think you deserve a medal.'

'What, for services rendered in the battle against crime? Or perhaps you speak in jest, *mon ami*?'

Redmond stopped at the hotel on the way back from the pier, trying to decide whether to join a few garda colleagues inside for a drink. As he stood in the shadows near the smoking shelter, he could hear a group of journalists in full flow.

'You mean, I'm taking the piss, Jack? Just because you're smirking to yourself for doing your bit to supply us with today's colourful splash, if you'll pardon the shameless pun?'

'I'm glad you think I did something useful, but of course—'

'Of course, you won't actually write it in cold print, will you? That it was your exclusive feature interviews on Sunday that drove Dominic and Maureen to try to kill themselves today, conveniently providing us with such drama this morning?'

Redmond pressed himself against an ornamental pillar, watching and wishing he could step out to spit in their faces. But his colleagues at the bar were probably trading their own black-humoured banter about the day's events.

'I may have eased the story along a little,' said Talbot piously. 'But I could hardly foresee how Dominic's conscience would affect him.'

A curly-haired woman cut across him. 'You're so full of

shit, Jack, you must be paralysed with constipation. One week it's a sinister Russian conspiracy, and now listen to you taking credit—'

'Ah, fair play, Jay, all the same,' said a fourth voice. 'The only headlines that matter are tomorrow's, isn't that it? Sure who wants yesterday's cold porridge for breakfast?'

Redmond was fairly sure that the woman in the group was Conor's friend, the reporter in a local radio station. He wished the sergeant was not confined to a hospital ward, and that they could stroll in to the hotel together, tossing a few pointed grenades amongst the hacks who supported Talbot.

He fumbled with his mobile, in case anyone looked in his direction and realised he was eavesdropping. He told himself that he was too tired to join his colleagues. He should go home to bed, that was his best option. He had been given a couple of days off, but he wanted to be at the garda briefing announced for eight thirty in the morning, when the next steps in the investigation would be discussed.

He returned to his car, as indecisive as before. After the day's great surges of adrenalin, he was afraid it would take him hours to get to sleep. His mind would be churning: remembering how Maureen fell because he failed to help her in time; wishing he had spotted Darina O'Sullivan as soon as she got hold of Maureen; wondering again and again whether Dominic had intended to drown himself as well as his wife, for fear of Maureen giving evidence against him in court.

Redmond tried a few radio stations, but he was not in the mood for cheery music or the predictable rantings of phone-in shows. As for news bulletins, he could recite them off by heart, including references to the heroic role ascribed to himself and to Conor. Darina O'Sullivan was also praised widely – in an internet piece Redmond read earlier, she was called 'Maureen's guardian angel', for saving her life twice. Darina's own comments were more muted, simply confirming that she went swimming in the same place most days, and had done as anyone would when she heard shouting from the pier.

At a garda press conference in the afternoon, praise had also been spread around liberally and Redmond had felt his heart gladden at every mention of his name. He was on a high at the time, feeling he had done something worthwhile at long last, which the super could not fail to notice. Most of all, he had been there for Conor when it mattered.

But as the day advanced, his doubts grew. His deeds were a hollow success if Dominic suffered brain damage because he was under water too long. As for Maureen, it was plain to everyone that it was not him who had saved her, but Darina. He resented her now for depriving him of the full glory of his actions. She was not even the type of person to relish the spotlight as he would.

He went over the opposite arguments in turn. If he had reined in his pride and allowed her to help Conor with Dominic, she might have done a better job at that too. She was clearly as strong a swimmer as he was, and more used to the local conditions. He subjected each incident to the pitiless microscope in his head, and ended up scourging himself as always before.

He told himself now that he should act like a normal person and go home with a few beers and a DVD. But he knew that drinking alcohol would send him off on another well-trodden path – brooding over his father's addiction and his own fear of succumbing to the same weak genes, asking the unanswerable questions about how his life would be today if his parents had taken a different road home on that awful evening.

He could hear music from the hotel as he drove away. He was glad he had left. It would give him a headache to sit in a bar straining to chat above the din. Instead, he would go somewhere quiet, to sort out his thoughts for the morning's meeting. Scannive Strand would be a good spot, and he might walk along the beach to help him sleep later.

Trevor had told him in the afternoon about the latest information from the pathologist, that Oscar's body had been placed by his killer or killers in a double layer of plastic bags, before the stiffening effects of rigor mortis had set in. The pathologist had also commented on another important process known as livor mortis: this showed how the blood had settled after his heart stopped pumping, including purplish discolouration where the heavy red cells had sunk by gravity to the lowest areas of his body, and blanched whitish skin wherever it had been pressed directly against another surface. In Oscar's case, the pattern provided evidence that his body had not lain prone in a car boot or ditch, but rather that it had been pushed, feet first and knees jammed to his chin, into a restricted container such as a box or tub. A new search would have to be made throughout the area to try and identify a likely container.

Redmond sat in his car, watching the sea's rhythmic flux. No matter how hard he and his colleagues worked, it seemed that they had barely advanced in their task. And now there was a serious risk that the biggest questions would remain unanswered. Even if Dominic survived, he might well be unable to face trial. He could certainly not be questioned in the near future about the incriminating strands of wool. Redmond could see himself being moved back to the tedium of routine duties – checking driving licences, maintaining public order and following up on complaints of violence in the home, many of them crimes and rows that were the everyday consequences of excessive drinking as practised by too many people in Ireland.

He had formulated a few specific questions of his own in the course of the investigation, but had been unsure about pursuing them. He was too cautious, too willing to take his lead from others. Jumping into the sea in an emergency was all very well, but presenting original information to his superiors would be better still. The morning's action needed a sequel. And if he failed to make a move before he was taken off the murder team, he would have long months in which to castigate himself.

The clock told him that it was twenty to nine. He procrastinated a few minutes longer, before turning the ignition at last. Reversing out of the parking area, he took the narrow road to the holiday houses at Carraig Álainn. It was time to trust his own judgement, just as Trevor had counselled him to do.

NINETEEN

Thursday 1 October, 9.00 p.m.

Redmond opened three drawers in turn, his hand covered with a cloth so that he would not leave any prints. Marcus was careless, he thought, to have left the cabin of his boat unlocked. Unfortunately, there was nothing of interest in the drawers. A pack of cards, a few old sailing magazines, a small box of headache pills and a curl of withered orange peel.

He switched off his torch for a moment. He had seen two cars parked at Marcus's house, and a light on inside. If Marcus happened to step out to the edge of his patio and look down, he would realise that an intruder was snooping about on his boat. If he came down to investigate, Redmond would have nowhere to hide.

In any case, it was hardly acceptable garda behaviour to trespass on private property and carry out a search without a warrant. Even if he found a stash of illegal drugs on board, his evidence would probably be thrown out as inadmissible. Redmond's only excuse would be that he had suspected Marcus since he first laid eyes on him – but as to why, or what he suspected the young man of doing, he could not explain convincingly. He wanted to propose to his superiors that Carraig Álainn should be searched from top to bottom; but his real reason for sneaking onto the boat was to check in advance what might be found by such a search.

He opened a cupboard door quickly and flicked on the torch. Clothes in a heap. A pair of women's tights, rolled up in a ball. On a shelf above them, two boxes of condoms, one empty. No surprise that Marcus kept himself busy in that department. Redmond spotted a mini-cupboard by the door, and tried that too. A few packets of crisps and peanuts in a plastic shopping bag, plus a bottle of water. Some electrical items in a shoebox

– a few timers for a central heating system, used plugs and a bit of cable, probably spare stuff for the holiday houses. No sign of what Redmond secretly hoped for, such as blocks of cocaine wrapped in cellophane, or a notebook conveniently listing prices, weights and importation dates. Oscar's name jotted in the notebook too, as clear evidence that he and Marcus were up to their necks in it together.

Redmond kept the torch up his sleeve as he moved around. Another few minutes was all he needed. The boat was a cabin cruiser, maybe twenty-five feet long and fitted with an engine. One main room under the deck, with a tiny kitchen in the corner, a pullout sofabed and a sliding door into the bathroom and toilet. Redmond had noticed the GPS steering system by the wheel upstairs, which probably had a computer record of all journeys. He was fairly sure that the boat was not big enough to make it across to France or Britain, but shunting twenty or thirty miles along the coast or out to sea should be no problem.

Finding valuable drugs on board was just a fantasy, as he soon admitted to himself. That sort of thing was usually the result of painstaking cooperation between Irish and other police forces, assisted by customs officers and sometimes paid informants. Carraig Álainn was ideally located for drug smuggling, however. The boat was part of its tourist offering, available to guests for sightseeing and fishing trips – and it could also be used by people posing as guests, to make a scenic trip out to sea where a consignment of drugs awaited collection from a larger boat.

Redmond left the cabin cruiser and clambered up the cliff-side steps in the darkness, holding onto the handrail all the way. He should leave Carraig Álainn too. Marcus would be absolutely delighted to catch him creeping around, and could even claim that Redmond had planted false evidence against him.

A light was still on in the house nearest the cliff, so he stayed in the shadows of the trees. When he reached the middle house, he stopped for a few seconds to calm his breath. The house was as dark as ever, without a glimmer from its shrouded windows.

He was about to set off when he heard a sound. He crouched behind a large shrub and watched as two people came out of the darkened house. Marcus and the woman who fitted Katya's description, according to Conor's information. Perhaps they had switched off the hall light before they opened the door, or had been romping together in pitch blackness.

They paused on the pathway, lit by an outside light, and he got a good view of them. Katya was slim and sleekly dressed, her fair hair draped down her back. She said something to Marcus as he turned to open a garage door. He laughed in reply and called back over his shoulder. 'Wait till you see the place. It's perfect for us.'

Redmond made a decision on the spot. He could stay at Carraig Álainn, and hope to get into one or more of the houses while they were gone. But that was the kind of crazy risk he had just taken on the boat. Instead, he would slip out the gate and drive ahead to await them at the nearest secluded junction. There was no law against following them along the public roads, in order to find out where their so-perfect hideaway was.

The speedometer climbed rapidly. Well over the speed limit on the twisting main road towards Kenmare. Easily over seventy-five an hour. The needle danced above the eighty-mile-an-hour mark as Redmond's car jolted on a pothole. Marcus was in a hurry – just like so many young drivers who rushed pell-mell to an early grave.

Redmond eased his foot on the accelerator. He hated fast driving. Fifty million people around the world killed since cars had become lords of the roads, a vast battlefield of pain and loss. That was of no concern to Marcus, of course, as fire sparked on hot metal and Katya admired his manly feats.

It was impossible to keep up with them. As soon as they overtook another car, they went out of sight. Redmond would prefer to be accused of burglary than of driving at an outrageous speed. Let them go and good riddance.

He parked in Ardgroom village. He would buy three cans of beer to take home. Total abstention from alcohol was taking things too far, after all that had happened earlier, and he could watch some silly film on television to calm his thoughts. It was none of his business if Marcus snogged a different woman every night. Even if he had a brothel on the go down at Carraig Álainn, well, that was a problem for Trevor or Conor as far as garda action was concerned.

He was about to drive off again when he saw the young pair stroll out of the pub. They must have been in the lounge having a quick drink while he made his own purchase in the bar. Katya was munching crisps out of a bag and Marcus was carrying a few bottles, that same sly smirk on his mouth that made Redmond's blood boil. Strutting about as he pleased, daring anyone to get in his way.

Redmond released the handbrake and drove out of the village. He had to do it. Follow Marcus and his lady friend, and find out why his gut screamed at him that they were up to no good. The morning's heroics had ended in self-doubt. He could not succumb to fear or caution now.

The road north soon narrowed and twisted into the night. Redmond kept ahead of the white car this time, keeping strictly to the speed limit and making it impossible for Marcus to overtake. He eyed the rear-view mirror with satisfaction, sure that he was being loudly cursed from the other car.

Just in time, he spotted them turning off the main road. Redmond drove on until he found an opportunity to make an about turn, and back to the side road taken by the Mitsubishi. He had lost a few minutes now, and would need a dose of luck to catch up.

He rounded a bend and saw red lights at a distance. When he came to a small crossroads, he was unsure of his bearings, but decided to go straight ahead. He glanced at several houses along the way, to check whether the white car was parked beside any of them.

At the next crossroads, he almost drove into the Mitsubishi. Marcus and Katya must have stopped to decide which way to go. Redmond turned down his lights as soon as he spotted them. When they set off, he followed slowly. At the next bend, he decided to switch off his headlights altogether.

The night was quite cloudy and he could barely decipher the landscape's outlines. He was in a maze of small hills and thickets. Every now and then, he caught sight of their rear lights flickering and leading him on.

He was moving through the night in an invisible tin box. Trees grew close to the road in places and he had to flick on his sidelights to avoid plunging into a ditch. Once, he drove through a pitch-black tunnel of foliage, guided only by a red pinprick at its far end. He could hit a wall or a hedge at any second.

When a car approached from the opposite direction, he had no choice but to light up properly and pull in to let it pass. He noticed grass growing in the middle of the road. He drove down a fairly steep slope, wondering if the shiny surface he glimpsed off to his right was the sea. The white Mitsubishi had disappeared from view.

As the road curved uphill again, Redmond saw movement in the corner of his eye – a gate being closed, a swish of blonde hair. He found a small space for his own car on a laneway nearby.

He took several deep breaths before he opened the car door. He remembered to check that his phone was on mute and that his torch was still in his pocket. A great surge of gladness welled inside him, adrenaline gushing through his veins as it had done that morning on the pier.

The old house was almost surrounded by fir trees. Redmond watched from behind one of them. Almost half an hour since he had arrived, and his feet were seizing up from the cold. The white car was parked by the side of the house, there was a soft glow from one window, and Marcus and Katya were inside.

Redmond had tried taking a few photographs on his mobile phone, but it was too dark to get much of an image. A window on either side of the front door, dirty paint on the walls and an air of decay about the place. Redmond shone his torch on a pile of moss-covered concrete blocks he noticed behind the parked car. Somebody had planned building work that had never taken place.

The house was a bungalow, but a wooden staircase at the side led up to a door that presumably gave access to a loft or attic. Perhaps the idea had been to make two separate holiday apartments, one above the other, but then the money had run out. Unlike the newer houses at Carraig Álainn, there were no upstairs windows here.

A thought struck Redmond as if it had hit him over the head. It was so obvious that he was amazed it had taken him so long. Darkened houses with heavy blinds on each window, a telltale sliver of light at one Velux edge, and spare electrical fittings in a cupboard on the boat.

He crept up the wooden staircase, straining to hear any sound from the front of the house. He tried the upper door but it was locked. He gave as hard a push as he could manage quietly, but when he could not shift it, he hurried back down to his hiding place in the trees.

Perhaps he should leave now and alert the inspector to his suspicions. A search warrant could be issued and a full investigation conducted. He could find his precise location by turning on his GPS. He tiptoed between the trees, making for the gate, aware of every slight swish of his waterproof jacket.

He stopped and broke into a sweat. Something had moved beside him. A quick darting sound, followed by a thud or two. Noises that were magnified in the darkness, his nerves on edge in unfamiliar surroundings.

It was nothing, just a small animal or bird frightened by the arrival of a human at close quarters. He was stupid to be startled by such things.

He heard another sound just then. Not a scuttling creature but a loud voice as the front door was opened. Marcus ran out of the house, swearing angrily. He ran up the wooden stairs and fumbled at the attic door. He disappeared into the upper area for a few moments. Katya came out the front door, heels clacking as she went towards the car.

Redmond tried to melt into the trees, while keeping Marcus in his sights. The young man seemed to be unsteady on his feet. He pulled open the driver's door of the car, but Katya was already sitting there. She held her ground as they argued over who should drive. Redmond waited in the shadows until Marcus opened and closed the gate, his laugh jangling in the dark night as he got into the passenger seat.

Redmond flew up the wooden stairs as soon as they had driven away. The door did not budge but when he shone his torch around him, he saw that the key had fallen on to the top step.

There was a narrow corridor inside, separated from the attic room by a heavy-duty curtain. Redmond tugged at the curtain, and was almost blinded by the lights in the room. His heart thumped against his ribs as he took in the scene.

He took seven or eight pictures on his phone, shifting position to try to avoid the glare of the lights. The phone signal was intermittent, but he tried emailing the photos to his home computer. He stooped down to take a few closer shots without stepping into the room.

Redmond did not hear the footsteps that came along the narrow corridor. He did not realise that another person was behind him until he heard a low voice in his right ear. The voice told him that a sharp knife was pointed at his spine and that he would be very sorry if he did not do as instructed.

Beara was as quiet as a graveyard. In the grey dawn of day, nobody stirred. A line of cloud hovered offshore, waiting to make landfall.

On a minor road beside a boggy pool, a small bird hopped down from a bush. She picked at the damp earth here and there on the verge. She twitched lightly as she kept a sharp eye on all sides for predators.

There were fresh tyre marks in the damp earth, made by a car skidding to a sudden halt. The car's bonnet had rammed into an old hazel tree. Its occupant lay slumped inside against the door, his left hand dangling off the steering wheel.

The bird hopped to and fro in search of food. The sun gained strength in the eastern sky. All over the peninsula, people awoke and set about their daily tasks.

Inside the car, Redmond shifted his hand. As he stirred into consciousness, he felt pains all over his body. An ache in his neck and a sharp stab in his ribs. His skull was like a steel helmet clamped on too tightly, and blades of pain pierced his eyes as he tried to open them.

An old house hidden behind black trees. Steps leading

upwards, and lights dazzling in a room. Images flickering in his memory, like faraway stars in the night sky.

A while later, another car drew up beside his. But Redmond's eyes had closed again and he did not see the driver looking in at him anxiously. His deadened senses failed to register the elderly man's knocks on the car window, before he drove off to a neighbour's house to phone the gardai. The sun rose and fresh layers of Atlantic cloud piled up offshore.

When Redmond awoke a second time, shafts of sunlight bored into his eyes. His mouth was as dry as sand and tasted foul. He realised that it was the taste of stale alcohol. He felt sick all of a sudden and lifted his head, hoping to get a door or window open. But instead he found himself throwing up violently onto the clean floor of his car.

He had to get out. Find a clump of grass to cover the mess. Find water. He was thirsty as hell. But he was terribly stiff and sore, and bending over had brought on new spasms. He thought his shoulder was broken.

He looked around and saw an empty bottle jammed down beside the passenger seat. A half-bottle of whiskey. Panic hit him. Even if he was not injured, he would be unfit to drive.

He looked out the window at a bleak mountain view. Fissures of purple-grey rock breaking through the heathery grass at steep angles. A few cottage roofs in the distance. He could be anywhere.

He had to open the window to let in some air. He was drenched in sweat and about to be sick again. At least the key was in the ignition. It felt like a big achievement to operate the electric windows.

The night's events resurfaced in his memory. A knife to his back, forcing him to walk all the way to his car. Redmond tried to fight back at one stage, but a sharp nick on his cheek convinced him otherwise. There were two of them, that was what made it impossible to resist.

Two men wearing dark glasses, one with a baseball cap and the other in a hoodie. Identical voices. One of them got into Redmond's car, bursting into raucous laughter as he ordered him to drive. After a mile or two, he was told to stop and the second guy, who had followed in his own car, joined his brother in the back seat.

Marcus and Carl, no doubt about it. They spotted the beer cans Redmond had bought earlier and gulped them greedily.

His memories of the night throbbed uncontrollably. Redmond put his head to the open window and sucked in the mountain air. He closed his eyes for a few moments, trying to remember everything.

Marcus was the worst of the two, he was fairly sure of it. He was the one with the harsh laugh, who produced whiskey and took a slug or two himself before he pushed it up against Redmond's ear, telling him to drink. When Redmond tried to ignore him, he waved the knife in the rear-view mirror and shouted at him to swallow every drop. Carl laughed too, but he also made a few attempts to calm his brother's aggression.

They got out of the car at last. Redmond remembered sitting on his hands to stop them from shaking. He tried to steady himself to walk away from the car. Then he heard a shout at the rear door, followed by a string of filthy language. He was ordered to drive again or he was dead meat.

He had only a hazy idea of what happened after that. He drove as slowly as he could, churning with fear. Headlights appeared in his rear window but he did not know whose they were.

The night got darker, that was his impression. Trees swayed towards him. The thought swirling in his head was that he should kill himself before he rammed some other poor sod into a ditch.

A lone tree had rushed out of the gloom. He hit the brake, or maybe the accelerator.

The sun climbed over the mountains. Redmond dozed for a while. Insects and birds flitted about outside the car.

When he came to again, he remembered his phone. He dug into his pockets but they were empty. Marcus or Carl must have found it. But if he had managed to email the photos he took in the attic, it might all be worth it.

He had to get out of the car, away from the smell of vomit. He could walk to the nearest house and ask for help. Conor was in hospital, of course. It felt as if weeks had passed since they had both jumped into the icy water to rescue Maureen and Dominic.

He had to phone Trevor, that was the only option. The grotty bungalow had to be searched as soon as possible. Marcus would be nailed once the attic was opened and Redmond's discovery revealed to his colleagues. A large room full of cannabis plants, arranged in long rows under powerful heat lamps. Equipment set up to produce the maximum growth in the shortest time – timers to control heating and lighting, and spares kept in the boat if Marcus had to replace a few of them.

It was a valuable haul. No wonder Marcus and Carl had turned violent in order to protect it.

Redmond opened his eyes properly. Somebody was speaking to him. A jolt of terror shook him at the thought that the brothers had returned.

Then he recognised the inspector's voice. Trevor O'Kelleher was trying to open the passenger door.

Redmond saw disgust in his eyes. Disgust, surprise and, most damning of all, disappointment.

TWENTY

Friday 9 October, 5.15 p.m.

ancelled. A cold and unforgiving word, Nessa thought, as she marked it on her screen. Six bookings cancelled for the October bank holiday weekend, which should have been their final flourish of the season. Customers who had seen the name Cnoc Meala in the headlines once too often, and did not want to spend their hard-earned holiday cash in the shadow of death, wondering if a crazed murderer lurked behind the next rock.

'We have to make a decision soon, you know that, don't you?'

Patrick did not reply immediately. He was frowning at his own computer screen, his desk at right angles to Nessa's in the small office between the kitchen and the family living room. He flicked through a sheaf of papers set neatly beside his computer. By contrast, Nessa's desk was covered in disorderly heaps which she swore at least once a week to sort out.

'We'll have to call off the weekend very soon, Patrick, if we get one more cancellation. People who are still booked in will need enough time to make alternative plans.'

'I'm sorry, love, I'm trying to contact the lawyer in Lilongwe, so I can't—'

'Oh, never mind, we can talk about it in a day or two. Maybe everything will work out of its own accord.'

She knew that her voice betrayed her frustration. For the past week, she had tried hard to make allowances for Patrick, and all the pressures that had followed his aunt's death. But she also suspected that he kept his mind on matters in Africa in order to avoid the problems at home.

'I don't think we should worry unduly about one weekend,' he said then. He turned to face her and Nessa noticed the tiredness in his eyes. 'The public's memory of these events will fade sooner or later, and we'll be back on our feet by next spring, I promise you.'

'I wish I could believe that, but even if Oscar's killer is caught, things could drag on until a trial takes place a year or two later. Meanwhile, we could find ourselves out of business.'

'It's far too soon for that sort of talk, Nessa. You told me yourself last week that we got goodwill messages from some of our best customers.'

'Yes, but goodwill won't pay the bills, will it? And our finances are pretty fragile.'

'Would you prefer me not to send money to Esther's grand-children? I know we haven't discussed it properly, but if you're worried about helping with their school and medical bills, you should say so.'

'That's not what I meant at all, Patrick. Of course we should help them, because we live in the lap of luxury by comparison. But it's just, I don't know . . .' Nessa stopped as several papers toppled off her desk. She had a habit of gesticulating extrava-gantly when she got frustrated. She bent to pick them up. 'I feel as if we've been in limbo for weeks now, with no word of progress from the gardai.'

'I told you I saw Sergeant Fitzmaurice in Castletown the other day? Unfortunately he had no news about the garda checks on me. He looked uncomfortable when I asked him about it, which was not like him.'

Nessa glanced out the window. 'It's like the weather we're having, drizzle and low cloud day after day, and not a puff of wind to bring hope of a change.'

Patrick attempted a lame smile. 'I suppose Beara has had some extra visitors recently, though. Day-trippers, you know, who walk around the area expecting to see smears of blood on the roads.'

'I'm sorry, love, I can't . . .' Nessa rubbed her eyes. She seemed to get less sleep each night that passed. Raging fury and grim determination had given way to weariness after three weeks of the murder investigation. Patrick got up and stood behind her, touching her neck gently.

'We have to believe it will be solved,' he said. 'The gardai are under huge pressure to get the killer, and it's probably best that they move cautiously.'

'What upsets me most . . .' Nessa allowed herself to breathe in deeply as Patrick stroked her skin with the tips of his fingers. 'It's not just that I want it to be solved,' she said then. 'That's only part of why I feel so chewed up. The other part is that I've begun to think that whoever killed Oscar did the right thing.'

Nessa turned as Patrick stopped his gentle massage. 'Can't you understand that?' she asked. 'I mean, the evidence that's coming out now tells us that he was a complete bastard.'

'The latest accusation of rape, you mean?'

'Yes, and I bet you there's more to come too. First, there was his housekeeper, and this week there's a young woman who got her first job in the marketing section of his company, saying she had to leave the job after he raped her. Oscar had threatened to blacken her name if she reported him, and then he and his admirers in the gossip columns spun the story as another of his broken-hearted conquests. The same thing may have happened to other women he claimed to have seduced.'

'I agree with you that it's very nasty. But I suppose we rarely hear the unpleasant secrets of our guests.'

'Jesus, I bloodywell hope we haven't harboured rapists here on a regular basis. It's all very well to be a charmer, as we took Oscar to be, but it makes me ill to remember how we kowtowed to him. In fact, Dominic was the only person who wasn't taken in by him, and that's not easy for me to admit.'

'But you can't seriously say that Oscar deserved to be murdered? The justice system is there for people like him. Otherwise it's the law of the jungle.'

'I know that, Patrick, but justice can't always be relied on, can it?' Nessa leaned back her head, closing her eyes to hold in her tears. She felt she understood for the first time how vicious life really was. Lying awake in the lonely hours before dawn, she could wish for the whole human race to be swept away, with all the infinite suffering and tortures that so many people inflicted on others, or tolerated in the world.

She had a few new leads in her researches on Oscar, but no clear answers. Mounting evidence of his cruelties was not the same as finding out who murdered him. She could not sit on her hands doing nothing, but uncovering a snake pit was taking its toll too.

Patrick held her head in his hands, stroking her temples slowly. The phone started to ring, but they ignored it. After a moment, the answering machine clicked into play, and they heard Trevor O'Kelleher's soft voice saying that he would like to call at the house that evening, to discuss a few matters relevant to the investigation.

'I don't want to go tomorrow. It's going to be boring, I know it is.'

Ronan was seated on the stairs when Nessa left the office. She thought she could escape upstairs, to make a few phone calls before Trevor arrived. She put down her laptop and sat beside her son. She had enrolled him on a sea-kayaking course, to try to get him out among his own age-group more often.

'Do you remember what we said the other day, when we talked about this?'

'Not really. I didn't say for definite that I'd go.'

'You said you'd try the course if you knew someone else who was doing it. So last night, I made a few calls—'

'But it'll be too cold. And too wet. Anyway, you know I don't really like team things.'

Nessa sat with him for a while, cajoling and encouraging. In the end, Ronan agreed not to disappoint his school pal who had also enrolled on the course, and in return, Nessa promised to buy him a new Playstation game after the first two sessions. The bribery school of parenting, as she muttered to herself.

Up in her bedroom, she opened a file named 'B-Z' on the laptop. It contained copies of the material Ben and Zoe had found nine days earlier, as well as follow-up information. Nessa re-read an email Zoe had sent at the start of the week.

> Your idea of checking out arms brokers has paid off. Ben's told me all about these people who buy and sell weapons for their own grubby profit. He's found out that Oscar got into this in the 1990s, when his respectable operations were going through a bad patch. So much for his entrepreneurial genius!

I can't believe how easy a business it is. All Oscar
had to do was buy a supply of hardware from one crowd,
say in China or Kazakhstan, and then sell it on to someone
else. He never got dirt under his shiny fingernails, of
course, and he could do it nice and handy from Ireland
in spite of our great claims of neutrality and suchlike.
He was the middleman, you see, and once the internet
came along, he could just watch the money pour in.

Meanwhile, the business journalist friend of Nessa's was
looking for links between Oscar's investments and the Russian
ship, but to no avail so far. One of Stella's contacts had
confirmed Oscar's links with military and intelligence figures
in Saudi Arabia and in Egypt. Nessa had also decided to contact
James, Patrick's friend in Bandon, to ask if he could find out
anything about Oscar's investments in eastern Europe, via the
organiser of Patrick's trip to Moscow. It was a delicate request,
because she reckoned the recent publicity about the trip could
have rekindled bad feelings among that group. So she had said
nothing to Patrick about it. But her risky request had paid off,
if information relayed to her that morning by James proved
to be true.

She hesitated before she picked up the phone. Perhaps she
should wait to find out if Inspector O'Kelleher had news of a
breakthrough. On the other hand, Oscar's vile business dealings
should be exposed, whether they had contributed to his murder
or not. She decided to talk directly to Ben. Her difficulty with
Zoe was that she did not fully trust her to keep her mouth shut,
or to distinguish fact from feeling. Finding Oscar's killer seemed
to be rather less important to her than denouncing a rich entrepreneur to the world and its mother.

Nessa noticed her own reflection in the darkened window
– the auburn glow of youth in her hair disguising the grey
underneath. She wanted to keep Zoe at arm's length, but she
also envied her vigorous certainty about right and wrong, and
her sense of life's endless possibilities. At the end of her email,
Zoe mentioned that she would stay on in London for a while,
to get to know Stella properly and to take up Ben's offer of
regular volunteer work in his office.

'I'm glad we've been able to help,' he said, when he answered the phone. 'It's a pity we didn't learn about Oscar Malden while he was alive, but better late than never.'

'You know that his products in Russia and Ukraine were described in the business media as "security systems", which could cover a multitude of purposes. Well, I've heard this morning that he supplied equipment for use in prisons, including restraints that can deliver an electric shock to unco-operative prisoners.'

Nessa let out her breath as she awaited Ben's response. She had deliberately used the most neutral words she could think of, to allow him to interpret them on his own terms.

'The word "restraints" certainly covers a multitude,' he said slowly. 'It could mean a type of cable or chain to prevent a prisoner from moving around, or else something bigger, such as electric fences or gates protecting an exercise area.'

'Not fences or gates, no. Whatever precisely his company makes is packed and exported in packages that are smaller than shoeboxes. Or so I've been told in relation to one of his factories in the Ukraine.'

'Well, he could be making stun guns, Nessa. They're used all over the world as a defensive weapon in security situations, but unfortunately they've been known to cause very serious injuries. That's just a guess, though, and there is another possibility.'

Nessa braced herself. She remembered the photo of Oscar at the arms fair, next to the thin Englishman. Patrick's account of the sharp pains his aunt used to suffer had been on her mind all day.

'Restraints that deliver an electric shock suggest torture to me,' said Ben. 'There's a big market out there for such products, I'm sorry to say, considering that torture is used regularly in at least sixty countries around the world, and electro-shock devices are the most common method used. They include stun guns and they're made all over the world, the United States being the leading producer as far as I know, and certainly not associated with Ukraine in particular.'

Nessa had to stop herself screaming out loud. 'Torture devices is just what I was afraid you'd suggest. But all I have at the moment is third-hand information, and the company involved is not registered directly in Oscar's name. It could take months to get proper details, including photos of these products, and a paper trail of documentation.'

'Are you going to tell the Irish police about it? They must be asking some of these questions themselves by now.'

Nessa studied her reflection again in silence. Perhaps she was holding back out of pride, in case she became the laughing stock of Bantry station, scrabbling for crumbs of information about companies that Oscar had nothing to do with. Or perhaps she feared the glee with which Jack Talbot would rework his depiction of Patrick as a stooge of Russian gangsters, if she gave him half an excuse.

'I'll give it another week before I tell them,' she said, surprising herself by saying it so firmly. 'But if you've any more ideas . . .'

'One possibility would be to check the patents for the products manufactured in the Ukraine, and elsewhere in eastern Europe. I know someone who's an expert at that kind of thing, and may be able to trace ownership of the patents.'

'That would be really great. I know you've a million other things to do . . .'

Ben laughed, and his tone became a lot warmer. 'I've a new volunteer to call on, you know. Do you mind if I tell her about this? It may also be useful to talk to her sister, Stella, with her enviable network of contacts.'

'I'd really prefer to keep it quiet for now.' Nessa tried to choose her words carefully. 'I don't know Zoe or Stella well, and I hardly know you at all, Ben, but at least you've worked on these issues for several years. I feel I'm stumbling around in a minefield, and there are other allegations.'

'That's OK,' he said quietly. 'Zoe has already filled me in on the rape stories, and if Oscar Malden was as truly evil as we now suspect, we'll get the full story out eventually.'

When Patrick showed their visitors into the sitting room, Nessa was glad to see that Inspector O'Kelleher was accompanied by Sergeant Fitzmaurice and not Garda Joyce. She did not feel able for the younger garda's supercilious airs. Caitlín had told her he had not been in Derryowen all week, so perhaps he had been taken off the team.

'The first reason for coming to see you both,' said O'Kelleher, 'is to update you on those matters that affect you personally.' He smiled as if to apologise for speaking in officialese, and turned to Patrick. 'I'm referring to our inquiries into your movements on Thursday 17th September last, and indeed your own statements about your meeting with the deceased man, Oscar Malden.'

Nessa glanced at Conor Fitzmaurice to check his demeanour. Unlike the inspector, he was a familiar and friendly presence in the area. But he stood with hands clasped on the navy cap he had removed at the door, shoulders straight and eyes to the floor. She began to feel nervous of what was to come.

'We've found two pieces of evidence to verify what you told us,' said O'Kelleher. 'Your mobile phone signals on that day place you in the Bantry area by one o'clock, so while we cannot confirm every minute of your journey, you certainly do not seem to have delayed en route, or had time to engage in any unexplained activity. In addition, we have a CCTV recording of your presence in Bantry town, where you stopped off to buy a bottle of water in a shop.'

'I'd forgotten about that, inspector,' said Patrick. 'I should have included it in my statement, but my aunt's death was so much on my mind.'

O'Kelleher smiled gently, and said he'd prefer to be called by his first name. Nessa relaxed a fraction. 'It's not a problem,' he said. 'Most people forget large chunks of their day-to-day activities, unless they live by a very fixed routine.'

Fitzmaurice looked from Nessa to Patrick, hardly a glimmer of a twinkle in his eyes. 'If I may put in a word here,' he said, 'what the *cig* has given you is the good news. But unfortunately, it doesn't amount to conclusive proof that you were in Bantry before Oscar felt the smooth pull of a cord on his neck. It's still not impossible, you see, that he went off in your car and you managed to kill him and hide his body somewhere between Derryowen and Bantry. In other words, it's very hard to prove a negative in this situation.'

'What you mean,' said Patrick drily, 'is that it's a pity I

didn't pick up a hitchhiker at Scannive Strand and have him watch me while I put his rucksack into the boot of the car. Then he could swear in court that I hadn't hidden a trussed-up body under my own luggage.'

'That's about the size of it,' said O'Kelleher. He lapsed into silence, as if he was pondering how to continue. Both he and Fitzmaurice were more soft cop than hard cop, Nessa thought to herself, but there was still an air of wariness in the room. Their message was that while Patrick was not a lead suspect, they could not yet say so in plain words.

She broke the silence by offering them something to drink. After a few rounds of refusals, Fitzmaurice agreed to tea and O'Kelleher conceded a fresh apple juice. When she returned from the kitchen, both men were sitting upright on a sofa, making polite small talk with Patrick. The inspector resumed business fairly quickly.

'We've another reason for calling in this evening,' he said. 'We'd like to ask for your assistance with some filming for television, for the *Crime Scene* programme. We've asked to do a reconstruction of Oscar's murder.'

'When will that happen?' The news was unexpected, and Nessa was unsure how to react. 'Would you like to film here in the house?'

'The production team will have to speak to you about that, but one or two short scenes may be helpful, yes. I think most of the filming will be outdoors, though, along the cliff path near the hotel, around the Briary and up to the Coomgarriff Walk. It'll happen in a week or so, we hope.'

'By all accounts this kind of thing can have a dramatic effect on people's memories,' added the sergeant.

O'Kelleher sipped at his juice before he continued. 'The production team will bring in a few actors, but we'll also ask some of your guests to return to the area – Fergus Malden, certainly, and two or three others who were around Derryowen that Thursday. We'll encourage local people to take part too, and indeed the process of filming itself might jog a few memories.'

'What about Maureen, inspector? Are you considering . . .?'

'I think she'll be invited, yes, but I doubt if she'll be up to it. And unfortunately, there's no question about Dominic. The actors will have to cover his part as well as Oscar Malden's.'

Nessa decided to venture a few questions about the investigation itself. 'Can you confirm yet whether Maureen's incident on the Thursday evening had anything to do with Oscar's murder?'

'Or whether she was actually assaulted?' Patrick put a question that he had asked Nessa several times since his return home.

'I'm afraid we can confirm very little,' said O'Kelleher, 'one way or the other. Either Maureen genuinely doesn't know what happened, and gives us a different version each time we ask, or she doesn't want to tell us.'

'We've heard that Dominic is still in hospital,' said Patrick. 'Is there any word?'

'He'll be staying in hospital a fair while,' Fitzmaurice added. 'And he may never be right in the head again, God help him.'

Nobody spoke for a few minutes. Nessa wondered whether gardai had decided on the television piece because Dominic's condition left them with little else to pursue.

'I know you're constrained in what you can tell us,' she said then. 'But is Dominic still suspected of killing Oscar?'

Trevor O'Kelleher held his hands to his lips as if in prayer. Unlike most people, he was at ease with silence.

'I can tell you one thing,' he said eventually, 'provided it stays in this room.' He waited until Nessa and Patrick nodded their agreement. 'We got some information this week that supports Dominic's alibi for the day in question.'

'Is this the boat he's supposed to have seen while he was fishing?'

'Yes, his story was that a group of tourists who were out on the bay watching seals waved at him a few times, and that they were within view of his rock for a number of hours. However, he couldn't tell us the name of the boat, and as a result we were unable to send out a VHF message to track it down.' The inspector weighed his words carefully. 'All he told us was that it was flying the French flag.'

'Which narrowed down the search to one or two hundred boats,' said Patrick.

'Exactly. We sent a description to all the marinas on the Irish coast, but got nothing useful back.'

'It was very unfortunate for Dominic,' said Fitzmaurice heavily. 'It turns out he told us the truth about the boat, but the French group on board went off the next day on a tour of some of Ireland's remotest islands, where there are no marinas to deal with.' The sergeant glanced at the inspector and got the nod to continue. 'They arrived in Donegal four days ago and mentioned their visit to Beara to someone in a pub, whereupon they heard about our alert for French boats who'd been in this area.'

'And they confirmed that Dominic stayed put at Pooka Rock all day?'

'They did indeed,' said O'Kelleher. His eyes met Nessa's and Patrick's in turn. 'As I said, I'm relying on you not to broadcast it, but as Dominic was your guest . . .'

'We're very grateful to you,' said Nessa quickly. She was anxious to get in another question while she had the opportunity. 'We also heard that there was forensic evidence against Dominic. Something about threads of wool, was it?'

'Something of the sort, yes,' said O'Kelleher. 'But there was nothing to indicate what time of day they got snagged on Oscar's jacket, or precisely why. So that's another mystery we may not solve, I'm afraid.'

'What's more, I doubt if we'll ever find out what was in Dominic's mind when he drove down that pier.' Fitzmaurice spoke in a tone usually reserved for someone who had just died. 'Maybe the truth is that Dominic himself had no idea what he was doing. He was a fragile individual in the first place, as his wife was, and people like that can fall apart completely in the face of a public and media hullabaloo.'

The four of them fell silent again, and Nessa wondered whether to risk the inspector's forbearance with more questions. She would love to know what the gardai had found out about Oscar's business dealings, to help her decide what to tell them about her own investigations. But before she had formulated what to say, a loud thud came from the direction of the kitchen, followed by a wail and a string of expletives from Sal.

'Excuse me a minute,' said Nessa. 'I'd better check what's up.'

'We were hoping to speak to your daughter,' said O'Kelleher, smiling a little. 'But if this isn't the best time . . .?'

Nessa hurried out of the room. She found Sal in the kitchen staring at the coffee grinder lying on the floor amid scattered beans. Her lower lip was trembling like a child's.

'You sit down, Sal, and I can clear this up.'

'Don't pretend to be all sorry for me.' Sal's tone was bitter. 'I'm sure you're thrilled to hear that Marcus hasn't phoned me for over a week. I think he's left Derryowen, and no wonder.'

Nessa found a brush and dustpan in the cupboard. 'I'm not thrilled that you're upset, of course I'm not. But maybe Marcus had to go away for some reason. Have you asked Darina about him?'

'Yes, as it happens I asked her yesterday but it was no use.' Sal sat hunched at the table, cradling her phone in her hands. 'She was all, like, terribly busy with some art exhibition abroad that she's getting ready for, so she couldn't be disturbed for long. The only thing I know is that Carl asked her to drive the hackney one day earlier this week, and that means that Marcus wasn't around.'

'I'm sure she's genuinely flat out for the exhibition, Sal. It's a big opportunity for her, and it's also a hard time of the year, with her mother's commemoration coming up.'

'Yeah, well, that's all fine but I'm having a hard time too.' Sal lifted her head and looked defiantly at Nessa. 'And maybe Darina should count herself lucky in one way, not to have a mother who shouts at people in the middle of the night. Can you not understand how totally humiliating that was?'

'Sal, you can't speak like that, as you know well.'

They both turned at a soft knock on the door, which was opened by the sergeant. 'I'm sorry to bother you,' he said, but stopped when he realised that Sal was staring at him.

'Is there bad news?' She spoke in a strangled voice. 'I just knew it, I told Darina that Marcus wouldn't go away without telling me.'

'I haven't any bad news, thank God,' said Conor. 'But we're anxious to have a word with Marcus O'Sullivan as soon as possible, and we've found it hard to contact him. So if you had an opportunity . . .?'

'I've heard nothing from him in the past week. Not a single solitary text, and he's posted nothing on Facebook or Twitter either. Something awful has happened to him, I'm sure of it.'

TWENTY-ONE

Saturday 17 October, 1.30 p.m.

Filming was well underway. The TV crew and actors had installed themselves at Derryowen Hotel the previous night, and got to work after an early breakfast. They recorded a scene on the coastal path and another at the hotel. Nessa and Fergus Malden were filmed driving off from Cnoc Meala and passing by Scannive Strand. Then Ambrose exerted his theatrical talents to the full, telling the actor in Oscar's part the precise tone of voice needed for the encounter by his gate. He was back on form after the attention lull of the previous two weeks.

Nessa became rather less enthusiastic as the day passed. There was no guarantee of a breakthrough in the case, and the television broadcast would stir things up anew, reminding the country of how Oscar Malden arrived at Cnoc Meala on holiday and left in a coffin. The blemish left by his murder could only deepen.

She had begun to understand why people wanted to hide such traumas from the public gaze, and closed their doors to journalists when shocking events struck their home place. No matter that she bore no responsibility for Oscar's death, she still felt guilty and ashamed of it. Her guilt was irrational, of course, and the truth had to be sought, but she found herself wishing hard for the quiet life she had come to enjoy.

In the end, only two of the guests had returned to Beara to assist with the reconstruction. Fergus asked to stay at Cnoc Meala in order to avoid prying eyes at the hotel and, after consulting with Trevor O'Kelleher, Patrick and Nessa agreed. Zoe was also keen to return, but luckily she opted for a hostel in Castletownbere. She would hardly make good company for Fergus, spitting fire at him over his father's sins while he sank further into nervy silence. Stella was too busy to travel, it seemed, so her restraining influence was absent. As for

Maureen, she had declared to gardai that she would never set foot on the peninsula again, but then she had helpfully suggested which well-known actors might suit her *Crime Scene* role.

Nessa allowed Ronan to watch her own short scenes being filmed. Afterwards, she stayed on chatting in a huddle of neighbours near Ambrose's gate. It was a good opportunity to pick up on the local mood, but by lunchtime, Ronan was getting impatient. She looked around for Fergus, to check on his lunch plans, and saw Zoe beckoning her urgently.

'Ben's just texted me,' she said. 'He emailed you an hour ago but heard nothing back. It's something about a patent, if that makes sense?'

Nessa quickly checked her phone. She had switched it to mute earlier, and saw now that she had missed two calls from Ben. His news was that his expert source had found a record of a patent taken out by Oscar Malden on a particular electrical device made by his firm and installed on high-level security gates. Repeated attempts to open the gates without a required code would cause an electric shock to be delivered to the culprit. According to Ben's contact, the same patent was being used by the company in the Ukraine that manufactured prison restraints.

'Has he got the evidence we need? Ben was a bit vague the last time I asked him what he'd found out.'

Nessa signalled to Zoe to keep her voice down. She spotted Fergus across the road, hands gripped tightly in his armpits.

'I think it's a step forward, yes. But I'll have to phone him back about the details.'

'So is it time to break the story? Should we go directly to the media about it, Nessa, and bypass the gardai? If Oscar was involved in something illegal . . .?'

Nessa glanced around again. Patrick's friend James had forwarded two photographs to her the previous day. She might show them to Zoe later in the afternoon, but for the moment, she would say just enough not to appear cagey.

'I don't think the business we've tracked down was illegal. But it may have been very nasty, because my fear is that he was making money from instruments of torture.'

'Oh Nessa, surely we must expose this now? I mean, rape and warfare often go together, as I'm sure you know, but now you're saying he made it an unholy trinity by including torture as well.'

The photographs had shown two items, and were accompanied by some marketing blurb translated from Russian. One was a chain with which to attach prisoners to a wall. Taking a step too far from the wall would set off an electric shock from a device integrated in the chain. The second item was a stun gun in the shape of a mobile phone, capable of discharging an electric shock to a person at a distance of up to five metres away. By pressing a switch on the gun, a narrow cable was released, to enable convenient restraint of uncooperative prisoners.

'I'm still trying to verify the details,' Nessa said, keeping her emotions carefully in check. 'I've been told that the company involved had a contract with security forces in Saudi Arabia, and maybe other countries that have no qualms about inflicting torture.'

'So Oscar may have been killed by someone who wanted revenge, is that what you think? Someone who suffered as a result of his horrible products . . .?'

'The problem, Zoe, is that we still have no idea how his business relates to his death. That's why I've been holding off telling the gardai.' Nessa lowered her voice again. She noticed Ronan eyeing her, signalling his boredom. 'The thing is, there are thousands of people tortured in dozens of countries. Most of them are accused of ordinary and not political crimes, and there are plenty of vile ways of hurting them without technology, such as solitary confinement in a darkened cell inhabited by rats, or burning them with lighted cigarettes, or any damned thing. So no, I think the motive must have been more personal than you've suggested.'

'Well, it's time we got it out. If the TV crew include this insight on Oscar in their story, just imagine the reaction!'

Nessa sighed and nodded to Ronan. He was shifting from foot to foot, a sure sign that he wanted to make a move.

'Let's decide later this afternoon,' she said quickly. 'The crew still have several scenes to shoot, and we'll have to discuss it with Inspector O'Kelleher first, not to mention clearing it with Ben himself. So it's really important to keep it quiet for now, OK?'

She dropped Zoe at O'Donovan's pub on her way home. Something had been bothering her for days about Zoe and Stella and she asked Caitlín quietly to try to get into conversation with the young woman about her family background – how she had found her sister, whether Stella was in touch with her father, that sort of thing. If anyone could ask personal questions without appearing rude, it was Caitlín.

Back at home, she tried Ben a few times but got no answer. After a quick toasted sandwich for the two of them, Ronan drifted off to the living room and she had an opportunity to look again at the photographs. She needed to act quickly before Zoe lost patience or Patrick found out that she had contacted James without telling him. But she also needed time to think everything through. Patrick had just left the house to meet the crew and actors at the Briary, and would drive Ronan to his afternoon kayaking session as soon as he returned.

But really, it was not about practicalities. Nessa's biggest worry was her gut instinct that she was on the wrong track. She had uncovered new and chilling information about Oscar, but it told her nothing about why or how he had been murdered.

She slipped out the back door and up beyond the gate at the top of the garden. It was a beautiful autumn day and a golden light shimmered amidst the trees. She looked back at the house, where orange-red flames of colour danced on the clambering ivy. All around Cnoc Meala, the hillsides sloped in folds and rucks towards a triangle of sea. A glorious afternoon, as nature wove its radiant tapestry for her eyes. A moment of peace, a chance to feast her senses as if nothing in the world could trouble her.

As if. As if there were a single quiet corner of the world free of the shadows of evil and calamity. As if scenic loveliness existed in pristine isolation, unsoiled by nature's rotting carrion. We could enjoy our moments of peace, she reflected, indeed it was essential to enjoy as many moments as came our way to make life worth the bother; but while we might forget the weight of death's noose around our necks at those times, we could never cast it off.

She opened the gate to return to the house, but froze as

something stirred beside her. She looked around warily at a rambling blackthorn tree near the gate and the walls of an old stone outhouse beyond it. Cats and other animals made a habit of sheltering under its eaves.

'Shhh!' The sound came from the shrubby tree, where a pair of dark eyes stared back at her, like deep brown pools rimmed by snow.

'You bold thing, come out of there this minute! You gave me a fright!'

'I've been hiding for ages, and you'd no idea I was right beside you. See, I told you I'd make a good secret agent.'

Ronan slid out between tangled blackthorn branches, as lithe as a cat. Nessa picked stray leaves off his shoulders, and reminded him that he had to get ready for sea-kayaking.

'But I'd prefer to stay here,' he pleaded. 'I heard the TV people say that they've more filming to do when it starts to get dark, and that's the best time for spying on people. I did it yesterday evening.'

'What do you mean, spying on people?'

'I followed that man, Fergus, that's all I mean. It was when he went out for a walk, just after it got dark. He's kind of like a spy himself, isn't he, the way he creeps about?'

'I hope you didn't leave the garden, I've told you before—'

'I know, but I don't think the murderer will come near us while the TV crew is here, because otherwise he might be spotted by the camera. Anyway, I hid behind the front wall and watched Fergus when he went down the road. Sal went out a while later and she didn't see me until I sneaked up on her on her way home.'

Nessa steered her son into the house as she listened to him. She was surprised to hear that Fergus had been out for a walk – she remembered him telling her that he would rest in his room before dinner.

'Sal is so cross these days, isn't she? Just because that guy Marcus won't phone her, she thinks everyone should feel totally sorry for her.'

Nessa glanced at her watch. She hoped Sal could cope with her own filming bout later, when Maureen's incident on the

boreen was to be recreated. Another week had passed and still
no word from Marcus.

'Anyway, I think Sal is just jealous. When I asked her
where she was last night, she said she wanted to talk to Darina
but couldn't, because she saw Darina and whatsisname,
Fergus, on the Briary together, and she thought they were,
you know . . .'

Nessa looked at him with curiosity. Like most boys of his
age, any mention of personal relationships left him tongue-tied,
so she kept her own voice in neutral.

'How do you mean, "they were, you know"?'

'Nothing really. Just that Sal said they were standing very
close and she saw Fergus kind of . . . I think he put his hand
on Darina's shoulder or something, but Darina was cross
with him and pushed him away. So Sal thought they were
having a row and she came home again without speaking to
Darina.' He paused and looked embarrassed. 'That's all Sal
told me, and then she banged the door and went up to her
room.'

Patrick and two of the television team arrived into the kitchen
at the same time as Nessa and Ronan. She offered them coffee,
but her mind was on Ronan's rigmarole.

'The director wants to check something with you,' said
Patrick, 'about the scene you'll be filming in a while. I showed
them the spot where Maureen was found.'

'I wanted to see it in advance, to work out the lighting we'll
need,' said the director. She was a lively young woman, tall
and quite dark, and looked as if she had Spanish or Mexican
origins. Nessa had noticed some signs of rivalry between
herself and the cameraman.

'I'll leave the discussion to yourselves,' said Patrick. He
called up the stairs after Ronan. 'Once I get our young sailor
out to sea, I'll phone you to check how things are going.'

Nessa followed him into the hall for a quiet word. 'Have
you seen Sal this afternoon?'

'As it happens, we met her while we were filming. She
was on her way to Darina's yet again, same old story, but
the latest news is that Carl, Marcus's brother, is coming to the
Barn with his van. I believe he's going to make the trip to

France, to bring over Darina's pieces for her exhibition. So poor Sal is hoping to get an answer out of Carl about his absent sibling.'

Nessa returned to the kitchen and made her apologies to the director for ignoring her question. She was trying to juggle three or four different conversations in her head.

'If I could explain my colleague's question about the lighting,' said the cameraman quickly. He had a world-weary air, although he looked younger than the director. 'The issue is how bright or dark it was when Maureen was found on the ground. It's not a problem of filming per se, because of course I can make adjustments to the exposure. But we've been told it was twilight, and yet your husband said she'd been lying in the shadow of the stone wall, which didn't quite tally.'

The director took her turn to speak. 'I was surprised, you see, that Maureen could be seen at all in the twilight. We've been told that the woman who found her, Darina, had stopped at the top of the track, quite a distance away, and I couldn't quite imagine how she saw her.'

Nessa poured coffee, wishing she could sit and think in silence. She suddenly had an image of herself in a darkened room, watching a reel of film over and over again. The film had been out of focus from the start, but now she could grasp a few scenes, even if she did not know how they fitted into the storyline.

'It was fairly dark when I arrived at the boreen,' she replied then. 'And I remember Sal saying that she and Darina had tried to take photos, maybe five minutes earlier, but that daylight had already faded. There had been a delay, though, after Darina found Maureen, because she couldn't get a phone signal on her first few attempts.'

'On a fairly good September evening, I'd expect up to half an hour of twilight,' said the cameraman. 'We can ask your neighbour Darina about these details when we get to the location, but she was hardly delayed all that time by signal problems.'

Nessa did not reply this time. She would like to pay attention to the discussion, but something far more urgent had to be done straightaway. She looked from one to another, and made a vague excuse about having to go out for a while. They were welcome to do the exterior shots of the house they had mentioned earlier, she said, and she would get back before the filming session on the boreen. Her heart was pounding as she hurried towards the road.

Redmond pulled his jacket zipper up to his chin. The afternoon was bright and sunny, but he felt cold, even after walking a few miles. He felt cold all the time these days. Perhaps lack of sleep had that effect, or eating only a few mouthfuls instead of proper meals.

Conor had taken time to meet him at Scannive Strand, when he got a lunch break from his work with the television crew. The sergeant's job was to observe the participants and take note of any unusual comments or interaction. He told Redmond that it was about as exciting as watching grass grow. Every second time the crew set up to do a shot, the cameraman seemed to go into slow motion, looking anxiously at the sky, muttering to the director, and then shifting the tripod a footstep to the left or a centimetre backwards. But the sound recordist had told Conor that the cameraman was highly regarded, and saved a lot of editing later on by getting consistently good takes in the can.

Redmond would have paid to watch grass grow, if it had meant being on duty. But he had been suspended from work a fortnight earlier, while an official investigation took place into the events of the night he crashed his car into a tree. He was ill for days afterwards, and then spent hours answering questions at Bandon station. He had to hand in his garda ID, and pass his time as best he could while others decided on his future.

His home computer had no record of the photographs he took that awful night, showing rows of cannabis plants in the attic room of the old house. As for the phone itself, it had disappeared. So he had no evidence to support his story, and the longer he tried to explain it, the more sceptical the two senior officers questioning him became. Redmond could see their eyebrows almost hit their hairlines when he could not even confirm where the house was located. The only question that was not in doubt was the high level of alcohol in his own bloodstream.

He spent a long time driving up and down minor roads, looking for the accursed house. When he finally found it, he noticed signs of recent activity on the gravel and rough grass by the gate. He phoned Trevor to report its location, remembering just in time to address him as Inspector O'Kelleher. The days of easy familiarity had not lasted long. The inspector thanked him politely and said that he could not say for certain whether gardai had valid justification to search it. But in any case, Redmond was sure the attic would be empty. Meanwhile, he learned that Carl and Katya had both stated that they had spent that evening together at her apartment. As for Marcus, nobody seemed to know where he was.

Back in his own house, a letter from Inspector O'Kelleher lay in a drawer, like a phial of poison gas whose fumes had seeped into every corner of Redmond's life. It outlined the possible consequences of the incident. Witnesses were being sought who may have seen him driving to the spot where he was found. If the evidence against him was borne out, both garda disciplinary action and criminal charges could follow. The letter's bland, bureaucratic language allowed him no false hope or comfort. As it concluded:

> A thorough investigation is taking place into all of the issues that have arisen in your case. If you have any queries, you may contact the Garda Síochána at the divisional headquarters in Bandon, either directly or through your solicitor. Otherwise, you will be contacted in due course about the outcome of our deliberations.

He sat on a wooden bench which gave him a wide view of Derryowen and its surrounding countryside. After meeting Conor, he had walked up the trail from Scannive to Coomgarriff, and down the other side as far as the bench. He had checked his newly replaced phone a few times, and noticed that the signal was very weak on the Scannive side of the hill. So Oscar must have been closer to Derryowen when he had made the final phone calls of his life.

But Redmond knew it was futile for him to speculate on such matters. Walking the trail was just a form of killing time. It would have been better, he told himself, to go to the Buddhist Centre on the other side of the peninsula, which he had visited twice since he was suspended, hoping to snatch a whisper of peace there. He had resorted to sleeping pills to get him through the nights, but even so, he rarely slept more than three or four hours. Some days, he was numb; others, he felt as if a wild animal was clawing and tearing him apart from the inside. His greatest fears were that Inspector O'Kelleher had lost all faith in him, and that one day soon, Conor would not believe him either.

He looked out at the Atlantic's wide plain stretching to the horizon, as empty as the life he saw ahead of him. If he was convicted of drunk driving, his shame would force him to leave Ireland and never return. He would go to one of those teeming cities he used to enjoy visiting, take a new name and endure a low-paid job that demanded no references.

Loneliness, his companion since childhood, would follow him across the seas. Regret would lurk at every corner too. Instead of accepting the gifts of ordinary life offered by Conor and Trevor, he had thrown them away in one stupid night, desperate to be singled out for applause instead of learning how to work as one of a team.

He hung his head over his knees, pain burning in his belly. It was a mistake to come to Beara. The shapes and colours of the landscape looked radiant rather than bleak, as they used to appear to him. But now he had no right to gaze at them. Up on the hillside, he was like a rapparee of former times, brooding over the land of which he had been dispossessed.

He lifted his head when he realised that someone was nearby, a woman who had her back to him. He rubbed his eyes quickly, in case it was obvious that he had been crying.

He was taken aback when she turned her head. Nessa McDermott stared at him with undisguised hostility.

'Do you mind? I was hoping to sit.'

Redmond stood up awkwardly. He may as well be helpful. He was unlikely to meet her again.

She stepped towards the bench. 'I'm sorry to bother you,' she said brusquely. 'I don't have a lot of time right now.'

Redmond could not quite make sense of what she said. Perhaps his brain had stopped working. If she was in a hurry, why did she want to sit at all?

'I'm surprised to meet you up here,' she said, in a politer tone. She was breathing hard, as if she had been running. 'I imagine you must be very busy with the film crew.'

Redmond looked around distractedly. The crew could be on their way to Coomgarriff. If he went downhill, he was in danger of meeting them.

'I thought . . .' She took a step closer to him. 'Yes, I thought I heard Inspector O'Kelleher mention a briefing this afternoon, down at the hotel?' She looked at him as if he was an obstinate child. 'Something about one of the scenes with Oscar, that's what I understood.'

Redmond tried to sound normal. 'Which scene was that?'

'I'm not sure. Down at the Briary, I think, after Oscar left Ambrose and got a phone call from someone in France or whatever it was.'

Redmond moved away, mumbling a reply. He could not tell her he was barred from the investigation. But she was behaving strangely. Was she just trying to get rid of him, going on about a briefing at the hotel? Conor had said the *cig* was going to Castletownbere for the afternoon, and there was definitely no mention of a briefing.

He turned to look back at her, his mind racing. She was on her hunkers at the back of the bench, searching for something.

'Why did you say—?' He ran towards her. 'Who told you that Oscar got a phone call from someone in France?'

She pulled herself up, eyes flashing annoyance. 'What do you mean, who told me?'

'Please, I'm not asking you lightly.' Redmond looked at her steadily, hoping to calm himself as well as Nessa. 'I think you've said something that could be really important.'

She looked down at the bench, as if she wanted to begin searching again. 'As far as I remember, it was Fergus Malden who told me. But you know all about that already, don't you? We were on our way to the pharmacy when he got a text from

Oscar, saying he'd got a call from France and was changing his plans.'

'Fergus got a text from his father's phone alright, but there was no mention of France in it. The link with France is that Oscar had received a mysterious call a while earlier that lunch-time, and we discovered that the phone in question was purchased in France. But information about the call was never released by the garda team, as far as I know.'

'So why did Fergus say it? Perhaps it was just a mistake, unless—?'

Nessa and Redmond stared at each other, as hostility gave way to urgency. He was first to finish what she had begun to say.

'Unless Fergus knew in advance that he was to receive a text from Oscar's phone, in which France was supposed to be mentioned. But if that happened—?'

'If that happened,' Nessa interrupted, 'Fergus must have been in on a plan to kill his father, and part of the plan was to create the impression of a business quarrel in France that led to his murder. But then Fergus said it to me even though it wasn't in the text.'

'And the purpose of the text was for us all to believe that Oscar was still alive at a particular time.'

'Instead of which, the text was sent from Oscar's phone by his murderer.'

Nessa took hold of Redmond's elbow and sat him down clumsily on the bench. They stared at each other again, before a stream of explanation poured from her.

'I lied to you about a garda briefing, I couldn't think how to get rid of you and I had to find out . . . I had to look at this bench, you see. It seemed so silly when I thought of it first, but I had to find out if Fergus Malden had been hiding notes here for someone else to pick up. There had to be a split or a niche in the wood for that to be possible, so I wanted to look.'

'And what made you think of that, or who . . .?'

'It was my son, Ronan. He told me he'd spied on Fergus yesterday, and then I remembered something else he'd said ages ago, about hiding secret messages up here. But I thought at the time it was just a childish game he'd invented for himself.'

Redmond nodded, looking around at the bench. 'Whereas leaving paper messages would be a very useful way to avoid mobile phone contact or emails. Any electronic communication leaves a permanent record that can be examined by gardai.'

'In that case, the whole thing was planned in detail, down to finding the right place to hide the messages.'

'But who was the accomplice? The person who exchanged messages with Fergus?'

Nessa did not reply immediately. Her brain felt like a battle-field, flashes of fire and confusion all at once. She took her phone out of her pocket and stared at it, as if willing it to speak to her.

'Ronan said something else today,' she said then. 'He told me that my daughter Sal went out last night, and saw Fergus and Darina together. They seemed to be intimate, or that was the impression she got.'

'You mean, they were together as a couple?'

'Yes, but I was deaf to what that meant. I didn't think it through right away, because I'd a different notion, one about Zoe and Stella, and how they might be the guilty ones.'

She got up and pointed down the hill. Redmond saw terror in her eyes. 'Sal went down to the Barn this afternoon,' she said, 'hoping to find out where Marcus is. I tried to phone her but she hasn't—'

'Do you think Sal will ask Darina if she's involved with Fergus?'

'Yes, she might. That's what frightens me now.'

'Because you think Fergus and Darina were in it together?'

'I can't make sense of it any other way, Redmond. And that's why I'm so frightened. Because if Sal tells Darina that she saw her with Fergus, what will happen? Will Darina say yes, and admit that she conspired with Fergus to do terrible things, or will she ensure that Sal can't tell anyone else about the two of them?'

TWENTY-TWO

Saturday 17 October, 4.15 p.m.

Nessa tried Sal's phone again while Redmond examined the wooden bench. He found a gap between one of the vertical supports and a decorative post on top of it. After poking in it for a few moments with a sharp stick, he extracted a small scrap of paper and showed it to Nessa.

'It's hard to be certain,' he said, holding it carefully. He wished he had a proper plastic evidence bag to keep it safe. 'This could have got snagged on the wood when the rest of the piece of paper was pulled out. I think there was something written on it, but it's damp, which doesn't help.'

They both examined the scrap of paper, which was barely the size of Nessa's thumb.

'That could be Darina's writing,' she said. 'I can make out the letter "Y", and even though it's written as a capital, there's a kind of flourish to it. The word could be "y-o-u", couldn't it?'

'Did your son actually see Fergus leaving notes here in September? Could you phone him now and ask him?'

'No, he's out in a kayak right now. And really, the whole thing seems unbelievable. But all the same, I have to go to Darina's now.'

'I'll go with you. It might be best not to be on your own.' Redmond felt as if he had been given a blood transfusion, filling him with energy. 'I'm not . . . I'm actually not on duty this afternoon.'

Nessa nodded absently as they set off. She still felt wary in his company but that was irrelevant now. All that mattered was to make sure that Sal was safe.

Redmond hurried to keep up with her. 'Had you any inkling of a relationship between Fergus and Darina?' he asked. 'Weeks ago, I mean, while Fergus was on holiday at Cnoc Meala.'

'No idea whatsoever. And the only inkling I have now is thirdhand, so it's hardly reliable.'

'I remember that Darina told us in her witness statements that she had a short conversation with Oscar on the Thursday morning, outside the shop in Derryowen. Her line was that Oscar was interested in calling to her studio at midday, but that he never arrived. There seemed to be no reason to disbelieve her, but of course, if he did in fact call in to the studio . . .'

'But surely your garda colleagues questioned her about how she spent the day? She told us she was sick and tired of being questioned, that's one thing I remember very well.'

Redmond ignored her barbed tone. He had been too quick to take offence in the past, and to cloak his insecurities with a veneer of pride.

'Yes, of course,' he said evenly. 'We interviewed her twice and she came across as a very helpful witness. She told us in detail what time she called in to Ambrose with his eggs, for example, and who else she called to before she went for a swim near the hotel.'

'So can you work out . . .? Can you say now whether she could have, you know, carried it out?'

Nessa could not bring herself to say aloud the stark word that pierced her every thought. She still hoped for another explanation, one that would not point unremittingly to the conclusion that Darina had murdered Oscar.

Redmond also found it difficult to speak directly. Instead he tried to make his bland reassurance sound kind. 'It's OK, it must be really difficult for you. But we'll be at the Barn in a few minutes, five or six at the most.'

She nodded again and Redmond continued. 'If she was involved, she must have set out to confuse us about timings on the day. She would've had access to Oscar's phone once he was dead, to send a text to it from a phone she had purchased in France, and then to send another message from Oscar's phone to Fergus.'

'It wasn't unusual for her to come and go from the Barn at irregular times. What's more, she made sure that Ambrose saw her, which probably made her own statements more credible.'

'I could never understand how Oscar had been swallowed

up by the hills soon after leaving Ambrose and meeting your husband at midday.' Redmond and Nessa had reached the bottom of the hill, close to the old man's house and the small road leading to the Barn. 'But if Oscar went off to Darina's house, how come he wasn't spotted by Ambrose, who was still standing guard at his gate?'

Her own experience of dodging over walls with Ronan came into Nessa's mind. 'It wouldn't be impossible. He'd spoken to Darina earlier at the shop, and she could have suggested a shortcut across a few fields.'

Nessa stopped, short of breath. She would like to be silent, alone with her thoughts. Against the clear sky, every familiar detail of the landscape stood out in sharp relief. Any minute now, Sal would appear on the roadway. She and Darina would saunter along, chatting on their way to meet the TV crew.

'Are you OK? Things could be dangerous with Darina, so perhaps we should wait and get help.' Redmond wished he could explain his situation to Nessa, but he was afraid she would just walk off without him if she understood that he had no garda authority. He paused long enough to send a quick text to Conor, to say he had new information about Fergus and Darina, and would text again soon.

'No, let's go ahead. Better just the two of us than a squad in uniform. Once I know Sal is OK . . .'

Nessa stopped again to open a new text on her phone. It was from Caitlín, telling her that she had probed Zoe about her family. She had learned that Stella's father was a Catholic priest who had a feverish affair with their mother while at home on holidays from missionary work in Africa. He was back in Zambia when the pregnancy was confirmed, and was told nothing about it, and he had died by the time Stella and Zoe started asking questions about him. It had been a farfetched idea, Nessa reproached herself, that Oscar might have been Stella's father and that the two sisters had set out to expose his business secrets after killing him. If she had only grasped the truth earlier, her daughter would be safe.

'Is it possible,' Redmond asked suddenly, 'that Darina hadn't planned to kill Oscar? Suppose he went to her studio and attacked her there, just as he attacked other women, and she acted in self-defence?'

'I wish I could believe that. But if Fergus was involved in advance, it had to be planned before they ever arrived in Beara.'

'Yes, you're right. Perhaps Darina had met Oscar at an art event in Cork or somewhere else, and he promised her his patronage but attacked her instead? And somehow she persuaded Fergus to help her?'

'It's plausible but we don't know, do we? We know so little, that's the bloody problem.'

They stopped at Darina's gate, and Nessa was tempted to phone Patrick or Caitlín or Trevor O'Kelleher – someone she could trust to make the right decisions in a crisis. But she could not risk more delays, so she steeled her nerves and stepped past the handpainted sign advertising portraits, drawings and small sculptural pieces to visitors.

'Darina gave a card to Fergus,' she said quietly. 'She spoke to him about it in our kitchen that Thursday night, making out it was a drawing she'd done for Oscar.'

'What kind of card? Did you see it yourself?'

'I saw it the next evening. She'd done an impression of Oscar's face on one side, which I thought was a sketch for his portrait. And on the other side, she drew a view of Beara, with a standing stone in the foreground. I just took it as a touristy image, but now . . .' Nessa's voice hardened. 'You see, a standing stone could be an image of death, like a headstone.'

'You mean it was a message? Once she'd done the job, she didn't bother with notes hidden in the bench, and gave Fergus a message openly, in front of other people?'

'She told him on Thursday night that she hadn't put the finishing touches to her drawing, so-called, but would do it on Friday. Oscar was dead by then, but maybe she still had his body, and she was letting him know that too.'

Nessa rapped on the door of the house and then of the Barn, but to no avail. The studio was named after its original purpose as a farm building, and the windows added by Darina were high up on the old stone walls. Nessa and Redmond looked around the garden and then Nessa suggested they check if she was at the henhouse, down the pathway past the fuchsia hedge.

The hens were scratching on the open ground. Redmond put his head around the henhouse door, holding his breath against the rich smell of droppings and straw. He was about to retreat when he noticed something in the corner. He stepped gingerly towards it and pulled it towards the light. It was a wheelie bin, about as high as his waist and covered with an old cloth.

'You don't think . . .?' Nessa put her hand to her mouth as Redmond opened the lid, his sleeve over his fingers. An image came into her mind, of Sal curled up lifelessly inside the bin. But it was empty except for a few old towels and dusty sweatshirts.

'This is the sort of container that gardai have searched for,' said Redmond. 'According to the pathologist's report, Oscar's body had been pushed into a cramped space. *Livor mortis* is the technical term for the evidence that showed that.'

'On the Sunday, when news of his murder was just sinking in . . .' Nessa leaned against the wall outside the door, memories jostling for space in her head. 'I came here with Ronan that Sunday and we stood chatting to Darina right on this spot. She was washing out the henhouse, and she gave the hose to Ronan and told him to spray it into this same bin.'

Redmond said they should get off the premises immediately and phone Inspector O'Kelleher. He kept his eyes peeled as they returned along the path. Nessa was remembering what Darina was like two years earlier, while her mother was dying of cancer. After several months of caring for her day and night, Darina looked almost as emaciated as her mother, but a stubborn defiance shone through on her face every time Nessa called to visit. Had she become so close to Fergus that the same fierce loyalty pushed her to carry out his murderous wishes?

Darina's blue van was parked at the side of the studio. Nessa signalled to Redmond as she went towards it. Perhaps Darina had gone off with Carl, if he had arrived to load some of her artworks for the exhibition. Meanwhile, Sal could be down in

Derryowen, buying top-up credit for her phone, or looking for Marcus at Carraig Álainn.

'What do you want?'

Darina came around from the back of the studio, carrying a large bag and other stuff. 'I heard a knock at the front door a while ago but I was too busy to get it.'

'I called over to look for Sal, for the filming.' Nessa forced a smile, hoping to look normal. She hoped Redmond had stepped back out of sight for the moment.

'As I said, I'm up to my eyes for the exhibition. It's not a good time.'

'I know that, Darina, but I thought you'd agreed last week to join in the filming. On the boreen, you know. It won't take long.'

Darina looked around and Nessa saw her eyes settle on a wide plank of wood propped against the wall. She had seen her neighbour use it as a makeshift ramp into the rear of the van, when she needed to load heavy materials. She was tempted to offer to help Darina, as if things really were normal. But it was clear that the other woman wanted her out of the way.

'What about Sal, have you seen—'

'No, not today. I told you, I'm busy right now.'

'I've phoned her so many times, you see.' Nessa took out her phone to try dialling once again. Darina gestured to her to move away, to make space for her ramp. A crazy thought came into Nessa's mind, that Darina was helping Sal to run away with Marcus.

'Just wait a minute,' said Darina abruptly. She dropped her bag on the ground. 'Come in to the studio until I'm done.'

Nessa did not respond. She was listening intently to other sounds. On her own phone, she could hear the unanswered peals of her daughter's mobile. But she could also hear a faint ringtone, one that was very familiar. She could not figure out where it was coming from.

Darina had a mobile phone in her hand too, a shiny black one. Nessa looked up at her and then over at the blue van. She saw Redmond coming towards them both.

'I can hear Sal's phone,' she said. 'The ringtone . . .'

Then she saw that Darina had raised her arm. She was

pointing the black mobile at her. Nessa recognised the device. The picture flashed into her memory. A photo she had seen on her computer just a day earlier.

'Get it off her!' She pulled at the van doors as she shouted at Redmond. But she was unable to open them. A sharp pain suddenly ripped through both her arms, leaving them to dangle uselessly, as if she had been shot, or hit with a heavy object.

The cheery ringtone was coming from inside the van. Nessa dived towards the driver's door and tried to clutch one hand with the other in order to give her the strength to open it. Another stabbing pain hit her, on the left shoulder this time.

She felt weak. Her body would not obey her will. Electric shock tingled through her veins. She fell onto one knee.

Redmond was struggling with Darina. He swung her arm upwards to grab the device from her.

Nessa could not quite focus on what was happening. Darina seemed to turn in slow motion towards Redmond, but then everything shifted, and they became small figures in the distance, wrestling together.

She bent her head to look at her hands. If she could concentrate on one single thing her brain might keep working. She tried to make a fist but could only manage a flabby movement. She flexed her fingers, counting them one by one.

Her thoughts began to clear gradually. A stun gun. That was the word. The device was called a stun gun.

Darina was firing at herself and Redmond. She could hit them even though she wasn't standing beside them. It was something about the voltage.

She turned her head and saw Redmond slumped by the wall of the Barn. He was holding his shoulder. Darina had stepped away from him, still holding that awful shiny thing in her hand.

He tried to stand but his legs slid towards the wall again. He opened his mouth but said nothing. Darina pointed the stun gun at him again and Nessa saw how he was jolted by a spasm of pain.

He was paralysed, just as she was. The paralysis seemed to last for a minute or two.

The young artist's eyes were cold, venomous. 'Nobody

asked you here,' she said. 'Nobody asked Sal to stick her nose in my business either, blabbing about myself and Fergus. It's your own fault I had to hurt you.'

Darina's words hit Nessa like staccato bolts of lightning. But she felt stronger now. She had to keep Darina talking until Redmond could stand up. They could fight her together next time.

'Please don't hurt Sal,' she heard herself say. 'I'm begging you, just let her be. She had no idea . . .'

'Give me the time to get away and Sal will be safe. Keep your mouths shut, that's all you've to do.'

'For my sake, Darina, let her out of the van.' Nessa tried to look Darina in the eyes. 'I know you understand what a mother and daughter's love is. More than anyone . . .'

This time, Nessa saw the two prongs of metal that appeared just as a white spark flashed in the air. A low humming sound followed the flash. It was a kind of taser, that was another word she remembered. It could inflict a form of torture when it was used to hit prisoners over and over again. People could die from it, she'd read that somewhere.

Her eyes were losing focus again. Darina had pushed her back to the wall, before driving off in the van. She could hear the engine humming as it went out the gate. Or maybe the humming was in her ears, as if a swarm of bees was burrowing its way into her head.

TWENTY-THREE

Saturday 17 October, 5.20 p.m.

A woman lay sprawled on a rough track on the hillside. She was in the shadow of an old stone wall where it was difficult to see her. Night was falling and the surrounding hills had become black shapes hunched over the fields.

Nessa cried out at the sight – a woman on the ground, and two others standing at a distance, their heads bent together in conversation, just as she had seen them on the boreen over three weeks earlier, on the night of Maureen's incident. For a brief hallucinatory moment, she believed that everything was alright. Darina and Sal were waiting impatiently for the filming to start, one of them pale and slight, the other tall and dark-skinned, their features accentuated in the harsh glare of headlights and the deep shadows surrounding them.

At her cry, the two people on the boreen turned in her direction, and she realised her mistake. The smaller, paler of the two was Fergus, his hair light-coloured like Darina's, and his arms clutched around his chest as she had done that same night. The second person was the television director, whose stance had Sal's vivacious confidence. But as Nessa stared at them, she also took in how different they were to the image, filled with wild hope, that had leapt into her mind.

After a short silence, three voices broke out in rapid succession.

'The light is fading,' said the director, 'so we decided to get on with it when you hadn't phoned us.'

'There's a change of plan,' Redmond called out. 'There's no need for filming any more.'

'You must help us, Fergus,' Nessa pleaded. 'You must talk to Darina. She has a gun. She has Sal, she's hurt her already . . .'

Other voices joined in the commotion. Zoe appeared from

the shadows, and the actor playing Maureen's part got up from her position on the ground to go into a huddle with the director and cameraman. Redmond stepped close to Fergus – even without the authority to question or arrest him, he would make damned sure that the young man could not bolt into the night.

He had phoned Trevor and told him everything. Superintendent Devane had ordered gardai to cover the roads out of Beara, and had also asked Garda HQ for experts on hostage negotiations. Darina had to be stopped but not at the expense of Sal's life. If necessary, the blue van would be tailed discreetly until the right people were in place. Nessa and Redmond were unsure how long it took them to leave the Barn, but they reckoned that Darina had a twenty-minute head start.

'Darina will listen to you, Fergus, so please, please phone her now.'

'It's no good. She won't listen, I know she won't.'

'But you met her yesterday evening, didn't you? If Sal hadn't seen you both together . . .?'

Fergus, his face a ghostly white, clasped and unclasped his hands. Nessa thought distractedly that he and Darina were alike in their nervous intensity, which may have drawn them together.

'It's true, I went to see her yesterday, but she wouldn't listen to a word. She just did . . . She did whatever she decided. That's how it was all along.'

'Why did you keep your mouth shut, then? Were you too spineless to tell us the truth?' Redmond's anger at his own failure to stop Darina leaving the Barn burst through his questions, as well as resentment at being taken in by Fergus. He remembered how sorry he had felt for him at Oscar's funeral, picturing him as a solitary young man who had just lost a good parent.

Fergus turned to shield his eyes from the headlights' glare. When he began to answer at last, his voice was almost a whisper.

'You're right, I didn't stand up to her. I didn't stand up to my father either. Otherwise, none of this . . . But I was terrified my father would walk all over me in court if I tried to give evidence against him. Then Darina was so sure about the plan . . .'

His words faded and silence fell again on the group surrounding him. It seemed to Nessa that the world had stopped turning, as everyone waited for him to finish properly or to speak again. The silence became so intense that even the tiniest insects must have stopped shuffling in the undergrowth.

'We can't just stand here wringing our hands,' she cried out at last. 'Try to phone her, Fergus, please. It has to be worth a try.'

'I'm afraid . . . If I try that, Nessa, I think she'll go berserk. We had a big row last night. I told her I was afraid we'd be found out soon. But she wouldn't listen.'

'So you were struggling with your conscience, is that what you want us to believe?' said Redmond. 'And meanwhile, everyone else wasted time with pathetic filming reconstructions, and allowed Sal Latif to walk into the lion's den.'

Nessa gestured her impatience. 'We have to stop Sal being harmed, that's what matters now. So let's get the hell out of this cul-de-sac, in case people are trying to phone us.' She tried to ignore the anxiety that was swallowing her up from inside. The wind was rising and in the failing light, she could see a band of low black clouds rolling in from the sea. She felt trapped, closed in by stone walls and darkness and fear.

'Who else could speak to Darina, then? She must have other friends in the area.' Redmond stayed close to Fergus as they walked out on to the Briary. He could be making excuses for Darina, pretending they had fallen out in order to gain time for her to leave the peninsula.

'What about Carl?' said Nessa tersely. 'He was supposed to be at the Barn today, wasn't he?'

'She mentioned him yesterday,' Fergus replied slowly. 'He's driving to France with her art stuff tomorrow, or maybe even tonight. Do you think Darina would ask him—?'

'I'll tell Conor to phone Carl.' Redmond checked his mobile, and stopped on the Briary as soon as he got a good signal. Nessa looked at her mobile too, hoping for a message from Patrick. He was in Castletownbere when she rang him from the Barn, and arranged immediately for Ronan to go to a friend's house. He was going to ask Trevor O'Kelleher if he could join the gardai in their search for Sal.

'That evening, I knew already . . .' Fergus stopped alongside Nessa. 'That Thursday evening, when I heard about Maureen, I knew the plan wouldn't work out. I'd been sick with worry all day, even before that.'

'But how did Maureen come into it? What difference did she make to your plan?' Zoe had been walking with the television people, but now she pushed forward to face Fergus. Nessa was not surprised to notice the cameraman behind her, twisting the lens to re-focus it on them.

'Maureen turned everything upside down,' said Fergus. 'Not just on Thursday, but the night before, on Wednesday.'

'You mean the night Stella saw her going into Oscar's room?'

'Yes, she'd got it into her head that my father fancied her, and she practically threw herself at him on Wednesday night, I'm sure of it. He told me on Thursday morning that he'd had enough of her, and had decided to go home early.'

'She didn't just "get it into her head", as you call it,' said Zoe scornfully. 'Oscar flirted with her for days—'

'I'm not making excuses for him. I saw . . . I knew very well what he was like.'

'You made damn sure not to tell us what you knew,' said Redmond, putting away his phone. 'So would you mind explaining what your masterplan was – the one that Maureen threw into disarray, as you claim?'

'It was meant to happen on Saturday, two days later,' said Fergus flatly. 'Darina would invite him to the Barn in the morning, and ask to do his portrait. She'd already chatted to him when we went on that group visit to her studio earlier in the week.'

'In other words, she was going to seduce him, was that it, and then kill him? And that's what happened on Thursday instead?'

'She hardly had to seduce him,' said Zoe. 'If he was true to his vilest form, he'd be fired up for action anyway.'

'But one way or another,' said Redmond, 'by doing it on Saturday, nobody need have known that he'd met his death in

Beara, because his disappearance might not have been reported for days.'

Nessa was still clutching her phone as she tried to make sense of the exchanges. 'So Oscar's decision to leave on Thursday meant that Darina had to act quickly, and she talked him into coming to the Barn at lunchtime. But then all the hoo-ha about Maureen caused her a new problem that evening?'

Fergus just nodded, looking dazed as accusations and questions were flung at him in the deepening twilight. The circle of people seemed to have closed in around him, a crescendo of voices competing from all sides.

'My guess is that Darina was in a fix that Thursday night,' said Redmond. 'She had to get rid of Oscar's body, but when she stumbled on Maureen, she got delayed—'

'You're right,' Nessa broke in. 'She'd told Sal that she was planning to go to a pub in Kenmare, so I'd say that's when she hoped to get rid of his body. But then we called the gardai and it all got too complicated for her—'

The television director interrupted in turn, resuming her earlier argument with the cameraman. 'I told you Darina was up to something that evening, didn't I? There was a gap in her timing all along. She spotted Maureen on the ground while there was still plenty of light in the sky, but there was a half hour delay before she told anyone. She was up to something on that cul-de-sac – probably on her way to hide Oscar's phone and rucksack.'

'Yes, down the far end of the boreen, maybe, but then she saw Maureen as she walked right past her.'

'And her first thought was that it was Oscar who'd attacked Maureen, hours earlier.'

Nessa stopped as dazzling headlights approached the Briary. She looked so distraught that Redmond put his hand on her shoulder, hoping she would take it as a gesture of support. A garda car pulled up and Conor jumped out, to tell them that Patrick had received a text from Sal's phone. She seemed to have written it in a hurry, to tell them that Darina was trying to escape from Beara on a back road over the mountains, up north of the peninsula.

'Patrick has just forwarded the same text to me,' Nessa said, peering at her screen. She showed the phone to Redmond but most of the text made no sense to him: 'sos n mtn rd bunan cmhola.'

'We figure it could be an SOS,' said Conor, 'to say that Darina is taking a mountain road to Bunane, on the Kerry side of the road between Kenmare and Glengarriff. From there, there's a very minor road across the county border at the Priest's Leap and past Coomhola Mountain. That could get her past Bantry on back roads, and make it much harder for us to track her down.'

'Patrick says checkpoints are already up on the main roads. He's on his way to Glengarriff with Trevor. They think Darina must have boasted to Sal about her plans.'

The television people made for their vehicle, with Zoe in tow. Fergus still looked dazed, in a world of his own, and Conor murmered urgently to Redmond and Nessa, making sure the young man was out of earshot.

'We can't rely on it that the text is genuine. Darina must be very careless, if she's left Sal in possession of her phone.'

'But you won't ignore the text, surely? I thought—'

'We certainly won't, Nessa. All I'm saying is that we've to keep searching in this part of Beara too.'

'I know where we should look,' said Redmond grimly. 'Carraig Álainn. Not just the houses, but Marcus's boat too.'

The sound of waves beating ceaselessly against the cliffs rose up to the wooden railings. Both gardai strained to hear any other sound from the small pier where Marcus's boat was tied up. There were no lights on the boat and the evening was too dark to make out whether anyone was on board.

Redmond felt in his pocket for the torch he had taken from his car. Going down the steps to the pier would be tricky at night. He looked across to the nearest house, which was also in darkness. Nessa was out of sight, creeping around the bushes to check whether Darina's van or any other vehicle had been parked round the back. Conor had left the garda car outside Carraig Álainn's gates, and the three of them walked into the holiday cluster without using a torch, to avoid alerting Darina

or anyone else on the premises. A uniformed garda stayed in
the car with Fergus.

Redmond leaned over the railings as something new reached
him from below. A voice, perhaps, but it was impossible to
recognise if it was male or female. The swish of wind in the
trees added to the soundscape and he wondered if it was just
a seagull's whine wafting on the night air.

He turned again to see Nessa gesturing to him. He hurried
over to her and she whispered that Marcus's car was tucked
in by a hedge at the side of the garage. She had stepped towards
the front door of his house to see if it was open, but a security
light had come on and she had had to back away quickly.

Conor was crouched at the far corner of the railings. After a
few more minutes he joined them, to say that he had seen torchlight on the boat – just a pinpoint shifting about in the cabin.
Whoever was down there could return to the house at any time.

Nessa and Redmond moved in behind the nearest bush.
They heard a sound of footsteps from the top of the cliffside
path. Conor stayed in the shadows closer to the porch to see
who it was. Redmond had to dig his fingernails into his
clenched fist in an effort to stay still. Just walking around
Marcus O'Sullivan's property made his blood curdle.

They heard Conor's voice, firm and polite, and then a smoth-
ered shout as a scuffle broke out. The porch light almost
blinded Redmond when he rushed from his hiding place. He
was almost on top of the two people struggling at the front
door before he made out which was which. Conor was being
pinned against the door by a lanky dark-haired man.

Redmond caught the man by the shoulders and pushed him
away from Conor. Those hateful mocking eyes stared back at
him and he found his hands at Marcus's throat. He wanted to
kill him, to shake the life out of him in return for that glinting
knife in the rear-view mirror and the burning whiskey he had
been forced to swallow.

'In the name of God, don't do it!' Conor caught Redmond's
wrists in a vice-like grip and bent them away from Marcus's
neck. He nudged the door with his foot and pushed Marcus
inside. 'Let's find out what this fellow has to say for himself
before we've another corpse to deal with!'

'You bluebottle bastards, get the hell away from me!' Marcus glared from one to another. 'I'll have you fuckers up for assault and trespass.'

'Hold your curses, young man, and listen to what I said just a minute ago.' Conor kicked the door closed behind him 'Now, will you invite us into the kitchen like a decent citizen or I'll arrest you for obstruction of urgent police work.'

Marcus blocked his way, hands held out in front of him. Redmond, still trembling from the fit of rage that had overcome him, found it hard to take in what was being said.

'. . . This isn't a social call, Marcus.'

'Get the hell away, I said, you're the fucking lawbreakers around here.'

'Listen to me, Marcus, because we haven't a second to spare. We're looking for your cousin, Darina O'Sullivan, and for Sal Latif. It's a matter of life and death, and what's more, it relates to the murder of Oscar Malden. So just tell us straight – who's down below on your boat and what's going on?'

'Jesus, dude, is this some sick joke or what?'

'It's anything but a joke, I promise you. So just answer my questions now.'

Redmond took a step closer to them but Conor turned to him and whispered firmly. 'You'd better stay outside at this point, and put a lid on things. Anyway, you've no authority for this.' He turned back to Marcus quickly, leaving Redmond to stumble outside again, his cheeks hot from his own shame at losing control. Then he realised that by leaving the door ajar and standing just to the side of it, he could hear Conor's interrogation, which continued in the hallway.

'Listen to me now, boyo,' the sergeant was saying in a politely steely tone. 'We've good reason to fear that Sal Latif's life is in danger from Darina. So cut the crap and tell me whether they're here at Carraig Álainn.'

'I just got back here tonight,' said Marcus reluctantly. 'I've been away for a while, so I can't make sense of what you're saying.'

'Have you seen Sal Latif this evening? On your boat or anywhere else?'

'I told you, I've been away and kind of . . . Anyway, I haven't seen her for weeks, I promise you.'

'And Darina O'Sullivan, your cousin?'

'What makes you think she'd be here? And what in Jesus' name did you mean about Sal being in danger from her?'

'I meant what I said, so where is she? I'm in a hurry for an answer, so cough it up, you gligeen.'

Marcus mumbled in reply, and Redmond held his breath as he listened. When he spoke again, Conor's voice was low and deliberate.

'I expect your cooperation, Marcus, especially as you're already in trouble with us. We've been looking into an allegation of illegal activity at a house on the far side of Ardgroom that's registered in your mother's name. Just last week, we found some evidence that it's being used as a makeshift cannabis growhouse, and now we're due to take a statement from someone who claims to have seen you threatening Garda Joyce.'

Redmond leaned against the doorframe for support. Trevor had not informed him of any new evidence in his case, nor had Conor given him any inkling of a hopeful outcome when they had met all those eternal hours ago at Scannive Strand.

'Alright,' he heard Marcus say. 'And if I admit I've seen Darina this evening, what happens then?'

'So she's on the boat, you slippery bastard? Go on, say it to me.'

Marcus mumbled again, and then Redmond heard footsteps approach from the hall. He was already trying for a phone signal when Conor came outside to tell him to get on to Trevor immediately. Redmond cursed the mobile system for its blind spots, and ran to the gate to use the garda radio in the car. Fergus was slumped in the back seat, his eyes barely flickering as Redmond told his colleague who to call. On his way back to the house, he looked around for Nessa and found her at the railings, her face more drawn than ever. As he led her away, he gave her the news in a whisper.

'Oh God!' was all she said.

'We were right that the text from Sal's phone was a hoax,' said Redmond, just to fill the silence between them. 'So much for a wild goose chase in the mountains.'

Conor signalled from the hallway to join them in the kitchen. Marcus seemed very jumpy to Redmond, sitting on the edge of a chair, his right knee jigging constantly.

'Right, we've come up with a plan,' said Conor, 'now that his nibs here is prepared to cooperate.'

'Under protest, sergeant,' said Marcus, vainly attempting a lighter tone. 'I'm all for helping Sal, but it just seems ridiculous, what you said about Darina and a gun.'

Redmond spat his words at him. 'It's a stun gun. It burns your skin like a red hot poker. But amazingly, it leaves no mark afterwards.'

'Darina could strangle Sal with it,' said Nessa, just as vehemently. 'Oscar Malden designed the bloody thing, complete with a thin cable that can be released from the gun. I think that's how Darina killed him. She must have stunned him first, and then strangled him.'

'But do you actually know that, Nessa? I'm not saying it because Darina is my cousin, but it's just . . . she's not the type, is she? I mean, what did Oscar ever do to her, to make her a psychopath overnight?'

Redmond felt a new wave of hatred well up in him. 'You're the one who could tell us about psychos, you mad dangerous—'

'Listen, my friends,' said Conor briskly. 'We've no time for this. Darina was here at Carraig Álainn when Marcus got home a while ago. She gave him some sob story about owing a load of money and needing to get away for a while on the QT. So he agreed to bring her down the coast, and she's waiting for him this minute.'

'Where the hell is Sal, Marcus?' Nessa broke in. 'I'm terrified that Darina has killed her already—'

'I haven't the faintest idea, Nessa, I swear I haven't seen her.'

'Here's the choice,' said Conor. 'We've one extra garda out in the car, and if he stays here with Marcus as well as Fergus and Nessa, Redmond and I could go down the steps in the dark, and hope to overpower Darina on the boat. But if Sal is with her, the risk of your daughter getting hurt is substantial, Nessa, given what Darina said earlier about using her as a hostage. So the second option is for Marcus to go back down on his own and find out.'

'And you think you won't hear the boat chugging away to the far horizon?' Redmond found it hard not to shout. 'He's a lunatic, Conor, just like his cousin.'

'I understand the risks, believe me. But I don't think we can wait for the *cig*'s posse to come over the hill. So this is our best bet, and Marcus knows he's well advised to play it straight.'

'How will we know if Sal is on board?'

'Marcus is going to tell Darina that he has to test his supply of flares before setting off on a long journey. That gives him an excuse to check any floor cupboards that Sal could have been forced into. If the coast is clear and Sal isn't on board, he'll light the flare. Then Marcus will get Darina to us, in whatever way he can.'

'And otherwise? If Sal is down there?'

'We'll give it ten or fifteen minutes, and decide then. Meanwhile, we'll see if our Kerry colleagues can send a speedboat out of Kenmare.'

'Time to split.' Marcus ventured a quick smile. 'I came up to the house to get a loaf of bread and whatnot, but I'll have to tell Darina that I got stuck on the loo or something.'

Nobody smiled back and Redmond had to stop himself remarking on people who were full of crap. When Marcus had gone, Conor rummaged in a few drawers and found some keys. He handed them to Nessa and told her to try the garage, in case Darina's van was inside, and Sal imprisoned in it.

As they headed out of the kitchen, Conor put his hand on Redmond's shoulder and spoke quietly. 'If you overheard any of that blather I gave Marcus about his cannabis enterprise, just keep it to yourself. The *cig* wouldn't like me trampling on his prerogatives, especially as there was only a whisker of truth in it, as far as hard evidence goes.'

The sergeant crossed the path to the raised patio while Redmond accompanied Nessa to the garage. Sure enough, Darina's van was inside, locked tight. They found a sharp stone nearby and broke one of its windows. Redmond shone his torch into the rear space, only to confirm that it was empty.

They decided to try the houses, starting with the middle house near the garage. The rooms were almost empty of furniture, but as they raced around trying every door, Redmond noticed a mark on the paintwork in the hallway, where something heavy had hit against it very recently. He scanned the space and saw a second scratch on the paint above his head, at the edge of an attic trapdoor. There was no handle to open the trapdoor, but they soon found a ladder lying under a tree in the garden.

Redmond placed the ladder in the hallway and clambered up to get the trapdoor open. When it finally shifted, light blazed from above.

He hauled himself into the attic, and saw dozens of light-bulbs mounted on stands, shining onto rows and rows of cannabis plants. As his eyes adjusted, he heard a whimper from a hunched figure over by the attic wall. Sal, her face glistening with sweat and tears, lifted her head to gaze back at him.

Redmond heard large drops of rain pattering on the attic roof while he helped Sal down the ladder and into Nessa's arms. By the time he emerged from the house, the skies had opened and sheets of water drenched him to the skin as he ran to the raised patio to tell Conor the glad news about Sal. At the same moment, a flash of light illuminated the small boat tied to the slipway below them.

'This is our best chance,' he whispered to Conor, as they both backed away from the railing. 'If we go down now, we'll have them cornered on the boat.'

'*Whisht* a minute, my friend. I know this is hard for you, but we need to keep Marcus onside, instead of forcing him to defend his cousin.'

'But he'll spill the beans to her about us being here, I'm telling you, especially now that Sal is out of the picture.'

'Let's stick to the plan. Another five or ten minutes at least.'

'Conor, Darina is well able to swim off and hide in some cave, and we'll be stranded up here like fools.'

Conor put his finger to his lips, and they crept back to the railing. When they peered into the watery darkness, they saw flickers of torchlight close to the cliffside. The air was filled with a cacophony of wind and waves pounding the rocks. A violent squall had come in from the ocean in no time, attacking the land with all its force.

Suddenly a new sound reached their ears. Muffled voices from below.

Redmond moved closer to Conor as they strained to listen. Driving rain lashed against their faces and it was impossible to tell whether the two people below were on the boat or the pier. Redmond was assailed by a new fear, that Darina had turned on Marcus with the gun, having realised she could not rely on him. In her desperation, she might try to set off alone in the boat in the teeth of the storm.

He felt Conor tugging at his sleeve and they sidled around to the top of the cliff steps, concealed behind tall shrubs. Redmond's heart was thumping. He felt in his pocket for his torch just as a circle of light appeared out of the greenery. It was Marcus, lighting his way with his own torch, his lanky figure stepping onto the open path. Redmond counted slowly to five, but no Darina. Six, seven, eight. He was certain Conor was counting too, watching and waiting for the right instant to show themselves.

Marcus called over his shoulder. He turned and made as if to go back to the steps. Conor, who was closest to him, shrank back into the shadows.

Redmond was fit to burst from holding his breath. Had Darina pretended to follow Marcus, and then returned to the boat? Would Marcus exclaim out loud if his torchlight picked out a shiny button on Conor's uniform?

And then she came out of the shrubbery like a cat, wary eyes to all sides. Redmond pounced, a half second before Conor. He would make no mistake this time.

'What the fuck?' Darina shouted. 'You lying bastard, Marcus!'

Redmond locked his arms around her. He felt her writhing like an eel. 'You set me up!' she spat again in Marcus's direction. 'Telling me we'd to get water supplies . . .'

Redmond tried to push her towards the house but they both slipped on the muddy ground. As his shoulder hit the ground, Redmond felt a wrench of pain where he had been hurt earlier in the day.

He could hear other voices around him. A confusion of memories swirled in his head. Darina's strength that day as she pulled Maureen to shore. Her venomous eyes when she pointed the stun gun at Nessa. Electricity fizzing in the air as two metal prongs appeared out of the gun.

She was still trying to writhe out of his grasp. Something hard came against his shoulder. If she hit the switch she could disable him and make a run for it.

Redmond clenched his hands over Darina's wrists and pushed them up her back. He worked blindly at her fingers to loosen the cold metal object in their grip.

Conor was looming over them. Darina cursed loudly as he slipped handcuffs onto her wrists. As she was pulled to her feet, Redmond saw the glint of her stun gun on the ground. He set his foot firmly beside it, noticing absently that the rain had eased.

'You had an answer for everything, didn't you?'

It was Fergus who spoke from the doorway of Marcus's house. He seemed to have found a voice he'd lacked for weeks. Redmond scrambled upright, holding on to his shoulder. Wet mud seeped down his neck.

'It wasn't enough to kill Oscar, was it?' Fergus rushed forwards to confront Darina, pursued by his garda minder. 'You wanted more. The smell of his dead flesh in your nostrils was so sweet that you had to . . . You had to make a show of his body for the whole world to see, was that it?'

'You were lucky I had the balls to do it, instead of snivelling with self-pity like you.'

Fergus winced visibly but his hesitation lasted only a second. 'You promised you'd bury him where nobody would ever find him, Darina. He could just fade out of our lives, a missing person that we could pretend—'

'What, we could pretend he wasn't an evil bastard? So you could still hold up your head, proud of famous daddy?'

'It was enough to end his life, that was all it was to be. But then you couldn't even leave him in peace on the day of his funeral, with your vicious message to a radio station.'

'I was sick to my fingernails of all the media hacks praising him to the skies. And Jack Talbot started to smear Patrick.'

Darina stopped for a moment as Carraig Álainn was bathed in a wash of headlights approaching from the gate. She and Fergus stood facing each other, tense as caged animals, their pallid features almost translucent in the white glare. She looked around slowly at the surrounding group, and raised her voice as if for a speech from a podium.

'I did what I had to do. There are hundreds of people whose lives will be better as a result of my actions. Their judgement is what matters to me.'

'Jesus, Darina, will you get real!' Marcus cut across her in a low hiss. 'I can't believe you'd kill a man for the sake of people you've never met. I'm bloody sure you'd a better reason than that.'

Darina turned to stare at her cousin contemptuously, as a line of cars began to draw up on the roadway. Redmond was glad to see Conor keeping close to Marcus, and Nessa and Sal huddled together under an umbrella.

'You must have been seriously in love with Fergus,' said Sal bitterly, 'if the two of you planned the whole thing together?'

A curtain of fine rain hung in the air, glistening in the bright headlights. Nessa remembered the spotlit scene she had seen earlier that evening on the boreen, and how she had mistaken Fergus for Darina. She looked at them both again, their pale clenched faces and overwrought gestures, and saw with searing clarity what had eluded everyone from the start.

'I don't believe you were in love with each other, were you, Darina?' she asked. 'I think your relationship is a different one, and explains exactly why you killed Oscar.'

Her words seemed suspended in mid air. She had the same sensation she had experienced on the Briary, that the world stopped turning while everyone waited for her to continue.

'You found out that you're half-sister and brother, didn't you?' Nessa asked then. 'Because you shared the same father?'

A clamour broke out on all sides. Car doors were opening and what Nessa had said was passed on to Patrick, Trevor, Zoe and others who demanded to hear the news. As Redmond looked around, he noticed Fergus shrinking into himself, his moment of defiance ebbing and his eyes like black holes in which every spark of life had been extinguished.

Darina stood stock still opposite him, holding her stomach more tightly than ever. 'I never had a father,' she said bitterly. 'That's not what Oscar was to me, but a filthy infection that got into my bloodstream after he'd poisoned my mother's life. She was only eighteen years old when he raped her – the same age as Sal is now, so just think of that, Nessa.'

Darina took on her podium voice again. 'Just imagine it, all of you. My mother was working as an au pair with an Irish family in France when he came to visit, and then her life fell apart. It made no difference to him that he had a family at home in Ireland, or that my mam tried to stop him. For all I know, that could have spurred him on.'

'When did you find out?'

'I knew nothing until she was dying. She'd never said a word before about who my father was, but I knew she'd had to struggle to make a life for me, I'm sure that's what took its toll.' Darina wiped away a rivulet of water streaming from her hair. Her voice changed as she spoke of her mother. 'Maybe it was the drugs that made her delirious, so that she started talking about him. Or maybe she had to say it out loud before she . . .'

'And did she tell you his name?' Nessa asked softly.

'No, but afterwards, a month after she died, I went through her old diary. I had to do it, I had to know about him. And then I decided to purge his poison from my life.'

'But you were wrong,' said Fergus, his expression firmer once again. 'We were both wrong, Darina, because we had other choices. That's what I tried to say at the funeral when I . . . We set out to remove the stain he left on our lives, but it couldn't be done.'

He lifted his head and looked at her directly. 'The poison has spread, Darina, that's what we've done. Since his death . . . I could see you changing over the past month. You became like him, Darina – relishing the power you'd taken over other people's lives, and wanting to get your own way the whole time.'

TWENTY-FOUR

Friday 23 October, 6.30 p.m.

Nessa put her book face down on the counter. She was in O'Donovan's, sitting on a stool in her favourite corner of the bar. Cosy and secure against the wall, with a good view of the comings and goings. She could hear Caitlín chatting to customers on the other side of the partition between pub and shop. It was a genuinely old-fashioned place, complete with plain wooden furniture, original snuff drawers and a warm unaffected welcome.

Peace and quiet. Relief. A gradual return to ordinary habits, as the claustrophobic fog of public attention lifted day by day. Nessa still felt a little shy as she made her way through Derryowen, wary of a stranger's gaze or a neighbour's guarded comment. For once, she would be glad of winter's arrival, with its short days and stay-at-home routines. Time to gaze at the sky's wondrous expanse, and to be glad of all the good that was possible. Time to mull over everything.

A whole battery of garda interviews had followed the arrest of Darina and Fergus at Carraig Álainn. Sal spent two days in Bantry Hospital for observation but was recovering well, and Ronan was getting bored of stun gun games. On Tuesday night, Zoe came to dinner at Cnoc Meala and picked at every detail of the case, to figure out how they could have solved it sooner. She was as voluble as ever, declaiming about that day's news of an agreement with the crew of the Russian ship in Castletownbere, and how it just showed it was always worth fighting for your rights. By the time her taxi arrived after midnight, Nessa and Patrick were happy to wave her farewell, no matter how sincerely they admired her causes.

'So Sal's gone off for a heart-to-heart with Marcus, is that the idea?' asked Caitlín as she sat down slowly on her side of the bar. 'But not at Carraig Álainn, I presume?'

'Most definitely not. She says she'll never go near the place again. But in any case, Patrick and I wouldn't allow it. We took some persuasion to let her meet him at all, as you'd imagine.'

'Where's the romantic tryst taking place, then?'

'Down at the hotel, or most likely they'll go walking on the beach to get away from prying eyes.'

'God help her, poor kid, after all she's been through. Do you think she's wise to his charms by now?'

'I don't know, Caitlín. She says she just wants to find out why he disappeared without trace for a fortnight.'

Caitlín picked up a cloth and wiped the countertop absently. 'I suppose it's fair to say that Marcus did the right thing when it mattered most?'

'Well, that's true, but I don't think he'll get a free pardon for his growhouse operations, all the same.' Nessa dropped her voice, even though there were only a few customers in the bar. 'I saw Conor yesterday, and he told me off the record that all the attics had been used for the same purpose, and maybe the living rooms too.'

'The lure of quick money, and more exciting than plain old tourism?'

'No doubt. Conor said that the first time he and Redmond went to Carraig Álainn, Carl drove off in a hurry, probably with a van-load of plants.'

'They were up to the same caper in Clonakilty, according to a friend of a cousin of mine who lives near Carl's apartments in the town. She reckoned the furniture removal business was a handy one, to shift their products hither and yonder.'

'If Darina had copped what they were up to, she could have twisted their arms to make sure they got her out of Beara, and across to France.'

O'Donovan's door was pushed open and Sal walked in. She glanced around quickly before making a beeline for the corner of the bar. She was clutching a small red handbag which matched her woollen hat.

'He's such an eejit,' she said without preamble. 'Seriously handsome, of course, but a dimwit, all in all.'

Nessa murmured neutrally as she pulled over a second stool

beside her own. Caitlín poured a soft drink, guessing that Sal would not request alcohol in her mother's presence.

'Shrooms,' Sal said flatly. 'Mushies. Magic mushrooms, whatever you want to call them, that's what did for Marcus. Bad trip, surprise, surprise. He couldn't sit still or think straight, and then he got paranoid and horribly aggressive.'

'And how long did that last? Hardly a whole fortnight?'

'No, but it did last for days. He thought he'd calm down if he swigged vodka, but instead he just got worse.'

'And is that why he didn't phone you all that time, love?'

'He says he couldn't, Mam. He had panic attacks for a week, so he stayed in a darkened room in some mate's house, hoping he hadn't, like, lost his marbles for good. And then he didn't want to admit he'd freaked, so he lay low for another week.'

'Sounds like a scary experience for sure.'

Sal nodded, fingering her glass. 'Yeah, but it's a pity he went berserk with Garda Joyce as well, isn't it? He says he can't remember most of it, but I don't think that will get him off in court. Anyway, it serves him right for listening to his lovely friend Katya. She was mad keen to try the stupid mushrooms with him – said she'd done it before and it was amazing.'

Nessa smiled to herself. Clearly Marcus had decided to delegate some of the responsibility for his troubles to Katya. 'I remember you told me . . .' She paused to choose her words carefully. 'I got the impression that Marcus was against taking drugs?'

'He was against putting chemical substances in his body, that was his line. But his razor-sharp logic was that mushrooms are natural plants that grow in our very own Irish woodlands, and therefore can't possibly do us any harm.' Sal shrugged and rolled her eyes. 'He can be a right nitwit at times, like I said.'

'Well, at least he didn't try to get you to join in, did he?' Caitlín had a way of asking sensitive questions in an innocent tone of voice. 'Unless he was handing around platefuls of the stuff at the party in Castletown?'

Sal's expression changed and Nessa thought fleetingly that Caitlín had hit the mark. Her daughter had long declared that taking drugs was for losers, but teenage righteousness could change overnight.

'I don't want to think about that party,' Sal said then. She twisted a strap on her handbag to and fro. 'I don't mean . . . It's not over Marcus or anything, because he didn't hand around stuff, no way. But it's something else I've remembered.'

Nessa put her arm around her and was gratified that Sal leaned in to her for reassurance. 'It's OK if you'd rather not talk about it, love.'

'No, I'd better . . . I should have said it in my garda statement thing, but I've just been too tired to think straight. It's about Darina's van. That night, you know, when we drove to the party . . .'

Sal bit her lip and lapsed into silence. After a moment, Nessa realised what she was getting at. 'You're talking about the wheelie bin, aren't you? It was in the van that night, and that's how . . .?'

'Darina said something about bringing her work clothes to a launderette the next day. And then . . . Well, she left the party early, you know, saying she wanted to get up next morning for work.'

'But you believe she drove straight from the party up towards the Healy Pass?' Sal nodded and Nessa continued slowly. 'It would have been easy enough for her to dump Oscar's body that night, without even taking the wheelie bin out of the van. She could just open the back doors and tilt the bin against the parapet.'

'It was a hell of a risk,' said Caitlín, 'if another car had come along.'

'She could see headlights from both directions quite easily. And as we know, she'd decided by then that she wanted the corpse to be found in a very public spot.'

'I think we should stop talking about it now,' said Sal. She closed her eyes for a moment, frowning hard, and Nessa thought about her own night at the little bridge, and her sense of the murderer's abiding hatred of Oscar. But then Sal shook her head firmly and assumed a positive air again. 'Anyway, you'll never guess who was nosing around the hotel. We had to skip off down the coastal path in case he'd see us.'

'I think I saw his car earlier,' said Caitlín. 'A shiny silver Merc, by any chance?'

'Yes. Jack Talbot and a photographer. You'd think they'd be sick of the area by now.'

'I'd say they've heard the same rumour as I have,' said Nessa. 'I got a text from a media friend last night about it.'

'Go on then?'

'The rumour is that Maureen has sold her story to one of the big Sundays. Her line is that she's doing it for Dominic's sake, to pay for his longterm care.'

'Do you mean she gave it to Jack's paper?'

'No, no, she's turned against him completely, as far as I know. But if the rumour is true, Jack must be desperate for some new scoop.' Nessa laughed. 'You'd better watch out, Caitlín! He might write a feature claiming that you've powerful mushrooms on the pub menu here!'

Caitlín smiled, but her reply was in a serious tone. 'God help Dominic, all the same. It doesn't look as if he'll ever recover, does it?'

'No, and that kind of brain damage could make him very difficult to manage.'

'So you couldn't blame Maureen, really, for making what-ever money she can.'

'Hasn't she got her Lotto loot?' Sal looked from one to the other. 'Unless of course she and Dominic spent it all years ago. Anyway, the question is what she'll say this time about her little fall on the boreen. I'm sure she was glugging from her orange bottle all afternoon – and then she tried to climb a wall to see where she was, or something, and fell on her face. I told you from the start that I got a whiff of booze off her.'

'Conor says they're pretty sure that she wasn't assaulted,' said Nessa, 'so you're probably right, Sal. But I believe Maureen has taken on a PR company now, so who knows what they'll come up with to keep the readers excited.'

It was Sal's turn to laugh. 'This could be the start of, like, a whole new career for her. Next thing, I bet you she'll be starring in a reality TV show. Can you just imagine it? Celebrity ladies compete to get into bed with the richest, sleaziest man?'

Caitlín smiled ruefully at her. 'Then again, we know she

failed in that particular contest when she ran into Oscar Malden. And it was just as well for her, all considered.'

Redmond was learning to cook his own meals. It gave him something to think about at home, instead of staring at the microwave while the latest frozen package whirred around. Not that he was trying anything complicated – grilled chicken with olive oil, lemon juice and garlic was enough to get on with. It would help with calorie control too, to understand what he was eating.

He heard a knock at the door while he was turning on the grill. He rarely had visitors, but he hoped to invite Conor and his wife for a meal, once he learned to make something present-able. He had also put his name down for a sailing course in Adrigole at the Halloween bank holiday weekend – anything to take his mind off his worries about the future.

He found Trevor O'Kelleher at the front door, smiling apolo-getically for disturbing him at home. Redmond had a quick look around as he led him in, checking that the place was reasonably neat. After a few declined offers of tea, the inspector asked to sit down. The room seemed very cramped as he stretched his long legs to the side of the table.

'I'll come straight to the point,' he said, 'because I know this has been an anxious time for you. We won't be able to give it to you in writing for a week or two, but you can get ready to return to work very soon. You'll be reprimanded for certain unauthorised actions, there's no getting away from that. But you'll be glad to hear that your mobile phone has been found. It was in Marcus's car, under the passenger seat, but he and Carl both claim they've no idea how it got there.'

Redmond was glad he had sat down himself. He felt as if his senses were filling with the most wonderful aromas, after spending weeks on a diet of bread and water.

'I'm unable to return the phone to you yet,' Trevor continued in his official voice. 'It's being examined, and I've been told that some deleted photographs have been retrieved. The date on the photos corresponds with the same occasion on which you reported visiting the old house in the trees, and they show the exterior of that house at night, along with some well-lit images of cannabis plants.'

Redmond sat back on his chair, letting his breath out slowly. If he had to swallow a gallon of medicine for his misdemeanours, he would gladly do it, just to wear his garda uniform again. Trevor allowed a pause of silence between them, and then gave him one of his penetrating looks. 'I'm sure you're dying to know whether we've learned anything new,' he said quietly. 'Especially now that Fergus Malden has given us the benefit of a full and frank interview.'

Redmond muttered something about better late than never for Fergus, before he remembered to offer his visitor a drink again. Trevor relented this time, and Redmond was glad to busy himself at the kettle to distract him from his own emotions.

'According to Fergus, he met Darina for the first time a year and a half ago. It was some months after her mother's death, and she'd tracked down where Oscar lived, out in the Tipperary countryside. It seems she arrived at the house on some pretext she invented, to do with a survey on broadband speed.'

'And was Oscar himself at home?'

'No, he was away on a business trip, which she may have found out from his office beforehand. So instead, Fergus opened the door to her and they got talking. In fact, they got on so well that they met a few times in the following week.'

Redmond put teacups and a jug of milk on the table, although he knew that Trevor drank black tea. It was difficult to concentrate on what was being said. 'But she hardly told him straightaway that she was his half-sister?' he asked after a moment.

'Not at all, no. However, she may have had to tell him quicker than she'd expected. It seems that Fergus found her rather attractive and made that known to her, so she had to scotch his romantic notions and take her chances with the truth.'

'Do you think they came up with their murder plan at that stage?'

'Fergus says no. But of course, it's possible that Darina played him along until she was sure he'd cooperate.'

'Is it also possible that Fergus is trying to minimise his own responsibility?'

'Well spotted, Redmond, that had also occurred to me. But I don't think it was hard for Darina to plant the idea in his mind, because Fergus hated his father too, and it must have been a huge relief to him to say it aloud. They certainly decided early on that Oscar should know nothing about Darina, and took care to communicate using only pre-paid mobile phones.'

Trevor gestured his thanks as Redmond poured tea. 'Fergus has told us that they made their decision last Christmas,' he said after taking a sip. 'His father had just gone away again and their housekeeper, Irina, broke down in the middle of a conversation with Fergus, and blurted out that Oscar had attacked her. Fergus tried to get her to report it, but she denied the whole thing the very next day. He was already aware of previous incidents in the company, when young women who had worked directly with Oscar left their jobs suddenly, and he remembered a heated argument between his father and mother about just such an incident, before his mother left them to live in Dubai.'

Redmond pictured the woman he had seen at Oscar's funeral, eyes veiled with alcohol and pain. 'Fergus may have wondered about her too,' he said quietly, 'and how often his father had raped his mother.'

They went on to talk about other aspects of the case, but when Trevor made a show of looking at his watch, Redmond did not press a second cup of tea on him. He was impatient to savour his own good news, in the happy knowledge that he would have plenty of opportunities to dissect the case again. On other occasions too, he and Trevor might talk over the great unanswerable questions raised by every murder inquiry, such as the nature of good and evil, and how free will could swing one way or another between them.

As he waved Trevor off, he thought of something he wanted to do the next day. He had been putting it off, but it was time to risk his feelings just a little. He turned the grill back on and picked up the phone.

Nessa had arrived early. It was a breezy autumn day, the billowing clouds brightened by sharp blasts of sunlight. From her vantage of the wooden bench on the hill, great sweeping arcs of mountains, headlands, inlets, islands and ocean waters could be seen, as Beara's greens and blues merged with those of Iveragh, its neighbouring peninsula famed for the Ring of Kerry. She gazed all round to her heart's content, until she spotted Redmond making his way towards her. His gait was athletic but awkward, she thought, and he never appeared quite comfortable in his own skin.

She felt rather awkward herself, unsure of why he had asked to meet her. He had said on the phone that he would like to see the standing stone drawn by Darina, and she had brought the card itself with her to show it too.

Redmond spoke quickly, once they had got over their first greetings. 'What I want to say to you, Nessa – well, it's probably quite simple, but I hope it comes out right.' He blushed and hurried on. 'Just that I'm sorry about how . . . I know I was rude to you a few times, and I really regret that. And I'm really grateful, more grateful than I can say, that you trusted me that day, when we met up here.'

'It's coming out fine, Redmond. I appreciate it, and for my own part . . .' She felt flustered as she added her own gratitude. She had a sudden urge to give him a hug but knew he would find it too much. She smiled instead and tried for eye contact. 'I'm afraid Patrick tells me that I sometimes intimidate people. Not intentionally most of the time, though I have to admit it came in quite handy when I worked as a journalist.'

Redmond seemed glad of a cue to get onto a different subject. 'Do you miss being a journalist?' he asked.

'Sometimes, as I found out recently when I got stuck back into my old ways. But if I'd stayed in that life, I'd have missed all of this.' Nessa gestured at the view and then pointed down the hill. She wondered if she was babbling too much. 'You said you'd like to see the standing stone,' she said then. 'I think the one Darina drew is just down here, in a field opposite the turn for the Briary. We'll have to clamber over the wall, but my son Ronan and I tried it recently, so I know it's not too hard.'

As they made their way to it, she told him about hiding behind the standing stone with Ronan, the day after Oscar's body was found. They exchanged the latest news on the case and Redmond appeared to relax a little.

'Have you heard anything about how Darina got hold of the stun gun?' she asked him. 'I've been wondering about that a few times.'

'The inspector told me – Trevor, that is – he told me that Fergus found four of the guns in his home about a year ago. Oscar had travelled on a private plane and managed to avoid being scanned at the airport. Then a few months ago, Fergus removed one of the guns and met up with Darina near Cork city to give it to her. It seems Oscar never found out.'

'I can't make up my mind about Fergus, whether to despise him or to feel sorry for him.'

'I know what you mean. Whatever spirit he had seems to have been crushed.'

Nessa showed Redmond the drawing when they were in the field, and they compared it to the single slab of stone, wedged into the ground and as tall as themselves.

'Yes, I can see how it makes sense as a headstone,' he said. 'I couldn't picture it before, because I didn't really know what a standing stone was.'

Nessa turned over the card, to show the impression of Oscar's face on the other side. It was done in a fluid and sensitive style and Nessa looked at her companion, realising that he held her gaze this time without shying away. 'What I find very hard to take in,' she said slowly, 'is that we know so little about most people. Oscar, obviously, but Darina too. She always seemed to me to be a gentle, diligent kind of person, and not at all capable of what she did.'

Redmond nodded silently and they stood looking at the view, as clouds and sunlight jostled above the foam-rimmed curves of the coastline. Nessa wondered briefly about inviting him to Cnoc Meala, but decided against it. He was also someone she had known and understood too little, and that would not change in one afternoon. After a few moments, they picked their way across the field, caught up with their own thoughts as they took turns climbing back over the wall.

ACKNOWLEDGEMENTS

Writing is mostly a solitary activity, but I could not have written this novel without the generous time and support of all the people I want to thank here.

For valuable help with research: Professor Marie Cassidy, Ireland's State Pathologist; Detective-Sergeant Brendan Walsh (now retired); and friends in Beara including Sue Booth-Forbes of Anam Cara retreat for writers and artists.

For great critical feedback and encouragement to get me to the final draft: Simon Brooke, Kintilla Heussaff, Ciana Campbell, Alison Warlow, Wendy Barrett, Kate Ruddock, Maeve Lewis, Mary Hyland, Eithne Bentley and everyone in my wonderful book club.

Finally, I want to thank Micheál Ó Conghaile, my Irish language publisher at Cló Iar-Chonnacht, whose advice, patience and hard work made this translation possible; and all at Severn House for doing such a great job, in particular my editor Anna Telfer and publisher Edwin Buckhalter.

GLOSSARY

amadán: fool

blather: from *bladar*, cajolery

bockety: from *bacach*, broken, halting, unsteady

boreen: from *bóithrín*, a country lane or narrow, often unpaved, road

buckshee: a wannabe detective; also, any garda officer who does a job without being paid the proper allowance. Its origins may be both British (and Persian 'baksheesh'), for 'something extra obtained free', and Irish, *bog shí* or *boige shíne*, for getting a free drink in a pub, or over-generosity

cig: abbreviation of *cigire*, inspector/police inspector; used colloquially among the police in Ireland to speak about or to an inspector

garda: a policeman, a member of *An Garda Siochána*, the official title of Ireland's national police force, which translates as 'The Guardian(s) of the Peace'. A police station is called a garda station; and an individual garda (plural, gardaí or gardai) is the lowest fulltime rank in the force, for which 'guard' is aso used colloquially

gligeen: from *gligín*, an empty-headed person who talks too much

mar dhea: as if it were so – used sarcastically about what has just been said

plámás: smooth talk, flattery designed to gain an advantage

rapparee: from *rapaire*, an outlaw or bandit of 17th and 18th century
                Ireland, often dispossessed as a result of colonisation

whisht: from *fuist*, hush, be quiet – used as an interjection

KE 11|14